THE
SUFFERING
OF
STRANGERS

Caro Ramsay is the Glaswegian author of the critically acclaimed DI Anderson and DS Costello series. The ninth book in the series, *The Suffering of Strangers* has been longlisted for the McIlvanney Prize.

caroramsay.co.uk

Also by Caro Ramsay

The Anderson and Costello series

THE SUFFERING OF STRANGERS

CARO RAMSAY

BLACKTHORN

First published in Great Britain, the USA and Canada in 2019
by Black Thorn, an imprint of Canongate Books Ltd,
14 High Street, Edinburgh EH1 1TE

Distributed in the USA by Publishers Group West and in Canada by
Publishers Group Canada

First published in 2017 by Severn House Publishers Ltd,
Eardley House, 4 Uxbridge Street, London W8 7SY

blackthornbooks.com

1

British Library Cataloguing in Publication Data
A catalogue record for this title is available from the British Library

ISBN 978 1 78689 644 5

Typeset by Palimpsest Book Production Ltd, Falkirk,
Stirlingshire, Scotland

Printed and bound in Great Britain by Clays Ltd, Elcograf S.p.A.

This book is dedicated to the memory of David Mitchell
3rd December 1935 – 12th November 2016

PROLOGUE

August 1992

This year was going to be different.

Every day was still a test; every day was a challenge.

It was a fresh summer morning, very early, not yet seven. She was not confident that her knee was ready for the hike to the top of the Whangie, with its unforgiving rock formation and steep paths. But she walked on, knowing the car park at the bottom of the Queen's View was empty. She was on her own, walking slowly but sure footedly, skirting her way round the far side of Auchineden Hill, then through the gash in the rock, the walls fifty-feet high on either side of her. This early there were no rock climbers, no abseilers, only the thud of her boots on the grass underfoot.

The injury had destroyed her pleasure in walking, in the open air, her lust for life. It had almost taken her degree and her career. She was reclaiming them now.

She zigzagged her way uphill on the rocky path until she reached the jagged crags at the top where she bent over and let her lungs take their fill of the cool fresh air. She drank, standing too long, deluding herself that she was taking in the view. It was not the majestic beauty that detained her, not this time. Today her horizon was filled with challenges. Loch Lomond, the southern highlands, the Campsies. She was determined that she would walk them all again.

She breathed deep, glad she had brought her wrap-around glasses, the thinness of the air emphasized the glare of the sun. Noises carried easily up here, the drone of a distant tractor, the bellow of a cow down in the green patchwork of fields.

And something else.

A slap? A clap? A sound that was familiar but discordant here on the hill.

She capped her bottle and pulled her sunglasses up to rest

on her forehead, listening and looking around for the source of that quiet, familiar noise, resenting it. She wanted, she needed, to be up here on her own. And she begrudged her companion their peace on the hill.

She pulled her glasses back over her eyes and started down the quickest way. It was steeper and more unstable but she wanted the challenge, her irritation pushing her on. She kept going, faster and faster, placing her feet carefully, twisting to the right to negotiate two huge boulders, then to the left to jump a deep crevice.

She glanced back. Glad to see and hear no one, she slowed down. They had taken a different path.

She walked along, looking up at the last minute as she heard something above her. That noise? Something that reminded her of her dad?

Clap clap.

Clap clap.

She ducked a minute too late as the coil of rope settled around her neck.

ONE

By four o'clock DI Costello was walking along Byres Road, her hands buried deep in her pockets, collar up to protect her from the sudden onslaught of rain. She was heading for Superdrug to buy some shampoo and deodorant. She had been using soap on her hair for the last fortnight and spraying a cheap perfume called Kabana over herself in any breaks in court proceedings. It made her smell as though she had just cleaned out the toilets, but it was worth it to be there.

To hear the word.

Guilty.

The look on Bernadette Kissel's face was *worth it*.

Now DI Costello wanted to celebrate, but only after spending an hour in a hot shower, washing the stink of the Kissel case off her skin, scrubbing those images from her eyes. She wondered if DCI Anderson had been following the case; it would have been difficult for him to avoid it. One day last week, she couldn't remember which day – the trial seemed to go on for ever – her face had been on the front page, sharp focus, her frown making the scar on her forehead pucker. Beside her there was a picture of Professor Jack O'Hare, or 'John' as they had called him. Unfortunate black and white pictures of them looking tired and ineffectual, taken as they left the court, one word underlining the images: MISTAKES.

She had been furious but the professor hadn't minded at all. Of course, mistakes had been made. But not by them. The pathologist had taken it all with the finality of one who spends most of his time with the dead.

Costello, hurrying to get out of the rain, paused under the emerald green and gold awning of La Vita Spuntini, her eye attracted by a familiar jacket with a small herringbone pattern.

She recognized the square head, the salt and pepper hair, the white shirt with ironed blade creases down the sleeves. She recognized the back of his neck.

Archie Walker, Chief Procurator Fiscal and her . . . well, whatever he was. They were too old to be 'friends with benefits'. He sat with his back to the window, studying a few pages of A4 paper. She waited for him to remove the staple, flatten the papers out to line them up correctly. Finger and thumb pinched the corners, like an entomologist selecting some rare species.

She was about to tap on the window when she noticed there were two glasses on the table, both poured. White wine. Archie looked up and smiled in the direction of the small, tanned brunette pulling down on the cuffs of the cream blouse that hung loose over her black skirt. She appeared to have been to the loo and had rolled up her sleeves to give her hands a thorough wash. Somebody who routinely touched something unpleasant and had learned to wash their hands scrupulously?

Pathologist? A lab technician?

But Costello didn't recognize her.

Archie slid his papers from the table back into his briefcase. He locked the case, spinning the digits. The brunette moved an empty glass from another table and set it in front of her, placing both full wine glasses in front of him. Had he ordered wine? It was lunchtime and Archie never drank this early. Now the brunette was moving all three glasses, so she could get closer to him across the narrow table.

These two knew each other well. They were very cosy.

And Costello had no idea who the woman was.

She was talking now, this brunette. Friendly, laughing slightly. It didn't look like two lawyers discussing a case, ready to take corners and argue the burden of proof.

The brunette was younger than Archie, in her thirties? Minimal make-up, a very good suit and a blouse that looked rather loose as if she had lost weight and classic high-heeled black shoes. Her long dark brown hair was perfectly curled into a French roll, a few loose strands falling over her face to soften the look.

Probably another fiscal, somebody from his office. Costello raised her hand to tap the rain-spattered glass, as the woman threw her head back to laugh.

When had Archie ever said anything that funny?

The brunette glanced out the window and caught Costello's eye, her gaze passing over her as if she was invisible. No recognition. Nothing.

Costello lowered her hand and tilted her head to look at her own reflection, red-rimmed, baggy eyes and spikey, wet scarecrow hair. She noticed her own fingernails, rough and bitten, as the brunette reached her manicured hand out to lay it gently on Archie's wrist. He leaned forward, looking as though he was whispering to her across the table. Then she laughed again. She had a long feminine throat, a finely crafted silver butterfly hung round it, the delicate chain attached to each upper wing.

Had Archie just kissed the back of her hand?

Bastard. Costello walked away, across the road, stepping into the puddles. As she splashed along Byres Road towards Superdrug, an Asian woman with a long, purple-patterned dirndl skirt and a washed out baggy, blue woolly jacket approached her, hood up against the rain. Under her arm was a huge Lidl bag bulging like a balloon. Costello noticed the rainwater running out the side of the woman's crocs. She had her arm up, palm out as if to catch hold of her as she passed.

'I've no spare change,' snapped Costello, automatically and sidestepped. She was not in a mood to be generous.

At five p.m. Roberta closed the door of the Duster and eased out the drive, phone on hands-free in case James had news about the new job.

She pulled out of Acacia Crescent heading down towards the Avenue. They could take a wee drive along the twisting farm roads around Waterside. The smooth rocking of the car had put Sholto to sleep at half two this morning and again at half five. God, she was tired, the back of her eyelids felt like sandpaper. The cold outside chilled her tired, weary bones in a way that no long soak in a hot bath could ease. She was in the permanent winter of a land somewhere beyond exhaustion.

Nobody told her it would be like this. She had spent hours at the hairdressers when she was pregnant, reading the celebrity magazines and she'd imagined she would be like Angelina Jolie. Have a baby, go back to work, get a good night's sleep, the house would stay clean, her figure would snap straight back into shape and bits of her anatomy would stop leaking. Nobody had told her that babies stay awake twenty-four-seven, and that for the first six weeks she would have difficulty remembering her own name. And there were a lot more hours in the day, long, long hours where the crying never stopped. And yet she never had enough time to do anything.

'Why don't you just sleep, you wee pig,' she asked. Her baby son looked comfortable enough in his new blanket, still clean enough to see the fluffy cream lambs round the bottom.

Sholto looked at her with big blue, tearful eyes, and for one short moment he fell silent, as if he was chewing the idea over, considering the concept in his tiny mind. He rejected it and started wailing like a siren sounding a red alert.

When the mobile rang, Roberta pulled over, put the handbrake on and stepped out the car to stand in the road, in the rain, so she could hear her husband properly.

James's voice came through loud and clear. 'How do you fancy a glass of bubbly tonight?'

'You got the job?'

'I did and the pay rise means you don't need to rush back to work.'

She pulled up her hood. 'And how do we celebrate with the noise of the jumbo jet on a test flight in the room with us?'

'A drink might help you sleep.'

'I don't need any bloody help sleeping. It's him that doesn't sleep. I need help to stay awake.'

'OK, maybe if you calm down, he might relax better and stop screaming.'

Roberta felt like screaming. It was OK for him, driving to work in a nice silent car, staying late at the office then going to the pub, engaging with grown-ups who talk rather than gurgle and who smell of aftershave rather than Nappy San.

'Calm *down*.' James repeated. 'Go to Barry's and buy a nice bottle of bubbly, push the boat out, thirty or forty quid.

Go home and stick it in the fridge and I'll pick up a nice takeaway.'

'OK. Congratulations,' she muttered and climbed back into the ear-splitting interior. She shoved a Kleenex in each of her ears and drove on.

Ten minutes later, she pulled up in the inshot outside Barry's. The sky was darkening, the temperature had dropped. As she removed her makeshift earplugs, she looked at Sholto, and his mouth was closed.

In the car there was only the quiet rattle of the rain on the roof, the gentle rumble of the engine, and the easy rasp of Sholto's breathing. Then the engine cut off.

He had stopped crying.

Actually stopped crying.

His blue eyes widened and looked up at hers, beguiling in their threat to start again.

She waited.

He remained quiet.

She reached to undo the seat belt and stopped as he opened his mouth. Moving him now might not be a good idea.

She looked into the shop window. Barry was visible through the row of hams hanging across the window, chatting animatedly as he wrapped something small in paper and placed it in a plastic bag. The queue was short. She caught his eye and waved at him. He waved back, recognizing the car, if not the driver. She watched him as he turned and said something to a customer at the back of the shop, pointing out to the street.

Slowly and gently, she slid out the driver's seat and eased the car door over, without closing it properly to avoid any harsh clicks. She dashed into the shop, scanning the shelves of sparkly, then making her way to the fridge at the back. This was going to be her first drink for a year. She could feel her taste buds tingling already.

Barry asked her how she was doing as she handed over the bottle of chilled Tattinger. He wrapped it slowly in tissue paper and tucked the ends in neatly. Roberta looked out at the car, checking that it was OK and that the monster was not awake and screaming.

'James got the job?' Barry asked.

'How did you guess?'

'You look happy. You had any sleep yet?' Barry took her credit card and wandered to the machine at the counter.

'Nope but he's stopped crying now so I live in hope.' She followed him, giving the car a glance over her shoulder. 'Last night he slept for a whole hour and a half. Imagine!' She listened to Barry telling her that his middle boy had been like that, but had grown out of it eventually.

'How long was eventually?' Roberta asked, hopefully.

Barry handed her the machine for her pin number. 'Well, he started sleeping then sleep walking, then not sleeping again, then coming into our bed every two minutes, then teething and screaming the house down. In fact, he has been a right pain in the arse from the moment he was born.'

Roberta played along, enjoying this adult exchange, being witty, using her brain. Something beyond 'The Wheels On The Bus'. 'And how old is he now?'

'Twenty-six. He still lies in bed all day, playing his Xbox. Still talks crap. But you've got to love them.'

Roberta smiled, took the bottle and the credit card in its little blanket of receipt.

She walked out the shop, busy holding the bottle, slipping the credit card safely in her purse, closing the clasp, watching her step on the wet floor, before she looked up.

The Duster was gone.

DCI Colin Anderson listened to Brenda's voicemail but didn't leave another message. It was after five, she was normally home with Peter by now, giving their son his tea. Reluctantly, he joined the queue at the water cooler outside the main investigation suite. His meeting at West End Central was running late, so he may as well stay on and work the rest of the evening. He had nothing much to go home to. He eaves-dropped on one of his new colleagues, Steve, talking about his vengeful ex-wife, his money-grabbing present wife and the wondrous tottie he had his sights on for wife number three. Anderson and Brenda – he couldn't even refer to her as an 'estranged wife' – had a very good relationship. In Steve's opinion that was due to the little matter of Anderson inheriting a million-pound house, despite him arguing, truth-fully, that it was the twenty-year marriage and two kids that kept them close.

And Steve had laughed.

Was it him or were all cops complete dicks these days?

Bruce, Stevie's partner in crime, took out his mobile and began scrolling. 'The jury in the Kissel case are back. Guilty on all counts.'

'Was there ever a doubt? That kid was dead in the flat for six months before anybody noticed. I'm surprised they are not asking for the death penalty to be reinstated.'

'And your old pal was front page news, did you see that? The old woman?'

Anderson tried to make the connection in his mind. He had seen the headlines. It was a long time before the penny dropped. 'Costello, you mean, my old DI?' he said, well aware that he hadn't spoken to her about it, even though the case had been all over the media. Not so long ago, she would have been his first call. He looked at his watch, she'd be off duty by now. Maybe better to leave it.

'Word from Govan is that she made mistakes, her and that old pathologist. He should be retired by now anyway.' Stevie offered his valued opinion. 'There's a nice new pathologist over at the QE, little blonde, Welsh. Got an arse that could make a vicar kick a stained-glass window.'

Bruce chipped in. 'Costello's been drifting for a while. She must have been a dead weight in your career, Colin. I mean you were really going places. At one point. Is she retiring now?'

Retiring? Costello was only a few years younger than him. It was a chilling thought. Anderson looked at his phone, scrolling, pretending that he was reading the news updates on the Kissel case. God, in the old days they had shared every-thing, sat on surveillance in frozen cars for bum-achingly tedious hours, sipping tea from a flask and eating cold chips. He knew her so well he could choose her as his specialist subject on Mastermind. She was one of the few women he knew who was happy to sit in silence. Why had he not phoned her? Was he jealous that she was still out there doing the job while he was stuck in here with the Versace twins?

And did they see him as they saw her, old with his career well and truly behind him?

Cold case units had so many different names to mask the reality of the bureaucratic game of pass the parcel. They opened files, a quick check to see if any advancement in forensics might help or if there was any nicely preserved, uncontaminated material to test. There rarely was. So the file was closed again and left for the next review.

He was going to be the sixth unwanted cop to review the Gillian Witherspoon case. What was he supposed to do? Go out and interview Gillian, so she knew she wasn't forgotten? 'Under constant review' sounded like good policing to some but to others making contact with the victim every three years only dragged up painful memories that prevented them from moving on.

He looked at the picture inside the front page of the file, a pleasant, totally unremarkable woman except that on the 15th of March 1996, Gillian, a young, busy mum of two, had nipped out to her local shop for a pint of milk at night after watching the ten o'clock news, full of the horror of the Dunblane massacre. She had pulled her coat over her PJs, slipped on her trainers and picked up her purse to walk down to the main road and the garage shop. It was well covered by CCTV, it was an unseasonably warm night, the area was well lit. Everybody knew everybody. Nobody saw anything.

But somebody had been watching.

She was found behind the bins, bleeding badly. She couldn't remember what she saw, or heard, or smelled, or tasted, only that she had been aware of somebody.

End of.

As the rage of Thomas Hamilton unfolded, Gillian got lost in the later pages of the press. She had been divorced in 1998. Anti-depressants followed. Not an unfamiliar story.

'Looks like we are reconvening.' Stevie crushed his plastic cup in his fist and tossed it into the non-recyclable. 'Yeeeees,' he said, 'got it in one.'

'You've still got the moves,' agreed Bruce, and they high fived each other. Anderson walked quickly away before they started French kissing.

* * *

Roberta stopped dead, the world stopped with her. For a stupid moment, she turned to glance behind her, thinking she had come out a different door of the shop. She looked up and down the street, but the Duster was gone.

The car parking space was empty.

The baby was gone.

Baby Sholto was gone.

She dropped the bottle. It exploded onto the concrete, feathering the streets with champagne.

She turned around to see if anybody was about. 'Did you see? Did anybody see? Where is my son, where is my baby?' She knew that the words were coming out her mouth but they didn't sound right. She was merely making noises.

Grabbing a pensioner in a grey raincoat, she screamed in her face, 'Sholto? Sholto? Sholto! Where is the blue Duster? There was a blue Duster parked right there.' She pointed, then grabbed the old lady again, this time by the shoulders, and began to shake her. 'Did you see them? Who drove my car away?'

Then strong hands were removing hers from the damp grey raincoat. Barry was out the shop, shouting at his assistants, sending one to run up the street, the other down. The Duster couldn't have gone far.

Roberta was aware she was screaming. 'Where did that car go?' she shouted in the woman's face, flecking her skin with saliva. She plunged her hands onto her pockets, grabbing only the silky lining and fresh air, frantically searching for her phone. It was on the dashboard of the car. James had called. She'd put it back in the cradle on the dashboard. After she had moaned about Sholto, about how horrible he was, how noisy.

Well, her world was quiet now.

She heard Barry on his mobile calling the police. The old woman was telling her to calm down.

'Where did it go?' She heard the screeching of a banshee. She knew it was her, but she couldn't stop herself.

Now Barry was stopping people, the woman at the auto bank, the teenager walking her pug, another customer. Roberta scanned them, her finger held horizontally, pointing at each one, thinking that one of them could have taken the baby;

one of them must have seen something they were not telling her. It was a conspiracy. They were all in it together. Cars do not disappear, not in that short period of time. How long had it been?

She heard the word 'Duster'.

'What? What?' She wiped the snot from her face.

The teenager with the pug pointed. 'Look, there's a blue Duster parked round there.'

Just as the man who worked the front till for Barry shouted something from the end of the road and waved up the side street.

Roberta ran to the corner, to the narrow road that led to the small car park behind the shops. Not somewhere to leave a car on a rainy, darkening night. Not somewhere she would have parked. She thought she had been careful.

The Duster was there. She looked at it and stopped dead, registering the number plate. Then began moving quickly again, almost laughing. Somebody had played a little joke and she had fallen for it. She could see the front seat, the outline of Sholto's car seat, still in its place. She ripped open the door. Wrapped up warm in his yellow blanket, the baby was there. He was fine.

He was quiet, he was gurgling and content.

She pulled down his fluffy blue coverlet trimmed with cream fluffy lambs.

And then she started screaming.

In the end, Costello decided to get into a worse mood. She had got soaked twice shopping. Having gone in for a two-pound bottle of shampoo, she came out having spent thirty quid. There was a special offer on a cream that would energize her skin, make her twenty years younger and a foot taller. It would make her wake up each morning at five a.m. and eat yoghurt. If she was lucky, it might make her look like the skinny Scandinavian twelve-year-old supermodel on the cover of the box, but she doubted it.

She was nibbling a blueberry muffin in the coffee shop, quietly drawing a blue Groucho moustache on the supermodel when they walked past on the opposite side of the road. Archie with the brunette on his arm, sharing his umbrella. She was slightly smaller than him, despite her strutting along in very high heels. Costello thought she could see a flash of red soles. A young woman pushed a pram towards them. They didn't break stride as they sidestepped, both keeping under the shelter of his umbrella. As if they were used to walking together. The muffin went dry in her mouth. The brunette had stopped and turned her face to Archie. He leaned forward. Had he kissed her in the middle of Byres Road? He barely spoke to Costello in public, never mind show her any affection. She growled inwardly as the brunette turned towards the kerb, holding up her car keys.

'Holy Jesus,' muttered Costello as the lights flickered on a Porsche tucked into the kerb. A black Porsche Panamera? Who the hell was she?

What was she?

With Archie's wife, Pippa, in a care home for nearly a year now, enough time had passed for him to bring along a lady companion to the Law Society events. Places he had never asked Costello to attend. Not that she would have gone.

Had she only been a stopgap in his life? An emotional Elastoplast until time healed the wound?

She had always appreciated his need for privacy out of respect for his profession. Maybe the secrecy was for quite a different reason.

Maybe he was a two-timing little shit.

Her thoughts ran riot. Was there a conspiracy? Did Anderson know about it? Was that why he had not been in touch? Bloody men sticking together as usual. If anybody was good at convincing themselves they were being benignly unfaithful, it was her ex-boss DCI Colin Anderson.

She studied Archie's face as the Porsche pulled away, his hand raised in the rain. He remained on the pavement under the shelter of his umbrella, watching the Porsche merge into the queue of traffic.

He had never stood at his window watching her leave.

Abigail Haggerty had been home from the surgery since half twelve and had been cleaning ever since. Now it was half

five and she hadn't finished. She still had the downstairs
bathroom to do, and she needed to vacuum the hall again.
George liked the pile on the carpet to lie the same way, like
a cricket pitch. That kind of thing made George happy. And
if he was happy with the house then he might be more
agreeable about her going out with her sister tonight. But
then it had been George himself who had suggested that
Valerie stay over, as she was in Glasgow anyway. He had
even given her some money to treat Valerie to dinner before
the theatre and that was a first.

It would be nice, like old times for the two of them.
Abigail felt a bit guilty about not getting the housework
done but instead, with the light dying, she stood at the
window and looked past the monkey puzzle tree that dominated the garden, down the avenue, scrutinizing the houses,
watching the sky change colour from blue to grey to black,
the dark clouds rolling in. She liked watching the goings on
in the street but was always careful to retreat behind the
curtain when anybody looked up. Abigail couldn't recall the
last time she had spoken to somebody in a non-professional
capacity, either 'That'll be four pounds twenty please,' or
'Can I have a line for another two weeks' but tonight she
could talk to Valerie, sisters together.

She had texted Mary-Jane to see if she wanted to come
along but there was no response. There never was. Her daughter
hadn't visited them for months now; she didn't get on too well
with her stepdad. There was no animosity. They just didn't
gel like a family. Abigail wondered, sometimes, where she
was, the older one. Always somewhere else. Like wee Malcolm
after school or at the weekend always somewhere better than
here. When Malcolm eventually returned, he'd refuse his tea
as he had 'already eaten'. Then he'd go upstairs and not be
seen until the next morning. So, she didn't cook for him
anymore. George said she shouldn't waste her time and money
cooking food that Malcolm wasn't going to eat. The boy kept
his bedroom door closed and left his bedclothes on the kitchen
floor on a Monday, his laundry basket outside his bedroom
door on a Friday. Each morning he took a pint of milk from
the fridge and wound his way down the avenue, waving at

Mrs Sinclair from number nine. Sometimes he met up with the man at number four. Abigail didn't know the tall, skinny man's name but thought he was the dad of the wee baby in the dark blue pram.

They had gone to the last parents' night. Abigail had sat clutching her handbag to her chest as George did all the talking, chatting away with relaxed eloquence as she had sat tongue-tied, wondering who this child was, this young man they talked about. He was bright, Malcolm, they said. He had a future. He could go to university.

Just like his mum with her medical degree. Just like Aunt Valerie with her law degree. The words had floated through Abigail's mind but she had remained quiet. Malcolm wanted to study engineering. Not law. Not medicine. What good had her degree done her, leaving her too scared to cross her own front door step.

Her husband had nodded in encouragement, taking some pride in his offspring. That might last until they got home. He certainly had no interest in Abigail's career, forcing her to cut her clinics until, like now, she was hardly working at all. And he had no interest in Mary-Jane and her dreams of being a singer. She would never make it, head up in the clouds, full of empty ambition. And maybe if Malcolm belonged to another family, a family that fed him, that saw to his haircut and his dinner money. Maybe if he had a father who would give him a laptop to type on, a printer to produce his essays, yes maybe he would make it to university.

But his dad wouldn't. Not George.

Abigail glanced back at the clock. Malcolm would not be home for a while yet. She was surprised he had stayed in school the way he had been coughing and spluttering that morning. She hoped he was OK, feeling a little better. She missed him. Even when he was upstairs, locked in his room, she could hear him moving around, the odd floorboard squeak and when she was allowed upstairs she would go and lean her head against the door, not really listening, but hearing his movements all the same, sensing that there was somebody alive in this bloody house. Malcolm could still make her smile. Sometimes, on one of her bad days, he would make her a cup of tea and bring it to her in bed. On Mother's Day, he had made her up a tray with a few colourful weeds out the garden, stuck in an old jam jar. There had been scrambled egg with lots of eggshell in it, and a napkin folded into a swan. She had kept that, for a while, under her pillow, unfolding it as far as she dared before she couldn't get it folded back up again. Then George had found it and threw it in the fire.

She looked at the clock again, rubbing her arm to ease her bruises. The anniversary clock on the mantelpiece was going on for six. George might be back soon, she had better get a move on and get the carpet vacuumed before Valerie arrived. She hated that clock and its perfect time keeping. Its message was always the same; that was another day of her life she wasn't going to get back.

It was getting dark, the rain shortening the day. It might have been her mood, but she felt daylight had somehow escaped her today. She wondered where Malcolm was. When was he coming home to confront her with those black empty eyes that so reminded her of George. He was so like his dad. Too like his dad.

Mary-Jane was lucky, she had grown up and slipped out of her stepdad's shadow before he had time to notice. But Malcolm was stuck. And at night, as she stared at the ceiling worrying about the man who shared her bed, she worried that her son might not be allowed to grow up at all.

The system had been updated with Gillian Witherspoon's number. Before driving out to the house, Colin Anderson had already read the notes of DCI Lennard, who Anderson did not know personally but he admired the man's style. The update was comprehensive and personal with paragraphs detailing the passing of Gillian's mother, her remarriage and the acquisition of a stepson to her own family of two boys. Anderson did a quick calculation. Her own boys would be in their early twenties now, her stepson about fourteen or so. Gillian had been his mother for most of his young life.

She now lived in a semi-detached in a quiet estate in Cardonald. He could have phoned first but a footnote on the file said that a cold call would be better, not giving her time to fret, which sounded to Anderson more like they were giving her no chance to reject the meeting.

It looked like he was in luck and there was somebody at home. Anderson saw the Corsa in the driveway. He walked up the path, seeing the backs of greeting cards, a series of white rectangles standing to attention on the windowsill.

The door opened at his knock, a young woman answered, looking like she had a cold, eyes red and running, a handkerchief jammed to her nose.

'Hello?' she sniffed.

'Hi.' He was wrong-footed, no idea who this woman was. 'Hi, I am looking for Gillian, if I could have a quick word?'

She stared at him, her little buck teeth opened, the hanky went up to her nose, and she slowly shut her eyes. And she closed the door on him.

He placed his finger against it. It had shut firm. So not simply away to get Gillian. He stepped back, casually looking in the window, trying to see if Gillian was going to appear, maybe curious about her unexpected visitor.

The door flew open again, an older man. Her husband? He was small and powerfully built, not somebody to be messed with.

'And what do you want?' His words were clipped by anger.

Anderson realized he had landed right in the middle of something. 'I would like a quiet word with Gillian please. Witherspoon was her maiden name, I know she has remarried.' He stood on the step with his sincere face on, hoping that his hint about the time that had lapsed might get his message across without him having to spell it out. He was not going to break Gillian's confidence.

'And who are you?'

'My name is Colin Anderson, though that might mean nothing to her.' He conceded.

'What do you want to speak to her about?' The brown eyes bored into his, searching.

'It's a personal call just to see how she was doing.' He again hoped that was enough, without going into detail.

'Not much of a personal call if she wouldn't know your name.'

'She'd know Bobby Lennard.' That got a reaction, a slight
withdrawal of the head. 'And who are you?' asked Anderson
pleasantly, looking at the bright white shirt, thrown into contrast
by the plain black tie.

Oh shit.

Anderson recognized the hint of resignation on the other's
face, so he kept his own voice polite and engaging as he lifted
his warrant card keeping it shielded by his palm, aware that
there were people behind the door listening, peering out the
window, watching.

The man closed his eyes and sighed, pulled his hand
over his face then reached back closing the living-room door
behind him so nobody else could overhear. Anderson noticed
the three people staring out the window were all dressed in
black.

'Could you come upstairs for a minute?' The man stood
back, backhanding a lock of grey hair from a furrowed brow.
He gestured to the steep internal set of stairs, resplendent
in a plush dark-red carpet. The downstairs hall was covered in
boxes, some open, some taped up, some with clothes piled up
on top of them. Women's clothes.

Were they moving out?

As he went up the stairs, one foot in front of the other,
thoughts darted into his head with every tread. The cars parked
outside. The cards on the window ledge. The red-rimmed eyes.
The gathering in the downstairs room. Why Gillian herself
was still to come to the door.

The black tie.

Black.

Shit. Talk about bad timing.

He had come at a very bad time.

Gillian had a father, who would now be an elderly man
and might now be lying in a wooden box in the room
downstairs.

'I am so sorry. I now realize that this is a very difficult
time to call. I apologize,' Anderson said when he stepped
onto the tiny landing, noting the small nest of tables. The
top was covered with a silver framed photograph of Gillian
and a younger version of the man now following him up the

stairs. She held a small posy of flowers in front of her light-blue dress, a matching group of flowers nestled in her dark hair.

'You have no idea how bad your timing is,' said the man. 'I'm Gerry. Gerry Stewart. Gillian's husband.'

'Glad to meet you.'

'I'm afraid your journey has been in vain.'

Anderson stepped through into the bedroom, noticing another photograph of Gillian on the pillow, only one half of the bed had been slept in.

The two men looked at each other. Gerry's eyes started to well up.

Shit. Shit. Shit.

'I am so, so sorry.' Anderson felt like a total bastard.

'Not your fault. She told me that she was expecting a review of . . . the incident. She spent her life waiting for that knock on the door.'

'I hope we were never intrusive.'

Gerry shook his head. 'No. No. She never thought that. She wanted the bastard caught. Not got him yet though, have you?'

Gerry sat down on the bed, Anderson leaned against the windowsill. The hopper was open slightly, the cool draft making him realize how stifling the bedroom was. They remained in total silence for a few seconds making the sound of approaching footsteps immediately apparent. There was a quick knock at the door before it opened.

'You OK, Gerry?' The slightly older one asked.

Not his son then. Anderson could see the resemblance, these were Gillian's boys.

'Yeah. I was telling Mr Anderson here what a great woman your mum was.'

'I am sorry, I had no idea . . .' said Anderson, not bringing himself to say that he was sorry for their loss, it had always sounded so trite.

'Looks like there was someone we forgot to tell. So, thank you for coming, Mr Anderson, I think you can update your records now. Gillian passed away last week. Monday it was.' He glanced at his stepsons for confirmation. 'Seems a lifetime ago.'

'I'm so, so sorry. I have been there. I know what you are

going through, time seems to slow down to the point of standing still. She couldn't have been that old?'

'She was 45. We were about to go to Dublin for her birthday but she was having an operation and died while under the anaesthetic. Routine, they said, but she never woke up.' He shook his head. 'Never had a chance to say goodbye.' He dropped his head into his hands, Anderson placed his own hands on the man's shoulder.

'I'll leave you to your mourning. I never met her but she seemed a fine woman.'

Gerry's hand slipped over Anderson's, a rough hand, calloused with the hard skin of one who knew manual work. 'You have no idea how strong she was.'

Anderson thought of Helena, riddled with cancer, stepping in front of Claire on a dark rainy beach, sacrificing herself to save his daughter. He too had known strong women.

TWO

Costello trudged up the stairs to her flat, trying to avoid disturbing her next-door neighbour. Mrs Craig, a lovely little lady, was recently widowed and had taken on the social grace of a huntsman spider, jumping out at anybody who happened to cross the landing. Costello was fit enough to use the stairs, but God help anybody who was caught waiting for the lift. If lucky, she got away with a five-minute chit-chat on the weather, if not there could be a summons to tea and biscuits and a request for a lift to the doctors or assistance with a light bulb that needed changing. *I know you are busy dear, aren't all the young people today, but it won't take a moment.*

Costello would always knock first thing to make sure that she was OK, and pick up a shopping list, and put it through the door of whoever was going shopping that day. The good thing about senior citizens was they were creatures of habit. Mr Simons downstairs drove Mrs Craig to her appointments and Mrs Armstrong from the single end flat on the landing did the evening gossip with digestives and soap operas.

It was going on for six, not Costello's duty, so she snaked past on tiptoe, looking forward to her shower and her pot of tea. She shouldered the door open, turning the key in the lock as quietly as possible, then slid inside, kicking her boots off and padding her way into the kitchen, wondering when it had turned into a bombsite. She had hardly been home in the last two weeks, so who had left all these empty tins of beans and breadcrumbs sprinkled all over the worktop? She scooped them into the bin, opened a few cupboards and found only a half empty jar of jam, mouldy, and a packet of cream crackers that had gone soft. She filled the kettle and then walked wearily into the bathroom. She had turned the shower on and taken out the pearl earrings she wore to work when she heard her mobile. A colleague she presumed, wanting a chat about the

Kissel case. She ignored it, flicking her fingers in the stream of water from the shower testing the temperature, thinking about watching *The Walking Dead*. She'd get halfway through one episode then fall asleep. She'd had enough death and desperation for one week.

As soon as her mobile fell silent, her landline started.

She walked barefooted back into the hall, leaning her forehead against the mirror as she answered the phone.

She listened for a minute, two minutes, then closed her eyes.

She uttered two words.

'Why me?'

DI Costello parked the Fiat behind the squad car, and pulled on her woollen hat and her heavy jacket that made her look two stone heavier, even though the rain was starting to ease. Strange. No scene of crime, all very low key. A small row of shops in Waterside, outside Lenzie, a posh sleepy village on the outskirts of Glasgow to the north and east, well known for a very good school and little else.

When the two cops on duty saw her, they pointed her down the narrow road to the side of the row of shops.

The older one approached.

'DI Costello, called out from Govan. What's happened? Child abduction?'

'Constables Kenny Prior, Donny McCaffrey.' He introduced himself and his colleague, rainwater dripping off his hat as he nodded. 'Child abduction after a fashion. Roberta Chisholm was driving around trying to get her wee kid to go to sleep.'

'Sholto,' added the younger one, McCaffrey, who looked as though he might be old enough to cross the road on his own. 'He'd been screaming the place down for hours, difficult baby, six weeks old. Hence the drive around.'

Costello nodded. McCaffrey looked empathetic. She judged that he was talking from experience. 'And?' She sensed more she didn't want to hear but wished they would get a bloody move on. Time was not the investigator's friend in child abduction.

McCaffrey continued, 'Well, the husband phones and says

he has landed the dream job, and the wife pulls up here to buy a bottle of bubbly . . .'

'And leaves the baby in the car?' Costello pulled her hat down over her sticky, dirty hair, marvelling at the stupidity of people. 'She comes out the shop, baby has gone.'

'Well, yes.'

Costello took a deep breath.

'And another baby left in its place.'

'OK,' said Costello, 'wasn't expecting that.'

'She left the car, a Dacia Duster, right there.' He pointed to where Costello's Fiat was now sitting. 'It's easily in view of the shop.' The windows were largely uncluttered between the hanging hams and strings of garlic.

'And when was this?'

'Back of five, the credit card machine said five eleven. It was still daylight but overcast.'

She looked at her own watch. Forty-five, fifty minutes ago. 'Cordon?'

'It's set up, got that up in ten minutes but we are only looking for the baby. The Duster was found immediately up that access road, it goes round to the car park. The local guys were on the scene straight away.'

'OK,' said Costello slowly, 'the Duster was found round there. But they had taken the Chisholm baby and left another.'

'Sholto, his name is Sholto,' corrected the younger officer, his face grave. 'And yes they left another baby in his place.'

Costello let out a long, slow breath. 'Jesus. Are we sure it's not her baby? Has she suffered some mental health issue?'

'The baby that was left is Down's Syndrome.'

'And Sholto is not Down's?'

'No, he's not.'

'Who calls their kid Sholto anyway? Bloody hell.' As she spoke she walked up to the corner, approaching the car, a Duster, the tiny car cot still clipped on the front passenger seat, facing backwards. It wasn't an easy get out. She could count four straps, four clips to a complicated buckle, on the first glance. 'Do we have confirmation he's not Down's?'

'The husband confirmed it,' said the older cop, walking in her footsteps.

'OK, we'll check the medical records anyway.' She stood back, as the young cop played his torch over the vehicle, pointing to where the mother, Roberta Chisholm had parked it then walked into the shop.

'She knows the guy who owns the place. They were both keeping an eye out, you know, watching the car.'

'Well, obviously they weren't,' yawned Costello, too tired to stop it. She walked towards the actual abduction site, listening to the story of the drama unfolding. She could have filled in the blanks herself. Roberta leaving the shop and starting to scream blue murder. She had, she thought, left the keys in the ignition, but she was so tired she couldn't recall. The Duster had automatic cut out, and automatic start up when the accelerator was tapped. Costello looked at the dark pavement still glistening from the rain, the orange glow from the street lamps. It looked so peaceful.

Nobody would hear a thing. But there was a report from an eyewitness who saw a man in an anorak, hood up, moving the car. She had presumed that he was putting the baby in it. Costello felt her spirits lift until she learned that the witness, Angela Carstairs, was seventy-eight years old. In this weather, at that age, there would be a suggestion of gender bias. If Angela had seen Costello standing here in her bulky jacket, flat boots and trousers, Carstairs would have presumed that she too, was male. But the old dear did say that the man did not come out from the back of the shops again on foot, so he must have had his own car waiting there. Costello thought for a moment. They might need to check the old biddy's eyesight.

She looked up, wishing she was back at her flat, standing under the shower instead of under this dark and rumbling sky. The dank, rich smell of autumn had given way to an aching chill in the air. She was cold. 'Once she has calmed down a bit, go and see her and check her eyesight, make sure she had her specs on.'

She waited until they wrote it down then asked where Roberta Chisholm was now.

'I sent the wee guy off to A and E to get checked over, he was coughing pretty badly. Mrs Chisholm looked shattered so we sent her as well. I expect they will just check her out and send her home.'

Costello nodded, thinking about some poor woman losing the plot after having a Down's child, a child that then got sick. God knows what she could be going through with hormones raging all over the place. She shouldn't be too difficult to track down though, a minor psychosis after delivering a disabled child. What went through her mind when she saw a perfect woman with a perfect child, and the perfect opportunity to take the child in some belief that a swap would make her life complete again.

She checked the house-to-house was underway around the village of Westerton and the Chisholm's exact address in the small development at the back of the shops. The house-to-house team had been detailed to ask subtly about any newborns in the area. She glanced at her watch. 'Can somebody give me an update at eight? Who's in charge here?'

PC McCaffrey shot a sidelong look at Prior, shuffling his boots nervously, making waves in the puddles. 'We were told you were.'

'Really?'

They stood in front of her. It began to rain again and she realized they were waiting for instructions. 'OK, so let's get the Chisholm's life under a microscope for me? See what you can get by eight?' And they walked off, McCaffrey with a spring in his step, Prior moving like he was walking to his own execution.

Anderson felt like a total bastard. He knew it was a stupid, knee-jerk reaction, not even under his control but he had made Gerry Stewart a promise that he would bring Gillian's rapist to justice, hence why he was back in the station, sitting in the quiet office looking through the case again, trawling through the same notes that many others had read before him, trying not to come to exactly the same dead-end conclusion. He agreed Gillian had not known her attacker, and rapists of strangers tend to be serial offenders. And serial offenders are exactly that. So, he had struck again? Of course, he had. If the evidence wasn't in this file, maybe it was in another. Two would be a coincidence, three made a pattern. All he needed was a suggestion of similarities between the attacks, a hint of consistency in the pattern then he could argue to have similar rapes reviewed. Computers nowadays could pick up even the slightest commonality as long as you knew what you were looking for.

At his desk, he typed up the notes and updated them, then put a request in for the sexual crime database to be searched. Gillian might have passed away, but her case would not die with her.

Wanting a break, he nipped out onto the stairs, thinking about going to the loo and hiding there for ten minutes. He strode along the corridor, head down, face tight in concentration, looking like a man with a mission.

'Colin, just the man I was looking for.' Mitchum, Assistant Commissioner of Crime, guided him to the side of the corridor, waiting until a couple of uniforms went past. 'How are you finding life at the cold case review team?'

The question was asking for reassurance not honesty. 'I think it will take time to settle in,' he said tactfully. 'We seem to move bits of paper about most of the time.'

The ACC gave him a conciliatory smile. 'We were a bit worried that . . . that there might not be enough danger in it for you. Then I remembered your PTSD and thought you would be glad of a quiet life. You are a danger magnet but at least you haven't sued us for failing in our duty of care.'

'Yet.' Anderson smiled.

'However, we are aware that we have a responsibility to keep you out of trouble, as it seems to be rather good at finding you. To be frank, Colin, I am giving you the heads up, off the record. You will be pulled into a meeting tomorrow.'

'Not another cold case review?'

'It is. After a fashion. We are under pressure. The sentencing of that sex offender last week? We need to be seen to do something about that.'

Anderson recalled his own anger when he had heard about the lenient sentence given out for a sexual assault. He could see the quote in his mind's eye: *'Miss C's skirt was too short, she was too drunk, she had been partly responsible for the assault upon her person.*' Anderson could sense that a can of worms was about to be opened and couldn't help himself. 'To be seen doing something? Rather than actually do it?'

'Look, you are reviewing the Gillian Witherspoon case. Can you sound her out for becoming a voice, a face for those who have been victims of sexual assault, heading up a media campaign to—'

'She's dead,' Anderson said bluntly.

'Oh shit.' The words were out before the ACC could stop them. 'Shit, shit, shit.'

'I'm sure she was more than a bit pissed off about it herself. It was totally unexpected.'

'Sorry, we had her tagged to approach about the SafeLife initiative, we just need a face for the campaign.'

'There are plenty of them unfortunately, sir. Miss C for one. I'm sure she'd waive her anonymity in anger.'

'No, we need one that will—'

'—tow the party line?'

'You know as well as I do, that it's not all down to us. We need the public, police and the fiscal's office to all pull together on this one, but that isn't going to happen. Therefore, we are left with making sure that our garden is clean, all clean and tidy. We need to respond to Miss C's rape and this ridiculous short sentence with a strong, empathetic voice and we had earmarked Gillian Witherspoon for that. She had a kind of mumsy appeal.' He raised an eyebrow, inviting Anderson to come up with a plan B.

'And how popular did you think that was going to be? Sir,' he added. 'Compare Miss C's rape with Gillian's.' Anderson resisted the urge to poke his finger right in the ACC's shiny buttons. 'Gillian was dragged across a car park with a rope round her throat. He dislocated her shoulder and punched her so hard he ruptured her spleen. She bled so much internally, they had to pump twelve pints of blood into her – all because she had nipped out to buy a pint of milk. Miss C was drunk, hanging around outside the pub and she went home with the man who raped her. She consented and then changed her mind. I know she has the right to do that. She was not "asking for it" but if you put them both in the hands of the media you

will get much more sympathy for the Gillians of this world
than you will ever get for the Miss C's. It might even create
a bit of hostility. Yes, they are both tragic, but they are not
the same.'

Mitchum nodded. 'I know, remember the fiasco of the Stay
Sober initiative. Not too difficult, you would think, in this
day and age of the nominated driver, for one person to stay
sober and look after the others but all it did was produce a
backlash.'

'We were condoning the evil of men.'

'We can't help it if people don't want to know the truth.
All stupid people do is hand the power to the predators among
us. You know that better than any of us. We'd better get back
to the drawing board. The meeting tomorrow will still be on.
I shall have to think of something else.' The ACC nodded to
him in dismissal and walked off down the corridor, his shiny
shoes clipping on the lino.

Colin Anderson was having a cup of coffee, sitting on his
favourite spot on the sofa, trying to read Garcia Marquez but
still thinking about the ACC and his new campaign and Gillian
Witherspoon. There was a knock at the front door and he
looked up, wondering when his house had become a hotel.
Nesbit was curled up at his feet, snoring softly and preventing
his owner from standing up, so Anderson was still sitting,
paperback in hand, when he heard the usual thump of Doc
Martin's on the stair carpet and a shout of 'I'll get it.'

Claire.

As usual she was dressed in black, in a skirt so short it
wasn't worth wearing and thick, black tights covering her long
slender legs that had made her the butt of teasing at school,
but which now signalled her metamorphosis into the kind of
girl that turned men's heads.

Anderson had no real idea when that had happened.

He heard the front door open, a muffle of conversation and
then Claire shouting, 'It's only David.'

It was always 'only David'. For Anderson, the father, 'the
boyfriend' was new territory. Was he supposed to stick
his head out the door and ask David in for a coffee, small

chit-chat that avoided the question, 'Are your intentions honourable?' Anderson knew his daughter better than that, and yet suspected they weren't doing anything that he didn't do himself at that age. Which was cold comfort.

And this house didn't lend itself to casual intervention. The living room was too big for a start, there was no incidental meeting at the bottom of the stairs, no way he could leave the door open and call the boy in without it appearing the summons that it was. So he sat there, impotent, listening to the quiet thump of Claire's feet and the painfully slow step of David. There was a blast of music as the bedroom door opened, abruptly silenced as it closed over again.

Maybe more prudent to leave them to it. David was still carrying the scars of a terrible and violent crime. The perpetrator was in Carstairs for the criminally insane, pronounced unfit to face trial. Detained under The Mental Health Act, he was locked up for much longer than they ever would be at Her Majesty's Pleasure. It was not the easy way out, there was no defined tariff which meant they could stay there, locked up for the rest of their life and nobody would bat an eyelid. But the fact remained, David was the victim of extreme violence borne of a deranged mind. Apart from that, he was everything that Anderson would want in a boyfriend for his daughter. But he still wished they weren't upstairs on their own. When Colin had mentioned it to Brenda, she had drawn him one of her 'well she lives with you' looks. Mum and daughter spoke, they went shopping and had lunch. Surely Brenda and Claire must have spoken about 'that stuff'. Colin thought that David Kerr was a lovely young man, kind, intelligent, obviously thought the world of Claire, but if he laid a hand on her, Colin would have him up against a wall by his throat and the boy would be singing falsetto in a Bee Gee's tribute band.

He picked up his mobile. Brenda would know what to do. She was a mum, it was in her job description. There was no answer, no opportunity to leave a message. The last time he had tried, it had been turned off. He dialled the landline but instead of voicemail, Peter answered, his voice full of 'just got out of bed' teenage enthusiasm. Colin managed to extract a little information from him, a few statements about school, homework and his upcoming work experience. After that conversation had run its brief course, Colin asked if 'mum' was in. Peter's answer was short and sweet. 'No.'

He didn't elucidate. No mention of where she was and when she would be home. So he left it.

Colin slipped back into the chair and went back to *Love in the Time of Cholera*, trying to enjoy it. He had some stats to look at for an early meeting tomorrow, and the outline of a development report to write to lend support to his opinion about the way money was being spent in the cold case unit. He needed to affirm that cold cases should be selected by the scientific support staff like Mathilda McQueen, those cases where there was a little bit of tissue evidence or a DNA stain, where science might have caught up and it took an expert to recognize what might be useful. But everybody had an agenda. Usually on someone else's budget.

And there was the knock-on effect of Gillian Witherspoon's passing and that meeting to look forward to.

He came out in a cold sweat when he thought of the way he had knocked her door, intruding on the grief of that family. Police Scotland had had their pound of flesh from him this week, and tomorrow looked like death by spreadsheet. He felt like he was the only one who did the job for the right reasons nowadays.

There was another burst of music as the bedroom door opened, more clattering of swift feet on the stairs, so that would be Claire going downstairs to the kitchen for a beer for David. Claire was very sweet natured and supportive – a word she used a lot – but Colin was sure David would get through his trauma with or without her. The boy had emotional and familial resources, an adoring mother, his estranged father was back on the scene. He enjoyed a wide network of friends, a good brain and career prospects. To be fair, Claire had been just as kind to the other youngster caught up in that horror. Paige Riley. The Paiges of the world usually slipped through the net but she and Claire had struck up some kind of bond. Claire had explained to her dad, with all the patience of a teenager to a stupid parent, that she knew she couldn't help them all. But she knew Paige and she could help Paige. Well, her dad could help Paige. He had money. It had been hard to argue and Colin had felt rather proud of his daughter and her passion for helping a girl who had not benefitted from all that Claire took for granted. Paige had been abducted and held captive for weeks. The only person who had noticed she was missing was the woman who put a pound coin in her begging bowl every day. Even now, the file had no precise date as to when Paige was actually snatched from the street.

Anderson got into a panic if Claire was half an hour late.

So, Colin Anderson and his socially conscious daughter had come to an agreement. Paige was to become David's carer, accompanying him to uni, carrying books, his laptop and helping out when Claire or his mother couldn't. Anderson paid her a wage so long as she stayed clean; one whiff of heroin, any return of her habit and she'd be out on her ear. He had taken her to one side and told her that in a language she had understood. He had then pulled strings to get her put up in a decent halfway house run by a priest he knew well. Anderson was aware he was conducting a social experiment. Paige was removed from her old friends, taken out of her environment and placed in another where she was made to feel welcome. And useful. Paige had had her moments but overall, she was doing OK. The priest said she was now thinking about going back to college. It had been her idea. Claire had asked her dad if he would give her an allowance to help her through college. He said he'd think about it, recalling that quote about saving a life and then being responsible for everything that life did. The last time he had set eyes on her, Paige had stood, rake thin staring at him with eyes that burned with distrust and abuse. It was all she knew from every man she had ever met. He had smiled, said hello and walked on as if he hadn't noticed.

But he had the money. Funny how it had always been an issue, Brenda and him as newlyweds, struggling to pay a heavy mortgage. Now he had inherited loads of it and seemed to be getting more and more with every day that passed. He knew nothing about art as commercial value; a painting was a picture that sat on a wall and you looked at it. Either you liked it or you didn't. What he didn't know was that Helena had rented out much of her work and it was becoming more and more in demand now she had passed on.

Oh, it was a very nice position to be in, another sip of instant coffee. That was symbolic of the issue. He still couldn't work out how to get a good cup out of the state-of-the-art black mega vanilla steamer hot squirt device that sat in the corner of his kitchen. It seemed to behave for other folk, but not him. He was instant coffee and Greggs, not fancy dancy decaff mulberry flavour shite with more stuff on it than a John Lewis Christmas tree.

He felt that this one, this life he was living now, was not his somehow. He had been derailed into a life of good suits and endless meetings with wankers like Stu and Bruce. He was now valued in Police Scotland as some kind of adviser as he had 'been there', 'done that' and had the mental health reports to prove it. He was not old enough to be shifted into retirement, and he suspected that his history of PTSD simply made him an asset, allowing his bosses to show they were considerate to their colleagues injured in the line of duty.

His trouble was, having seen it all and done it all, he wanted to see and do it all again. And soon, before he got soft and rotted away into this lovely sofa and started cutting his crusts off and eating goat's cheese. He was one step away from tasting wine before he drank it and using a napkin. It would be quinoa next.

He needed to get back in touch. He scrolled down his mobile, thinking about texting Costello, getting her opinion on this media thing.

Costello had an opinion on everything.

DI Costello was cold and hungry by the time she was waving her warrant card at the hospital reception and had been told to take a seat like everybody else. In the emergency department waiting area there were a few pale-looking kids, two adults holding towels to various bleeding parts of their anatomy and three drunks arguing about Glasgow Rangers and Theresa May, as if they were in some way connected.

Costello sat in a plastic chair bolted to the floor, glad to have a rest, and watched the Sky evening newsfeed on the overhead screen. The Kissel conviction had not made the national news, thanks to Brexit and a supermodel falling over. That wee kid didn't even warrant a few words on the rolling commentary across the bottom.

She wondered if Anderson had read it. Was he taking an interest? Did she really want him dissecting her case, making sure that any chance of an appeal would be squashed, ensuring she left no way in for an inventive defence council? She wondered where the old gang were now. Anderson living up in his posh house, and working in a nine to five. Mulholland stuck in his desk-bound job by default due to his leg injury. Some weird kind of fracture he had that had formed a cyst in the bone. Was he still convinced that he was Johnny Depp's better looking younger brother? She wondered if he had undergone another leg operation. It had seemed so simple at the time, a fall from a stone not a foot from the ground yet it threatened to end his career. In new Police Scotland, if you weren't fit, you were out. But then, just as one of the drunks, the one with blood all over his face, demonstrated how to take a penalty, she recalled a rumour he had been transferred to some intel unit that was so hush hush nobody knew anything about it. Although she didn't put it past him to be the source of that rumour, to add a touch of glamour to what was a job involving sitting on his arse and typing. She hoped that Wyngate was with him, they worked well together and Wyngate lacked the streak of meanness needed to be a really good detective. But give him a computer . . .

One drunk was now doing the rounds of his captive audience, asking if they had any spare change.

She looked at her watch. This baby abduction was going to take a lot of legwork, Roberta and James Chisholm's lives were being pulled apart as she sat here. That baby had been targeted, she was sure of it. She wasn't so sure of Prior and McCaffrey, especially Prior. Still in uniform and out on the street at his age showed a remarkable ability to avoid promotion. She could do with the technical support of Wyngate and Mulholland.

After collecting a cup of hot tarry tea from the machine,

she enquired at the desk if they had any idea how long it was going to be. Flashing her warrant card again only got her a bad tempered 'Can you not see I am busy?' Costello closed her warrant card wallet slowly, looking long enough at the nurse's face to let her know her features and her name were being mentally noted. Busy was one thing, rudeness was something else.

Costello settled down with a cup of sticky tea and a notebook, aware of the staff at the desk talking about her. One sharp look at the words 'snotty' and 'bitch' silenced them. She had very good hearing.

This baby abduction case was falling apart before it had got going. She didn't know how she was supposed to work it. Nobody official had told her that Roberta was still here. That had only come to light on her visit to the neat, brand new, three-bedroomed detached sitting in the cul de sac at the end of Westerton Farm Lane. Despite the Duster in the driveway, she noted the darkness of the property before she had got out of her car. No lights on, no police cars, no sign of anybody. She had called in again, thinking that Sholto had been found but was told no. Had Roberta gone back to her mum's for some emotional support? Costello was still in the car waiting for Govan to get back to her with an update when the cop's gift appeared: the nosey neighbour.

Costello got out of her Fiat, encouraged that the woman in the flowery pyjamas and thick fluffy housecoat might know something. Bobby, Roberta, she had corrected herself was still at the hospital. Had Costello any news, nothing as yet she assured her but took the chance to ask if there were any other young babies in this estate, less than a year old? There were not.

That would have been too easy.

Costello then wondered why the house-to-house had not contacted her yet. She'd ask that young cop McCaffrey when she saw him. He had sounded bright enough to spell his name properly, which she couldn't say about many of the new recruits who went home at five p.m. on the dot and complained about the pension scheme.

Fifteen minutes after she had finished her tea, she was still sitting in the waiting area having remonstrated with the drunks for annoying the queue. Then she started arguing with the desk staff. Then she decided on blatant queue jumping. Costello eventually wound her way round to the treatment area of the A and E and was walking up and down until a voice asked if she was looking for him.

It was McCaffrey, sitting on a padded blue chair with his back to the wall, playing solitaire on his phone. She mouthed hello before pulling back the plastic curtains by an inch and glancing into the cubicle; two nurses, a baby tucked under a blue blanket with a drip that wound down to his tiny chubby shin, tiny pads of a heart monitor taped on the visible portion of his chest. A woman with bad skin was lying on the bed, her forefinger looped around the baby's elbow while a smartly-dressed man stood to one side, an island of calm in a sea of chaotic efficiency. Costello registered the child's shallow epicanthic fold, the big forehead. She withdrew, sensing her relief. They had traced the mum, she would get looked after. Nothing here that needed her attention right now and she could go home and have a shower, climb into bed and sleep the sleep of the righteous. She turned and sat beside the constable, wondering if she could take her shoes off and give her feet a massage, her soles were burning. She didn't think she could make it all the way back to the car, it was parked miles away.

'We meet again.'

'How long have you been waiting here for?'

'Long enough, I've been waiting for somebody to come here and relieve me, I didn't think I could leave, you know. Got kind of involved with it all.'

Costello waved her hand. 'Oh, there's nothing wrong with that, but you can go now. The mum's here so as long as everybody is safe and well, the paperwork can wait. Who is she? What's her story?'

McCaffrey stood up, and rolled his shoulders, then cleared his throat. 'That's not the mum, that's Roberta Chisholm. She's here because the wee guy has a chest infection. She "needed" to be here.'

That explained the man's detachment. It wasn't his child.

'At least he's in the best place.' She pulled out her notebook, sitting with pen poised. 'But why is Roberta in there, doing all that? That's not their kid. What's happening with Sholto? And where is that baby's real mother? Uniform haven't even called at the Chisholm's neighbours yet.'

'They said they were short-staffed.'

'Christ.'

'Road blocks up but I'm not sure with all those fields and back roads it will do much use.' He lowered his voice. 'Nothing has come back to me yet.'

'Let me know as soon as it does. How is that wee guy? It's not serious, is it?'

'I've called him Moses, you know . . . out the—'

'Yeah, I know the story . . .'

'His body weight is low, he's only five weeks, still vulnerable.'

'Any sign of abuse?'

He shook his head. 'No, he seems very well cared for. I thought he was coughing too much, going a bit blue round the gills so sent him here. They are waiting for a bed in paediatrics, and the paediatrician to have a look at him. We have been waiting a while, no surprise.' He moved into the side of the corridor, indicating that Costello should follow. 'You know, my wife was a mess after the second baby. Neither up nor down after the first. Five weeks is a long time to bond.'

'And long enough to succumb to the psychosis of sleep deprivation.'

'Indeed. And maybe the mum was OK with that until Moses got ill and she panicked. Maybe it was one push too far. She could be an unsupported mother with no experience. So she sticks her kid on a mum who appears to be doing a better job than her. And Roberta Chisholm is fulfilling that role, cuddling and soothing that kid as if it was hers. Maybe Moses' mum knew Roberta would be like that?' He shook his head. 'It's understandable. The doc suggested we leave it for now.'

Costello was warming to this young cop. 'It might give us more time. If Sholto was lifted because he was healthy and Little Moses left because he wasn't, I don't see the abductor hurting Sholto. I need advice about the press release, can't afford to get that wrong.'

'Moses might be on the mend from the chest infection, the Down's is pretty permanent. If it was the Downs she rejected . . .'

She asked, 'Do *you* think it was a man who swapped them?'

'Maybe,' he said, but shook his head, the idea not sitting with his internal logic, 'and to mention something more weird . . . Mrs Carstairs said the man had the baby in a seat he was carrying. Like a car seat.'

Costello nodded, that would explain the quick in and out.

'And another weird thing?'

'Weirder than this?'

'I think I heard Roberta and James arguing. In fact they have done nothing but argue. She thinks the blanket round Moses is the same as Sholto's but is not his, not the actual blanket. James says she's talking crap.'

'OK,' Costello said slowly, letting the implications of that sink in.

'The blanket is in there, still round the baby.' He nodded at the cubicle. 'You might want to retrieve it as soon as you can, it's distinctive. Got lambs round the bottom.'

'You're good. You should have a future in CID.'

He smiled. 'I hope so. Do you want me to hang around? I should have been off duty an hour ago.'

'Yes, you go,' she said ignoring the protests from her feet. 'From the sound of it, your wife needs you more than I do. What age is your youngest?'

'Nathan? A year.'

'OK. Before you go, spare me a minute and give me a list of all the places your wife takes the wee one. Clinics? The yummy mummy's club? Yoga for the under twos. Baby juggling? Somebody knew Roberta, and knew the baby.'

He rattled off a list that was alarmingly long, stopping every now and again to think and then coming up with another few items, checking the calendar on his mobile. Nathan seemed to have a very hectic social life. It confirmed Costello's fear. Anybody who wanted to get near that baby could.

'And again, before you go, who is the paediatrician?'

'It's a Dr Hayman they are trying to get hold of, he's not around after hours. Dr Hogan is the guy dashing in and out the cubicle. He's good, come across him before. Been here a few times with injuries sustained falling off swings, one was breathing difficulties and one a bad donkey bite. Oh, and one broken wrist after bouncing off a trampoline. But that was the wife and doesn't really count. You got kids?'

'No. I prefer a good night's sleep. I bet you are on some social services list with that catalogue of incidents. But yeah, off you go, I'll get in touch with Hogan.'

He got up and swung his over jacket over his uniform, 'Keep me in the loop will you? I'd like to know how this pans out. I'll get back to you about . . .' He indicated those behind the curtain.

'Sure, I'm based at Govan, here's my mobile number and office email. It's the best way to contact me with my roving brief, that way you can be sure I have received it.'

She watched him go, young and enthusiastic, ready to tackle the failure of law and order. Police Scotland would soon put an end to that. She peeked through the gap in the curtain, Baby Moses was mouthing as though he had something unpleasant on his tongue, the little blue blanket gripped tight in his fist. She closed the curtain over again and sat back down to witness the comings and goings through the curtain as she slipped one shoe off.

A quarter of an hour later a large doctor, hirsute and smiling, steth swinging from his neck, strode purposefully along the corridor and entered the cubicle. Costello leaned forward, trying to listen but she could not hear.

After a few minutes, he emerged, 'Hi, I'm Drew, the baby is doing fine, we have him on some IV antibiotics.'

'How is Roberta?'

'She is very shaky, feels very guilty. I'd rather that you didn't disturb her. It's all very emotional, I'm sure you understand that.' He cupped his hand round her elbow. 'Can I have a word? I made a few enquiries as soon as I heard. There was a patient who gave birth to a disabled child five weeks ago. On the off chance I gave her a call, and she's at home with her husband, and the baby is there too. The health visitor has seen the baby, and I've asked her to check again tomorrow.'

'Thank you. Was there only one?'

'That recently, in this health board, yes. There are only two Downs born a day in the UK, it's not as common as it used to be, thanks to the tests available. And I'm not sure where my patient confidentiality issues start and end with this, but I was concerned about the mother's mental health. She was flagged on the system but I think she's a non-starter for you. But to keep things right maybe you should follow that up yourself,' he said. 'Notes can take a long time in this hospital to come online, we have a nine-month waiting list in maternity,' he joked, rather charming when he smiled, reminding Costello of some old TV programme about a giant of a man living in the wilds of Canada, who used to befriend bears.

He rubbed his beard, Costello could hear the prickling of the bristles. She wasn't the only one who looked as though a good night's sleep might be in order. 'I am more worried about Roberta than I am about the baby.'

'And how do you know them Dr . . .?'

'Everybody calls me Drew. Jimmy and I go to the same tennis club.' He shook his head. 'Have you any trace on Sholto?'

'Not yet. We need to find the woman who gave birth to that baby, and I'm sure she will be looking after Sholto just fine.' Costello smiled in what she hoped was a comforting manner. 'She saw a healthy baby and took it. I hope it is as simple as that.'

'Except Jimmy tells me it wasn't the mother who swapped them, was it? It was a man,' said the doctor.

Costello left the hospital with the keys for the Chisholm's house in the can holder on the console of the Fiat. She drove back to Waterside, back into the little estate, the neighbour flicked her window blind, still keeping an eye out and seeing that the family was not returning, she retreated. Costello let herself into the house. It was as if Roberta had just walked out, a pair of slippers at the door, two damp towels thrown on the stairs, her handbag sitting beside the two-seater sofa. The house was clean, a mismatch of style that showed two different people had set up home together. Mostly it was cluttered with the detritus of a new baby, including a huge pile of dirty washing sitting on a pink plastic basket on the

living-room floor. No doubt Roberta thought she would have
time to tidy up later, once Sholto had stopped crying. She
walked through the living room to the kitchen at the rear. On
the rack above the tumble dryer she had said. There were a
few keys, she picked out the one that was most like a car key
and two minutes later she was crouching beside the open
passenger door of the Duster, the torch on her mobile phone
focussed on the catch of the Car Easy car seat.

Roberta might be right about the blanket. Mrs Carstairs
might be right about the car seat, so she examined the clasp
that attached the cradle to the seat belt. It was scored slightly,
indented in a linear arc as if, Costello thought, it had been
adjusted while somebody had been holding a key in the same
hand. The mark did not carry over to the other part of the
clasp, leaving the score to come to an abrupt end at the junction. Carefully, she leaned over, trying not to touch anything.
The car, technically, had been impounded, but the car seat
could have very important evidence. The clasp next to the
handbrake, to the naked eye, was a perfect match, but micro-
scopic analysis would confirm the seat was newer than the
cradle it clipped on to. Not a match. This piece of information
was going to stay within the investigation. She left a note,
dated, timed and signed that she had been there and closed
up both the car and the house.

'You alright there, pet?' asked the neighbour through a
slightly open door.

'Yes thanks,' Costello replied, without looking round.

THREE

Driving home alone, Costello's thoughts drifted back to Archie and the mysterious brunette in the Porsche and got mad at the two-timing little shit. She was practising her deep breathing, forcing her fury to subside. It wasn't working. And the greatest hits of Beyoncé on the car radio wasn't making her feel any better.

She knew she wanted to be angry at something. At Roberta for leaving Sholto in the car. At Moses' mum for abandoning him. At the man, or woman, who facilitated it all. At herself, for getting involved in the case. She thought about getting angry at the long wait in the hospital corridor and the rude blonde nurse on reception, but she decided to save time and stay angry at Archie. Whatever was going on with him, the only thing different was that she had stumbled across it. It wasn't his fault that he was having lunch with a younger, smarter woman and had forgotten to mention it. But that suggested to her that she, the woman, was more likely to be a colleague. Maybe more than a colleague, but he wouldn't be up to anything, not behind her back. The brunette would be the daughter or the niece of a friend, a new graduate, a young lawyer trying to make her way in the legal world. Maybe doing some research for a case and wanted the opinion of the Chief Procurator Fiscal.

Costello told herself.

And yet rich enough to drive a Porsche?

He wasn't the type to cheat, he was an honest man. Archie was the type to have an affair only once his wife was diagnosed with Alzheimer's. And that was a different thing.

Or was it? And she didn't strictly know if that was true, she only had the lying bastard's word for it. There could have been a bus load of women before her.

Since her.

She parked the Fiat outside the deli, near her old station at

Partickhill, bouncing up on the pavement as she couldn't be
bothered walking to the car park, acknowledging that she had
criticized Roberta Chisholm for exactly the same thing. But
she didn't leave anything of value in the car. She was going
home, home to have her long shower, put on her jammys and
turn her phone off. She was going to enjoy herself with
CBS Reality, a few episodes of *Dr G* or *Killer Clergy Go Mad
On Cocaine*. If that was a true reflection of criminality in the
southern states of the USA, she was glad she worked amongst
the more usual, everyday jakey kind of Glasgow scum. Like
Bernadette Kissel.

She climbed out the car, aware of the deep itch in her scalp,
a build-up of God knows what over the last few days. She
stood at the window looking at a side of ham, lying on a bed
of slimy green lettuce as she had a good scratch, digging her
nails in until it hurt. It felt good. The anger. The pain. Fury
still bubbled inside her like a bad biryani. At least Little Moses
had been left somewhere safe. Maybe by somebody who knew
how Roberta Chisholm would react. Maybe the abductor had,
with the good but misguided intention of the not very bright,
simply gone out and got themselves a better baby. Maybe the
car seat being the same was a coincidence or maybe an igniting
factor; he saw that and thought 'that's the baby for us'.

That was still a million miles away from Bernadette Kissel
who had stood there and shrugged her shoulders when shown
the post mortem photographs of her own emaciated child.
Nothing to do with her. Her kid had faded over a period of
weeks, dropping to less than half the body weight it should
have been. The infection that ate into his skin because he never
had his nappy changed, the bruises, the broken and fractured
cartilage on one whose bones were not yet old enough to
calcify. Who knows what they had gone through? Nobody was
too young to suffer the rage, the drunkenness of others. Costello
knew that first hand.

And some believe it's only abuse if it's violent. Neglect is
as bad, she mused as a couple of teenagers walked past the
shop window behind her, their uniforms reflected in the glass,
and neglect is often unreported. It was subtle in its evil. Mental
health issues Costello could get her head round, that might be

somebody else's responsibility to intervene. But that degree of neglect because Kissel had a needle in her arm, well that was something else.

'Your own call, Bernadette, nobody else's,' Costello muttered as she regarded her own reflection. She was as tired as a Halloween ghost. She had listened to so much shite in the past few weeks she could sell it as fertiliser. All kinds of crap about trust, relationships, primary caregivers, stakeholders, core feelings and the responsibility of the caring society. By day two of the hearing Costello had realized what a dinosaur she was. She couldn't abide this 'we will get you all the support you need' crap. The only two people she felt any empathy for were the deceased, life taken before they had the chance to enjoy it, and that poor overworked social worker who would take the mental scars of her cross-examination to the grave. Linda? Laura? McGill. Lorna McGill? She'd be on the happy pills after the roasting the defence council had given her. No doubt her boss had done the same when she got back to the office, the poor lassie had scapegoat written all over her. The powerful had feasted on that girl, and they were not stupid people, not stupid 'men', she reminded herself – they knew the financial constrains the social services were under – yet they pulled Lorna McGill apart. Costello made a mental note to find out the reg of the Merc the defence council drove and get him nicked for speeding or driving while on his phone or picking his nose at the traffic lights. She had a few friends in traffic who owed her a favour.

Applewood cheese, red onion chutney. She thought, the sight of the dead pig putting her off the ham. She realized she had been standing there for a few minutes, lost in her mindset. The two school kids had disappeared round the corner of Hyndland Road.

She thought she heard the squawk of a seagull and looked around. Nothing to see. She was stepping into the shop when she thought she heard it again and stepped out, listening, waiting for a break in the traffic to hear properly. There was a something, not sure exactly what it was but twenty years of being a cop alerted her.

A something.

She stood down back on the pavement, making her way to the corner, the lane and the three wheelie bins sitting in a line, waiting for the refuse lorry. A green and white hooped top was visible in between, none too clean and not warm enough for a night like this.

'You OK?' she asked.

Anderson had intended to turn left to take Nesbit for an evening stroll round the Botanics, but he was late and they would be closed, so his feet turned right, down to the junction with Hyndland Road and the road to Partickhill Station, his old cop shop. It was a chilly, damp night, the air seemed full of the post-rain fecund scent of leaves rotting slowly in the gutter.

In the end he had got out of the house for the sake of his sanity, listening to every noise upstairs, distracted by the noise of the door opening and closing above him. The presence of Claire and David in the house, their togetherness had made him feel a bit lonely. He had never had any trouble attracting women, just the opposite in fact, so why was he on his own now? By choice? So why was it troubling him? Helena was dead. His wife was out most of the time. Costello was away with Archie. Mulholland had formed some kind of peace treaty with Elvie McCulloch, Wyngate was happily married and breeding like a little rabbit. Even Claire was pairing off. They were all with somebody else now, except him. He only had Nesbit, the faulty Staffie, a faithful and constant companion on his walk to clear his mind of the mundanely boring work, a job so tedious he had started to look forward to emails from his boss. He should have been going for walks years ago, all those difficult times when he worked like a mad man, when he grafted all the hours God sent rather than the nine to five he was trapped in now. In those days, he was so stressed he didn't eat or sleep. All that counselling and anti-anxiety medication? He would have been better taking the dog out. In those days he never had time to speak to his family. Now he had all the time in the world but had bugger all to say. And there was the sneaking sense that they were moving on while he was going backwards.

Oh yes, he was getting quite comfy with his slow strolls

round the streets and back lanes around Kirklee, or the other way if the traffic was quiet, up to the hospital, around the pond, where Nesbit could chase the ducks. At the far end of the pond it was easy to forget that the hospital was there at all, it felt a mile away from any drama. That walk was a long slow drag up a dark, tree-lined avenue. If he was feeling energetic, not a common feeling these days, Anderson would turn right off Great Western Road and then right again, for a leg punishing stroll through the up and down twisty turny streets of the big posh houses of Kirklee itself. Some deep part of his cynicism reminding him that his own house was one of the poshest of them all. There had been another offer in his inbox that morning. These properties, the ones like his that had stayed intact as three-storey townhouses, were in big demand and very rarely on the market. Most had been converted into flats and sold off or rented out. He had been offered £1.2 million. He already had enough money to do him so he didn't know what to make of that offer. He liked the house, but it wasn't his home. And he liked the money he had to be tied up in bricks and mortar. Claire and Peter were good kids but money like that could easily absolve them of the need to get out of bed in the morning. He didn't want his children to be damaged by the money he had been left. That offer in the email had been more than it had been last month. How high would they go? And did he care?

Anderson walked on, standing at the crossing. The Premier newsagents shop behind him was still open, that strange little red and brown shop standing in an island of blond sandstone, like a few Lego bricks in a house wall, too bright, too modern. Out of place, a bit like himself.

Would tomorrow be another boring day of sitting in meetings or would his chat with the ACC that afternoon spark something worthwhile rather than another knee-jerk response to a headline. The Kissel case? Or that woman killed by her husband in a dispute over *Coronation Street* where the police had been called but taken so long to attend the incident that by the time they got there it was a murder scene rather than a domestic violence report. The nine-year-old son had witnessed the murder. There had been two cases of child killing in the last three months, which the media had blamed on the lack of intervention of unspecified social services. The meeting might be about another bid by some MP or an MSP to try to get Police Scotland and the social services to work more efficiently by cutting their budgets and incarcerating them in meetings.

It would be Klingon Kirkton all over again. And that thought made him feel sick to the stomach. If he sold the house he'd never have to work again and never have to pander to arseholes like him. Who was he kidding; he didn't have to work now.

Without him noticing, his life had emptied.

What crap would he get involved in this time? He walked on, Nesbit the Staffie panting and grumping by his side, pulling on the lead whenever he scented another dog in the air. Nesbit should have been enjoying himself back at Brenda's house on the south side, lying on Peter's bed as his young master played some unfathomable computer game where he pitted his wits against aliens, assisted by an unseen partner who lived on the other side of the world. And ignoring his homework.

Peter was at that really awful teenage stage, communicating by grunts and snorts. Maybe Peter was spending too long with Nesbit? Usually Colin could talk the boy round with an offer of going to Xscape or out for a pizza, but not this time. Peter had remained monosyllabic. It had been another very short phone call.

Come to think of it, Claire had been a little quiet as well recently, not annoying him as much as she usually did. He had come to rely on her to give the big house its vibrant buzz of music and nonsense now that his own job was so boring. And why was interrupting the purvey of a funeral viewed as lifting his working life from the mundane.

And he had admitted that to himself.

Late the previous evening Anderson had left Claire and David his credit card number in case they wanted a Chinese takeaway, and he had watched some slow TV about a barge trip along the Kennet and Avon canal, a nice glass of red in one hand, Nesbit's head nestling in the other. Bored or relaxed?

He had watched two hours of that programme, seeing

nothing but the front of the boat. And the water. And more bloody water.

When was the last time he had had a good laugh? Gone out for a curry with the squad? Had a pint with some pals? Listened to Mulholland moaning about his leg, Costello sniping at Mulholland's moaning? Wyngate trying to keep the peace and changing the subject? What had happened to Wyngate in the end? God, he couldn't recall if his colleague had actually left the force or got divorced. When they last spoke, those looked like being the DC's only options.

That was bad, he'd phone him tomorrow. He might even phone Costello and get the goss on the Kissel case and any spare goss on what was going on at the fiscal's office. He found himself smiling, yes he knew where he needed to be. Back in the buzz. If the buzz would still have him. He couldn't thrive in this coffee culture, in pubs, going out on his own. And he was 'on his own'.

He walked past a beautiful three-story detached house, sitting a little high from the pavement, a crescent of a pebbled driveway cutting across the front of the two four-paned French windows and the stained-glass porch over the front door, partially obscured by a monkey puzzle tree he had always rather admired as it had seemed so at odds with the neatly trimmed row of conifers grown to cover the garage door. At the moment the door was open, a white Volvo was running, door ajar, waiting to be reversed in. The owner, a slight man in a huge woollen cardigan was bending down at the rear of the vehicle, illuminated by the security light as he examined a scratch or speck of dirt. As Colin passed he took out his handkerchief and started polishing. He looked up and caught Colin's eye. They exchanged greetings in a very West End kind of way; too polite to ignore each other all together, but resisting any real conversation. Anderson walked on, thinking what a boring git that guy must be.

And how quickly he himself was turning that way. It would be slippers and daytime TV next, Werther's Originals and the *Reader's Digest*.

Whatever the ACC offered him tomorrow, he was up for it. Disturbing people's funerals was better than this.

*   *   *

There was no answer. Costello pulled the wheelie bin out a
little and to the left, manoeuvring it gently from side to side,
wondering how many weeks it had been since this thing was
emptied. The boy sat there, on the coping stone, his tracky
bottoms five inches short of his ankles, his knees up to his
chin. The green of his Celtic top matched the snot streaming
from his nose. He had huge doe eyes, a brown mane falling
across his forehead. He looked like an angel, fallen out the
dark clouds above, to land in the bed of crisp packets behind
the bins.

'You got a cold?' Costello asked, trying for her smiley face.
'Fuck off.'

It had been a very long day. 'Oh, fuck off yourself. You're
not the only one having a shite life, you wee squirt.' She pulled
the wheelie bin back over and walked into the shop, aware of
a high-pitched sneeze behind her, sounding very much like a
seagull in distress. In her mind's eye she could see the forearm
being used as a handkerchief.

Kids.

She went into the shop, buying some extra strong Applewood
cheese, red onion chutney and tiger bread. She added a box
of man-sized tissues with balm, paid for it all and went back
out again. Pulling the wheelie bin back she saw the boy was
rubbing his nose with a fist of fingers that were blue with cold.
And dripping with snot.

'You'll be smiting everybody with a nose like that. Here.'
She handed him the box of tissues. He put his hand out, sniffed,
and took the box, ripping off the perforated flap and pulled
out a handful of hankies. His thank you was polite and automatic. He spent the next five minutes coughing and spluttering
into them. At one point Costello knelt down between the bins,
amongst the squashed beer cans and the used condoms,
thinking that the boy was going to stop breathing. He couldn't
get a breath in between the coughing fits. He was red in the
face, getting redder, tears coursing down his cheek, looking
over the back of the bins with rheumy brown eyes.

Dickens would have been proud of this urchin. Costello
wondered if kids nowadays got TB. That cough had a terrible
rattle about it.

'Where do you live? Do you want a run home? I have my car here.'

'You a paedo?'

'No,' said Costello, 'I'm a cop.'

From the look on his face he might have been happier if she had answered yes.

'You got an issue with that?'

He shook his head, but she knew. And he knew that she knew. Not him, but somebody close did have issues with the forces of law and order, like the sort of parent who was too stoned to know where their kid was at this time of night, hiding behind bins in a football top.

'Come on then, in the car, we will get you home. You should be tucked up in bed, not skulking about. What was your name?'

'Harry fucking Styles.'

'Fed up with the singing then? Fair enough.' She looked around. 'You want to try that again?'

His house was a surprise. He lived in Balcarres Avenue, which Costello only found out after she had driven him around for ten minutes with him only saying left, left and left, taking her round in circles. She then pulled back onto Great Western Road, turning towards the police station at Partickhill, threatening to leave him in the cells overnight for his own safety. As she took a right, she caught sight of a man walking along the pavement, a dark Staffie limping along behind him. The dog reminded her of Anderson's little Staffie, but she was caught up in the long line of traffic before she had the chance to check and by then he had gone.

'Harry's' house, indicated by a nod, was a beautiful detached sandstone, behind a pebbled driveway that cut across the French windows. The stained-glass porch over the front door was impressive, but not as impressive as the monkey puzzle tree in the front garden.

'Is this really your house? Bit posh, innit?' said Costello in her best cockney accent.

'It's shite,' was the boy's considered opinion.

She pulled up outside and asked the sniffling Harry Fucking Styles if he wanted her to come in with him.

The boy sneezed into his hanky and then had a good look at the contents, dark green and lumpy.

He shook his head, but he didn't try to get out the car.

'Do you like living round here, Harry?'

'Nope.'

'What school do you go to, Cleveden Primary?'

'I am at the high school. Glasgow High School,' he clarified.

Too thin, too frail, too unsubstantial. 'You don't look old enough to be out on your own, never mind at high school.'

'I'm fucking stunted.'

'You're certainly not tall enough to be using language like that to an officer of the law. Still, no school tomorrow. Not with a cold like that.' She sniffed. 'You've probably given it to me now.'

'Sorry,' he said, but still made no move to get out the car.

'I think your dad is watching,' said Costello, pointing to a twitching curtain behind the wide French windows.

'Harry' turned his head. 'Yeah.' Flat voice, no emotion.

'Shall we go in then?' She unclipped her seat belt. He did the same.

'I'll explain where you have been,' although she had no idea why he was behind the bins.

He sighed, a middle-aged weary sigh, like nothing she did or said would make any difference. 'Or we can lie and say you felt faint and had to have a sit down. What about that? That would explain why you didn't go home.'

'I ran away.'

'Well I guessed that. You didn't run very far though.'

'I felt fucking faint, didn't I?'

'What were you running from?' *Who were you running from?* He had still made no movement to get out the car, the seat belt now entwined round his hand.

He shrugged.

'Well, you ran away and felt too poorly to go home. But why did you leave in the first place?' She adjusted the rear-view mirror, pulling at her filthy hair, pretending not to be interested in the answer. The smell of the cheese was starting to fill the car, her stomach was rumbling.

He turned and looked at her, every inch the vulnerable starving orphan, save the Celtic top, this season's, expensive. And the fact he went to an exclusive private school, and he lived in the West End in a half-million pound house. But would rather sit behind a bin.

'You know I am a cop, you remember that? Just in case you have sneezed out your brains. There's all sorts pouring down your nose.'

He nodded, slid his seat belt back and opened the door. He moved quickly, silently like a feral creature and slithered out, onto the dark tree-lined street.

He stopped at the sound of the front door opening. The security lights came on, two beams joining to highlight him in a sphere of white light that seemed to pin him to the driveway.

Costello got out the car, walking round the back of the vehicle while the boy remained frozen to the spot. The door was only open enough for the person behind it to look out. She couldn't see them, or get a sense of them, the way the light was shining in her eyes.

'Malcolm, you get yourself in here. Now.'

'You wee liar, telling me you were Harry Styles. I wouldn't have given you a lift if I had known,' Costello said quietly, holding up her hand as she turned to stand with her back to the door, between the boy and the house. 'You take that, Malcolm, that's my card. My mobile number is on it. You keep that somewhere safe, somewhere only you know and if you want to speak to me, you call me.'

She held the card close to her. He took it, slowly, and felt it between his thumb and forefinger.

'Malcolm!' The voice called again. Not particularly male or female. It had risen slightly, a little bit of impatience already giving way to anger. 'And who the hell are you? Bringing him home in your car?'

Malcolm took the card and slid it under his top, or wrapped a tissue round it, a sleight of hand that impressed her. He gave a little shake of his head. Was he warning her? Telling her not to do it. Begging her?

'Do you want me to walk away?' she asked quietly.

He nodded.

'Oh, no problem,' she said loudly, turning round and smiling into the light. 'He isn't feeling too well and had a wee sit down on a wall outside work so I thought I'd better bring him home. No problem,' she repeated. 'There you go.'

The door said nothing as Malcolm slid through the light, swallowed by the darkness beyond.

'He has a right bad cold on him,' said Costello cheerfully, from the door of her car.

'Picked him up outside your work, you say? And where would that be, young lady?'

Male, definitely male, she thought, but it was the authoritarian 'young lady' that did it. The tone of it. It wasn't friendly, it was bloody sarcastic. The tone that told women that the world was too complicated for them and would they mind getting back into the kitchen where they might be of use.

She had already turned her back to the front door of the house but it didn't stop her. She didn't turn around either, just threw a casual remark over her shoulder, loudly. 'That would be Partickhill Police Station,' she said realizing that was not technically true. 'And it's DI Young Lady to you.' And after a slow count of three, she added very quietly, 'Wank.'

She got back into the car, leaning over enough as she tilted the mirror round in order to see the house, knowing a small figure would appear up at a bedroom window. Then she saw the outline of a head, two sticking-out ears, a white patch appearing as he pressed his forehead to the glass, what looked like a violent nod but was another sneeze. She thought she saw him wave slightly.

She released the handbrake and let the car roll back so she could execute a U-turn, easing it to a halt as a black sports car came round the corner at speed, taking a wide sweep and disappearing up the drive and into the shadow of the monkey puzzle tree. It might have been a Porsche Panamera, but she couldn't be sure.

She wasn't sure about Malcolm either. Was he such a poor wee squint or was she seeing stuff that wasn't there because of her immersion in the Kissel case? That dad had every right to be annoyed that his boy had run off, dressed so badly for this weather.

But that didn't explain that look in the boy's eyes. And she was sure about that. She had seen it so many times when she had looked in the mirror.

FOUR

Valerie Abernethy stepped out of the shower and wrapped a plush white towel round her before walking across the upstairs hall into the spare bedroom, a casual glance out the window to make sure the Porsche was still there. They were coming to take it away next week.

The shower had woken her up, and she had further endured a quick blast of cold to give her focus after a sleepless night. She had dropped off to a fitful sleep around midnight only to wake up an hour later as the little flicker of a flame burning in the back of her mind began to fire.

God, she needed a drink.

She was still mindful that she was in her sister's house, hearing the odd snore coming from a bedroom, a slight wheeze and a fit of coughing. Standing outside Malcolm's room and stealing a glance through the door, she recognized the Star Wars Lego; The Millennium Falcon, something from her era. She had built it with the family, when? Last Christmas? Kneeling on the floor, getting the small white bricks under her shins, it was very painful. All this family stuff was painful. Abby was a great mother and didn't deserve the way her eldest daughter had deserted her.

So Valerie had steered clear, she had preferred, until now, to be on her own, nice clean life, in nice little boxes. She saw Malcolm's babylike button nose sticking over the duvet, translucent eyelids flittering with the internal drama of a bad dream, a lemon drink sat on the carpet beside the bed, a box of tissues open. Her sister was a GP and didn't agree with cough bottles. Valerie couldn't recall a time when her own dreams were anything other than films of children, small children, other people's children who had been battered and burned, injured and bruised. In her dreams they always screamed. They existed in photographs, in computer files, in her cases. A name and a family incident number. The stack of files on her desk was growing by the minute. She worked fourteen-hour days to clear her backlog, only for it to get caught up on the next desk in the hierarchy. And then it wasn't really cleared, not really. It was moved onto another place. And they kept coming. The files got bulkier, the kids kept getting battered, the excuses got tired, the merry-go-round kept turning. Nobody getting off, nobody getting on. For years now, the children had spoken to her in her dreams, pleading that they don't get forgotten, asking that they were not allowed to drift away.

Now they were told to prosecute only twenty percent of cases. Everything else to be on a fixed fine. That 'everything' included those crimes that were gateways to violent escalation. And people wondered why she liked a tipple?

She pulled herself away, unpeeling from the white gloss doorway, instinctively rubbing where her hand had been with the sleeve of her dressing gown, wanting to leave no trace. Why not? This was her sister's house. She was a guest here. She had been invited. That didn't mean she was welcome. By Abigail, yes. But not by him. Never by George. He had seemed more wound up than usual last night, if that was possible. He had been agitated as he closed the gate, locked up the house and looked out the windows for some unseen intruder.

She walked back to the guest bedroom, where her suit for work was neatly hanging in its cover, to protect the fine wool from getting covered in Alfred's cat hair. Her black court Louboutins in a bag wound round the neck of the hanger. After a spray of deodorant and a good covering of Jo Malone's Wild Fig, she pulled on her fleecy leisure suit, and lifted up her trainers. She stuck the perfume in her handbag and draped her suit bag over her arm. She went downstairs. The grand-mother clock on the half-landing resonated on all three floors. It had been left to both sisters in the will, Abigail had taken it. It wouldn't have suited Valerie's minimalist flat anyway. The striking of the clock was one of those noises she only heard when she listened for it, like the gentle burr of a child snoring; her sister when she was growing up and then her daughter, and now her son.

In those days, when they were young, an argument at a chimp's tea party wouldn't have woken them up. Years ago Mary-Jane had dreamt about the ponies she thought she was getting for her birthday and then how she was going to be the next Adele. And Malcolm? Well, what was going on in his mind was anybody's guess? Even though he hadn't seemed well when he went to his bed, still sweating and shivery, Valerie had caught him reading his vintage Dandy comics at midnight, under the covers but hadn't told his mum. Valerie used to do that too when she was a kid. He was a little livewire, a kid the word rapscallion was invented for. He was bright and rebellious, a kid with scraped knees who would have perfect false teeth after getting all his natural ones knocked out. He was always covered in bruises.

But Mary-Jane and Malcolm were safe. Not like those victims sitting on her desk, little lives laid bare in black and white.

She scribbled a note for Abby and left it on the telephone table in the lower hall, saying she had enjoyed her night at the theatre and scribbled her goodbye. Then added, thinking of the foul mood George had been in after Malcolm had come home, 'Call me if you need me'.

She thought that sounded innocent.

As she unlocked the Porsche, the lights flashed.

It was five past five in the morning.

Costello had hardly slept that night. The time for sleep had passed her by the time she went to bed and she had lain awake, working through the mechanics of the abduction. The abductor had been lucky. More than that he had been organized. The one image she couldn't get out of her head was the way James Chisholm had been leaning against the wall of the cubical in Casualty, wearing his lack of concern like a suit of armour. Detached. She wondered what a DNA test on Sholto would show.

She got up early and made sure Mrs Craig across the hall had put her lights on. Then she logged on and checked the result of the door-to-door, nothing of much interest. She had ordered the phone records to be pulled for the mobiles and landlines of James and Roberta but she hadn't had time to go through them yet.

By nine a.m. she was at the Chisholm's house, niceties over, a cup of hot tea in her hand, she had watched James's face intently as she told him and his wife about her findings on the car seat, showing them the photos on her phone in extreme close-up. It was shockingly obvious. If anything, James was more shocked than Roberta.

And Roberta had turned on her husband at that point; she had known it wasn't his blanket, now it turns out it wasn't his chair either. Why didn't he listen to her? And then there were more tears.

James didn't react, this was not new.

Costello had studied them during this little exchange. Roberta was stressed, no doubt about that. She had a pale, puffy look about her, her body still in aftershock from the birth. She was on maternity leave from a reasonable job working for NHS 24. Their bank account was veering towards the red, but they had a nice little house, a nice little life. But there was something about James, aside from his reaction at the hospital. He was either detached or sniping at his wife, removed from the horror of his son being abducted. As if it was nothing. As if he had known.

And he had never asked, Why Sholto?

There was a slight reaction when Costello explained that the Duster was being impounded by the forensics team and they were not to go near it, while neglecting to mention that it would have been picked up already if not for an oversight the night before.

'We will run you anywhere you want to go. You do have Constable McCaffrey as your designated case officer. He's clearing other cases so that he can be solely yours. We need to keep tabs on you, and protect you from the media. It can get unpleasant, and we do need to use the media carefully so they stay on our side. We run the case, not them,' Costello said, following James Chisholm's eyes to the folded newspaper thrown onto the table. 'Sorry I've not seen the headlines this morning, only what was online.'

'They are saying Sholto was taken by a paedophile. Is that true?'

'I doubt it. He was taken by somebody who knew you and

knew you well. They have been in your company if they know what car seat you use.'

'Jesus Christ.' Roberta let out a small yelp. 'Please no, oh please no.' She started to cry and reached out to James who responded by shuffling along the sofa. Away from her.

'We have no reports, no spike in activity about paedophiles and our boys would know. We have a whole department tracking that kind of thing.' She hoped she sounded surer than she felt. 'And they would not have left "Moses" as Constable McCaffrey has called him.'

Through her tears, Roberta gave a wry smile. 'Moses. Wee Moses.'

'We are working on the theory that a woman has become fixed on Sholto, seeing him as her ideal baby, maybe emotionally rejecting Moses. So, I need you to talk through everywhere you have been in the six weeks, since Sholto was born. Your main contacts might now be with people that you only know because you have had a baby. Or it might be something simpler,' Costello threw in. 'Have you upset somebody recently, Mr Chisholm?'

Roberta looked up, throwing a sharp look at her husband before pulling her wet hair from her face, trying to think rationally. Her brain had something to work through, and that was much better than doing nothing. But she shook her head. 'No, he hasn't, not now. He upsets nobody apart from me. He's middle management and boring.'

'You have just been promoted, though, did you step on anybody's toes?'

'My firm isn't like that,' he said, eyes fixed at the carpet.

Costello let that go, the seed had been planted. 'OK. Where did you buy the car seat?'

'Mothercare.'

'Which branch? And was that type recommended to you?'

Roberta spread her hands out in a helpless gesture. 'Well, at the prenatal class, and then I checked some out on the net, as you do.'

Costello knew the women at that prenatal class had already been checked – no Down's syndrome babies in their immediate family.

'The Car Easy was on special purchase,' said James. 'We bought it at Mothercare. We drove down to Ayr.'

'And when was that?'

'Two weeks before Sholto was born.'

Costello wrote that down. 'And since then, you don't recall anybody taking special interest, asking too many questions, paying Sholto a little too much attention.'

'No.'

'Roberta, do you . . .?'

'Bobby, please, nobody calls me Roberta.'

'Bobby, how would you feel about doing a media appeal? It would be carefully scripted by our psychologist. Nothing of authority as that might scare the person who has Sholto. We don't want to frighten her into doing something. We would want it to be more of a "mother to mother", with little Moses, showing how lovely little Moses is, that he's better. An appeal from mum to mum, come and see how your baby is doing. No harm done, let's talk. We need to get her to engage.'

'Why would we risk that if there is a chance that she might harm Sholto?' James asked, rubbing his arms, conflicted already.

'The theory is that as we speak to her, everybody hears the story. It will be on the front pages of every newspaper and somebody somewhere will know the woman who had a Down's baby, and now does not have a Down's baby. It might be as simple as that. She cannot hide Sholto.'

'What happens though if she dumps him? You read about people doing that.' James was belligerent. 'And you don't really know who . . . who that baby is. Do you?'

'We will—' she looked him straight in the eye – 'we will.'

'Imagine feeling so awful about your own child that you take somebody else's. I know how that poor woman must have felt, the way they cry and cry . . .'

'Only last week you said you would have swapped Sholto,' said James, childishly petulant.

'Never!' she yelled at her husband, arms flaying.

'It wasn't that when he was screaming the bloody place down.'

Roberta shot him a look of sheer hatred and became very still. 'I think we should do an appeal.'

'I don't,' James said petulantly.

'It's a calculated risk, but it's worth thinking about. It's going to be in all the papers, all over the net so his abductor will know anyway.'

'I think I need another cup of tea,' said Roberta, getting up from the sofa.

'Me too, please,' said Costello, opening her notebook. 'Now, if you talk me through everywhere you have been since the baby was born . . .'

For over an hour they pieced together everywhere that baby had gone, everywhere the Duster had been with the car seat in place, who Roberta had spoken to, every hospital visit, every postnatal class, every antenatal class, her postnatal Pilates, her baby bouncers, the local coffee morning, the mother-and-baby group in the village. James kept getting up and going into the kitchen to collect a diary, a calendar, his phone. Her phone, the laptop. He was a very organized man. Roberta stayed on the settee and got more tearful, tiredness etched into her face. Costello looked at her notes, pages of them. She had enough to be going on with. This was only the start of the process, so she got up to leave, with Roberta saying she was going back to bed, pushing James out the way on her way to the stairs.

James got up to see Costello out the door. 'She's phoned the hospital three times this morning, she's worried about the other kid.' He cast a glance up the stairs, making sure she was out of earshot. 'She wants to go in and see him, but he is not our child.'

'She's thinking that if she looks after Moses then whoever has Sholto will be looking after him,' said Costello thinking how much worse McCaffrey had made it by giving the unknown baby a name, it made him seem more vulnerable. Harry Fucking Styles could look after himself. But Malcolm was vulnerable.

'But if they bought a chair the same then that is not the case, is it? They just want us to think that.'

She was glad she was saved from answering by her phone. She was being summoned back to HQ.

James saw the expression on her face change to a smile.

'News?' His face was pathetic in hope.

'Not for you, sorry. But I think they are already moving this up the food chain.' If she was being sent to West End Central then surely she'd be back with Colin Anderson and be able to get this case moving herself. 'But I think we should keep the knowledge about the chair being swapped to ourselves. Cases like this attract nutters, we need to be able to weed them out.'

James nodded.

'I know we already touched on it, but can you think of any reason why somebody would want to harm you – or want revenge on you for some slight, real or imagined.'

He was too quick to answer. 'No.'

'We have your phone records, all of them.'

He shook his head, but his insistence was gone.

'And what about other women in your life, any of them creeping around that we should know about. Before we find out.'

'Nothing like that.'

She stared him down.

'Do you think you will get my son back alive?'

My son. Not our son. She paused a minute too long before answering.

'OK then.' He closed his eyes slowly and swallowed hard. 'You had better get on with it.'

Anderson jolted his head up at the TV news bulletin, the words Glasgow and baby abduction catching the periphery of his consciousness. Or maybe it was the mention of a team from Govan. From Govan to Waterside, he looked round to see that everybody was watching even Stuart and Bruce. Baby abduction was thankfully uncommon. The story from the newsreader, a female with a homely face, was gentle and engaging. The image changed to show the small row of shops, couple of old guys standing outside the post office, talking about the previous night's excitement. But they were a generation that were wary of the cameras. The end of the item was a close-up of a little baby with Down's syndrome, smiling. He wondered if the dad had a good alibi, that was crime stat rule number one. Dead baby, suspect the man who lives with the mum and you couldn't go far wrong, He could read the subtext of the news item easily enough, hoping that the abductor wouldn't be put off coming forward by the social media fascists who were already talking about hanging the paedophiles concerned. The image changed to a healthy wee baby, lying in a cot kicking at a flowery mobile, laughing. It was unspoken but the genetic defect was there for all to see. This was a case of broken hearts, no crime intended, just some kind of desperation. The mother needed help. It was sad all round.

He turned his attention back to the cold case he was supposed to be reviewing in between meetings, now he had, reluctantly, put Gillian's rape back in the file. This was a murder 25 years ago, June 1992. It sounded so long ago: 25 years.

It had been a fine summer Sunday morning when a young man had been battered to death on the steps outside his own back door. Edward Nicol Wiley, a thirty-year-old supermarket manager with two young kids; the kind of guy who polished his Ford Escort every Saturday. Not the sort to have his skull smashed with a neighbour's claw hammer by person or persons unknown. And for an unfathomable reason words from his old DCI floated back to him, 'Too boring to be murdered'. Harsh, but they contained a simple truth.

Wiley had access to money, access to a safe. Was it some kind of kidnap situation gone wrong? A bad idea drummed up in the pub after a few pints too many? Wiley was not easy to blackmail. He had been investigated to the hilt, Anderson had gleamed that much, and was squeaky clean. This was a case where the evidence would lie with the victim, not with the person or persons unknown. And Mrs Wiley was cleaner than the convent laundry, a stay at home mum who taught in the Sunday school. The senior investigating officer had considered the attack a case of mistaken identity.

Boring men did not get their skulls battered in.

His first task was ensuring what little forensic evidence there had been still existed. All he was looking for was a starting point like some retained material from the head of the hammer that could be subjected to a new DNA exam. He sighed. He needed to order a search of the databases for attacks where a hammer was the weapon of choice. A hammer that had been picked up in the neighbour's garden. Handy. It was the only thing about the Wiley case that was not boring.

That and Wiley having his brains bashed in.

He felt a gentle tap on his shoulder. A young female civilian stood behind him, her huge earrings that clanked when she moved her head were as gaudy as her perfume.

'Oh hello . . .' He searched for her name. 'Vicki?'

'Vivien,' she corrected. 'DCI Anderson, you are wanted in the meeting room.' She smiled. 'Again. I thought you might be able to smell the big cheese from here.'

Not over the stink of your perfume, he thought. Her earrings clinked like Tinkerbell as she nodded her head, subtly in the direction of the corridor. Through the open blind, the one that covered the glass partition, he could see a procession of three men going through the door and taking their jackets off. He recognized the detective super among them.

He noticed how quiet the office had become. Stuart and Bruce were standing at their desks, pretending not to look over but listening intently. 'Am I in trouble?' he asked her.

'Not yet,' she said in a voice that was just husky enough to be sexy. If she had not been the same age as his daughter.

Colin Anderson took a deep breath and knocked on the door of the interview room, fully aware of the continued scrutiny of his colleagues. A quick response told him to enter, he stepped inside.

It was the big boss, the det super who greeted him. Four of them were seated round the table, sleeves rolled up, tucking into the coffee and biscuits.

'We need a word, Colin,' Mitchum spoke next, indicating that he should sit.

Anderson noted the use of the first name, nodded to the others. 'Why am I sensing that this is not good news?'

Mitchum waved his concerns away. 'What are you working on at the moment?'

Anderson put his pen down, thought about the Wiley file. 'Not much I can get my teeth into.'

Mitchum spoke, 'Well, you might be able to help us out.

We have been forced into a corner somewhat unfortunately. As you know, we had Gillian Witherspoon pinned for a new, low-key but wide-reaching campaign. And now that she has . . .'

'Died?' added Colin helpfully.

'We need to find somebody else quickly.'

'Why?'

They were silent for a moment.

'We need to reinstate the campaign,' said Mitchum reluctantly.

'Reinstate the campaign rather than set up a specialist cold case task force to review the evidence and maybe catch the perpetrator. He's still out there.'

'God, DCI Anderson, you talk like it's our job to solve crime!' Mitchum allowed himself a chuckle. 'No, not that, but we did stumble across something we found to be of interest. Something about you.'

'Intriguing.'

It was the ACC who spoke, 'Do you remember Sally Logan?'

'Vaguely,' he lied as his mind jumped back twenty years, twenty-five years. Sally with her honey blonde hair and endless energy. The first on the trampoline, the first to skip when she thought nobody was looking. She was a delight, pissed out her brain on the dance floor while Andrew Braithwaite bopped with her, a dancing bear with a beer in his hand. Sally with her long brown legs, the scar deep on the inside of her knee. 'I can remember I had to prove where I was at six o'clock on the morning of her rape.' Anderson felt a little uncomfortable, they were poking into his past to a place and time that he considered his own. A life before he wore a uniform. A time before he wore a wedding ring. 'Yes, I knew her quite well.'

'You were a person of interest,' smiled Mitchum. 'For about five minutes.'

He remembered now, she had lost a year at uni due to a knee injury, and she was so happy to get back on the hockey team, back on the running track and out onto the hills. Then the attack happened. 'Did you ever find her attacker?' he continued.

'No.'

'We never found the man who attacked Gillian either, did we.'

'No.' Mitchum caressed his pen, holding it under his nose as if scenting a fine cigar. 'Sally was, if you recall, very media friendly as we would put it nowadays. She was that bright, smiley, any girl type of victim.'

'Yes.' He remembered that smile well.

'She had agreed to waive anonymity and become the face of a personal safety campaign we had at that time. She had our photographer take pictures of her neck wounds, the bruises on her face, the damage to her shoulder. Physically, she was a mess after the assault and she would have been good in that role, an eloquent woman standing up, telling her story, her injuries visible. Telling other women that keeping safe was the better part of being strong.'

Anderson was confused. He would have known about that if it had come to pass, that was the sort of thing he would remember. She was not a woman easy to forget. 'What happened?'

'We don't really know. She backed off. She changed her mind. Suddenly.'

'Women have that right,' said Anderson.

'Indeed, they do. We want you to ask her again. Give her the same script you were going to give Gillian for the SafeLife campaign. You know, speaking out for the victims of violent and sexual crime.'

Anderson said quietly, 'Would that not be better coming from one of your specially trained media officers? You spend a huge budget training them, why not use them?'

'Because they are all on a bloody training course,' said the super with a flicker of a smile. 'But you have history with the woman.'

'Hardly, sir, we were at the same university. Twenty-odd years ago, but I have no problem catching up with her and having a chat. But if the answer is no, then the answer is no. I am not going to use any past acquaintance to persuade her.'

'Of course not. But just one more thing.' The detective super got up, sliding a file towards Anderson. 'We have contacted your old DI. She's in the building right now on another case but feel free to approach her if you feel it more prudent to do this with a female officer.'

'Who?'

'DI Costello.'

'Oh,' said Anderson, wondering what idiot would put the words 'prudent' and 'Costello' in the same sentence. 'Just as I was beginning to like the idea.'

Costello slipped her card through the electronic lock of West End Central, summoned to a meeting which she knew would be about the media fallout from the Kissel case, so on the way she had got hold of PC McCaffrey on his mobile, firing out instructions, passing on all the information she had about the routines of Roberta and Sholto Chisholm and asking him to get them cross-checked and dig deeper into the phone call records of James. He was up to something, she could smell it off him. The lives of the parents would now be subjected to intense scrutiny, him more than her. He had told Roberta to go to that shop, the remote way he stood in the hospital cubicle. It was too neat, but so far there were no red flags.

As she waited for the lock to recognize her, she ran through various scenarios for the meeting. She had no doubt she was invited here for a game of one potato, two potato with social workers, cops, doctors, health visitors; all the king's horses and all the king's men sitting in one room seeing who else they could blame. Responsibility for the death of that child would be bounced around between them. Ignoring Humpty who sat in the corner, quietly bleeding to death, or starving to death as he would have been in Bernadette Kissel's care. She thought of the wardrobe in the child's room, a single wardrobe with a solitary rail and on it hung one hanger. On the hanger was one tiny jumper, a small blue and white striped affair, a navy blue anchor sewn onto the bottom corner.

And that was all. The only piece of child's clothing in the entire house. And it still had its label on it.

The door, resolutely refused to open. She gave it a quick push but it remained firm, responding to her violence with a reproachful buzz. She swore, waited, looking round her. Standing in a doorway across the street was the beggar she had seen the day before, still looking for handouts. Everything that woman owned in the world would be in that big Lidl plastic bag. She was ferreting about in the bottom of it now, a large lady bending over straight over from the hips. Costello saw that she still had her Crocs on. Of course she would, how many pairs of shoes do homeless people have? Her feet would get cold in this weather. Although still raining, it was warmer today, but if that woman was sleeping rough or out on the streets begging tonight, then the evening chill would bite deep. God, nothing was going right in this world. She wondered if she should go across and mention the nearby hostel. She could try and get her a bed for the night. Suddenly the thought of Malcolm floated across her mind. Had he been fed last night? Was somebody taking him to a doctor or to hospital? Or was he sent off to school because there was going to be nobody at home to look after him? Although she tried not to, she automatically recalled the black Porsche that had driven into the house. She had clocked the plate, of course: VA 2661.

Costello had friends in traffic, a revengeful nature. And endless patience.

The door buzzed her in and she walked through, into the warmth of West End Central.

'We are being joined by a leading supervisor from Social Services, she's in charge of liaison between social workers and health visitors for the various child protection units around Glasgow. She has a multi-agency remit and is keen for her input to be heard right at the get-go.' Detective Super McGrath glanced at his watch and then at the clock. 'She seems to be running a little late.'

'Probably can't get in that bloody door,' muttered Costello to herself.

The room fell quiet, six of them sat, looking at each other and the two empty seats. Four of her colleagues had laptops or tablets placed squarely in front of them. Costello pulled out her battered black notebook and searched her handbag for a pen that worked. Aware the very well-dressed man who looked like the actor in the stairlift advert was looking at her, Costello looked out the window of the room, taking advantage of the good view of the corridor her position afforded her. She thought she had caught a glimpse of Colin Anderson going into the room opposite. If it was him, he was looking much better. He had either put on a little weight or had started working out. Or maybe he could afford a well-cut suit now. She wondered what his meeting was about. Would they bump in to each other later? Surely if he knew she was here, he would make the effort? Then again, when did men ever make any kind of effort for her nowadays?

And she was thinking about it, wasn't she? Considering it rather than making a definite plan to catch hold of him later. They had grown so far apart without either of them really noticing, maybe that was the way of things as people grew older, they were merely twigs floating in the stream. The door closed on their meeting room leaving her to look again at her colleagues, trying to read the agenda upside down.

She wondered if this meeting had anything to do with a rumoured convergence of the cold case unit and her domestic violence remit, maybe bringing some psychological insight to those who started with fists and ended up with knives. And stop them before they did it.

Nobody had said a word. Costello had a sudden impulse to burst out laughing. Mr Stairlift, she didn't know. Ditto the other police officer, looking like he'd put his hand up first to answer teacher. There was one nervous-looking civilian poised to take minutes. The well groomed man on the far side was from the fiscal's office. He looked too young to have an opinion about anything. He was here to report back to his boss, Archie the bastard, who wasn't here to see things for himself. Probably couldn't face her, in case she read the guilt written all over his face.

'I think that might be the head of the team coming now,' said the young police officer at the noise of clomping footfall along the corridor. Whoever it was was heavy and dragging their feet, or maybe burdened down. The young cop got up to open the door, Archie walked in. Costello refused to return his smile, giving him her thousand-mile death stare but he ignored her, standing to one side to let his companion enter the room. Their local head of child protection social work. As the woman came in the room, she glared at Costello as hard as she could with her soft brown eyes before she placed her bulging, Lidl bag on the table.

Costello found herself on her feet, her face fixed to conceal the conflict of her emotions: guilt, shame, embarrassment and disbelief. And she daren't look at Archie, in case the woman had mentioned that some stupid, racist, female cop had thought she was a bag lady, snapping at her that she had no spare change. God, she could be in all kinds of trouble now.

'This is Deliana Despande.' Archie introduced her, his careful enunciation making it obvious he had been practising.

She pulled a cushion from her Lidl bag then sat down on it, smiling her way round the room at the introduction. The smile got rather fixed and frosty when it came to Costello.

They sat down, Costello taking her time to pull the seat in under her, still not able to believe it. She really was up to her neck in shit now.

'Call me Dali, it helps.' Her accent was pure Glaswegian, slightly punctuated with harsh Asiatic consonants. She shuffled her heavy bulk down on the cushioned seat, adjusted the shoulder strap of her bra and slipped a dirty, bulky anorak from her shoulders. 'Sorry I am late, I am too fat to walk quickly.' She laughed as she pulled another file from the bag and opened it.

Costello, sitting at right angles to her, had a good view of the first and second pages, densely covered in an inky web of thick black italic pen.

She cast a glance at Costello, a small, fleeting smile that seemed totally without vitriol. 'And you are DI Costello?'

Costello nodded, wondering how fast her career was going to come crashing around her. She looked at Archie, the two-timing bastard gave her a sweet smile like everything was normal. Had Dali not said anything to him and she was waiting to make her humiliation public? Or was she going to be taken in to a small room and lectured before being suspended for abject racism?

Dali was talking, 'DI Costello. Yesterday you were sent to investigate a very strange crime indeed? One child, a baby was swapped for another?'

'Yes.'

'I know, I tried to talk to you about it twice but you were . . . busy,' she said.

'Yes.' That didn't sound enough. 'Sorry,' she added.

'It happens all the time, don't give it a moment's thought.' Her dark eyes twinkled. 'We need to get to the bottom of that incident, and given your circumstances, I think you can be of great help to me. And vice versa.'

Given your circumstances? Was that a hint of career blackmail? Costello, while resentful, couldn't help but be impressed.

Dali waved her arms about and pulled up her bra strap again. 'I need a team of people who are focussed and don't talk shite. My office is complete rubbish, too many chiefs and not enough Indians.'

Costello smirked, caught Archie's eye and received the hint of a grin. The bastard.

'We are under investigation, our investigators are under review from this agency and that agency. I really would like some staff to help my staff to do their bloody job and then,' she rattled her fingertips off the top of the table, 'you Mr Walker, might have less work to do. *We* are there to prevent the crimes, not solve them and then *you* do not have to prosecute something because . . . it has not happened. Why is that madness?'

Shocked, Archie opened his mouth, but she was talking, sweet and brown-eyed, chattering like a Gatling gun wrapped in a duvet before he managed to get a word out.

'We need to start doing something. And it starts now. With us. Here.'

And something deep in Costello cheered.

She had left the meeting enriched as if somebody had lit the fire in her belly. There was no doubt that Dali was a straight talker and took no shite from anybody. Costello had become aware, as the meeting had gone on, that the young fiscal wasn't getting a word in edgeways. The cop with all the right answers wasn't doing that very well either. In the end, she felt like Dali was talking to her and Archie alone. Maybe because they were the only two listening rather than typing and looking up various references.

The young fiscal argued that a point Dali was trying to

make was unlawful but she talked over him, her silky voice
had the subtlety of a snow plough.

'This bastard broke the child's arm, in three places, he made
the child sit in the house with pants on his head, pants that
were covered in shit and piss. Now, Mr Fiscal, if you tell me
that any intervention to stop that is unlawful then I suggest
you set about getting the law changed. Or you get another
job.' She didn't quite add the 'young man' but it was there.

Dali was proposing a unit that would actually get things
done. They had to report back to her wherever they encountered
problems. Why things were not getting done, and then, yes,
all they do is sign reports that sit on the fiscal's desk and
nothing happens, while the wee kid still gets to sit in the corner
with the shitty pants on their head.

'This is the now, it is in the present, it's not like a crime
that should be investigated after it has been committed. We
have to prevent those crimes from being committed and I
know that does not sit well with you legal people, but the
consequence of your reluctance to act is this.' And she placed
an A4 colour photograph in front of the young fiscal. Costello
could make out the boy's bare body, bruised, broken and
burned.

The fiscal looked away, towards Archie who offered him
no help.

'You can pretend you don't see it but we see it every day.
And now, I hope that image is burned onto the back of your
eyes. It'll make you better at your job. Now, who is in charge
of the tea here? I could do with a brew.'

And with that she had announced that while they were
waiting for the refreshments she was going to use the ladies.
She lifted her cushion and stuffed it back in her bag, a clear
indication that she considered the meeting over. Costello
watched as Archie stood up, trying to help her, and she gave
him her bag to carry as she put her jacket back on, then thanked
him and made her way clumsily out the room. They heard her
heavy footfall on the squeak of her Crocs on the lino floor.

Costello sat quietly, closing her notebook, thinking
about Malcolm. There was a case that was going to happen,
but the young fiscal was right. You can't act on a feeling or

experienced intuition. It was almost impossible to wade in before there had been an incident. Even if there was evidence of initial abuse, sending an official round might keep the child safe while the abuser was sober, and could apply reasoned thought, but once they were drunk or high or enraged, then it would be open season.

She found herself alone with Archie. The others had left, he was standing at the door. She wasn't sure if he realized he was holding it closed.

'So how are you getting on? I've not seen you since the Kissel verdict came back.'

'I've been busy.' And she added, 'And so have you.'

'Are you working on the Waterside abduction?'

'I am, and I seem to be a one-man band on it.' She folded her arms, waiting for Archie to open the door.

'You're a DI, form a team.'

'Aye right, meanwhile here in the real world.'

'Are you in a mood?'

'Why should I be?'

'Bloody hell, I only asked.'

Archie looked normal, he hadn't changed into a two-headed evil beast that dripped blood on the floor. He was the same Archie, neat as a new pin, sharply ironed creases and perfect salt and pepper hair.

'How is Pippa?'

'Not good, she's refusing to eat and that's causing issues at the home.'

She wanted to ask where he was on Tuesday afternoon but couldn't.

'Is Colin here?' she asked. 'I thought I saw him.'

'Yes, I think Mitchum has him next door. He's being collared into PR.'

'I'll go and find him then,' she said and reached round him to open the door, and squeeze past him before he could stop her.

Costello walked up behind DCI Colin Anderson but he was so engrossed in his phone and the outpourings of the coffee machine, he hadn't even noticed. She had waited until her lips were at the lobe of his ear, waited until she could smell the familiar scent of him, before she spoke. 'I thought I smelled you in the building.'

He turned. 'Costello, how are you?' He sounded glad to see her and thought about hugging her then remembered that she hated any physical human contact.

Her grey cold eyes were already on the file, honing in on the photograph that he had been examining before his phone went. 'I'm fine. Are you working here? Is that your case?' She nodded at the picture.

'Somebody I knew at uni. Is Archie with you?'

'No. Who is she?'

'Where is Archie?'

'In that room there, waiting to burn in hell so he might be a while.' She turned her head to look at the photograph the right way round. 'God, she looks good for her age, much better than you. Has she had surgery or did you go to a tough school? She's . . .'

'Absolutely gorgeous?' suggested Anderson, knowing the only way to avoid interrogation was to give her something. 'She was always a good-looking woman. Nice too. Not like you at all, she's one of these really healthy types, always climbing mountains at weekends and swimming across lochs at six in the morning.'

'Sounds a right pain in the arse. I bet she ate yoghurt.'

'By the bucketful.'

'Is she a cold case?' She plucked the picture from him, sticking it under her nose, so close to her face Anderson thought she might need her sight tested.

'She was raped. It was never solved, so yes, it might be a cold case. Or something.' He took the photograph back. Not wanting her to have possession of it. Of any of it. 'She got badly hurt.'

'Is she another one of your redheads?'

'No,' he said patiently. 'She ended up marrying the guy at uni who got her better after she was attacked. Her physio, I think he was. And he was a much bigger bloke than me so I wasn't going to fight for her. He would have crushed me like roadkill. What happened between you and Archie?'

Anderson lifted his paper cup of coffee from the machine and took a sip, but Costello was already going through the file, memorizing the names, seeing the injuries, the scar, the deep cut on the side of Sally's face, the swelling with the odd speckle constellation of scars around her shoulder, some of them forming perfect teardrops on her tanned skin. He let her look, then held out his hand to stop her at one picture, a close-up of the bruising around her shoulder.

'Does she know you are a cop now?'

'She will when I tell her. I am going out to see her later. Does Archie know you are back here?'

'Yes. Is she involved in SafeLife?'

'You seem very well informed.' His voice was curt.

'Tread carefully, my friend, fools rushing in, where angels fear to whatsit.'

'And what happened with you and Archie? Precisely?'

'He's a bastard. Precisely. I've never heard you talk of her before? What's her name again?'

'I didn't say. It's not a big deal, Costello. Brenda and I were not in their social league. They both had the sort of parents that . . . well, they had money, let's leave it at that. They lived a life we couldn't afford.'

'The sort of life that you can afford now, Colin? Or have you forgotten that? You could buy Claire a flat in the city centre if she goes to art school. You and your ex – Sally, is it? – might be in the same league now, you can easily afford to take her out to the fancy dancy places. She might be able to show you how to work that bloody coffee machine of yours.'

'Costello, I have no interest in working this case at all and Sally's not my ex.'

'Liar,' she replied sweetly.

'I have enough on my hands, with Brenda and Claire and Peter. Nesbit is the only one that doesn't give me aggro these days.'

'And David. And Paige.'

'Indeed.' He turned over the page, 'We didn't keep up with them, Sally and Andrew, but it will be nice to catch up with old friends. Brenda wasn't that keen on socializing with them, back in the day.'

His DI pursed her thin lips, not saying 'thou protesteth too much', but the silence let him know she was thinking it. 'Brenda doesn't really like anybody,' was all she said.

'Neither do you,' he snapped. 'And that is my file.' He turned away, pulling the file from her and closing it, wanting the conversation to be over. It had been about six months since he had last set eyes on Costello. Two minutes reunited and she was annoying him already.

'So why are you here?'

'At a meeting.'

'Me too.' She sighed, then bit her lower lip. She deflated.

That was a bad sign that he recognized. 'Are you in trouble? Do tell, are you on your final written warning? I could do with cheering up.'

'It could be serious.'

'Even better.' But he was looking at her closely now. She was thoughtful, and he felt guilty and concerned. They had been through a lot together, her distress already part of his territory.

'The head of a new unit from Child Protection for Strathclyde was at my meeting. I bumped into her yesterday. She approached me and, well, I told her I had no spare change and she wasn't to bother me.'

Anderson tried not to laugh. 'You thought she was a dosser. Why?'

'Because she looks like a supermodel? Why do you think?' Her voice dripped with sarcasm. 'Dali she called herself. Like the painter.' She rubbed her face, she looked worn out.

His eyes drifted over her shoulder to a door opening and an overweight woman of Asian origin was making her way towards them, dragging her feet along the corridor, her Lidl bag over her shoulder, the weight of it giving her gait a roll.

'Did you think the head of the new unit was an immigrant beggar?' He laughed, but he could see why. 'I wouldn't worry, if she has got that high in her career in this part of the world, she will have heard, and been called, much worse. She probably found it funny.' He turned away. 'Probably. But if she wants to make a thing of it, you could really be in deep shit.'

'Oh God, she's coming along here, isn't she? Is she stopping at the lifts? Please tell me she's getting in the lift.'

Anderson watched the overweight woman pass the small queue for the lift. She was coming directly towards him, her plastic bag tucked under one arm, her anorak swinging from her shoulders. 'Nope. She's right behind you,' he whispered.

'Costello?' Her voice held a hint of command.

'Dali?'

The eyes were calculating and intelligent. 'Excuse us,' she said to Anderson with consummate politeness. 'Costello, can I have a word, please,' she said, flashing Colin Anderson a smile of beautiful white teeth as she placed a puffy hand with gnarled joints on Costello's shoulder and guided her back along the corridor.

He wished he was a fly on the wall.

FIVE

Orla Sheridan lived in a small flat tucked away in one of the narrower side streets off Dumbarton Road. Wheelie bins were out permanently, two skips at the end of the street stuffed full with old sofas and carcasses of kitchen units. A row of three discarded fridges like decayed teeth was evidence that the students had started a new term and the detritus of the tenants' last clear out had not yet been uplifted. Somebody had left out a cheese plant, complete with ceramic pot, a sign round its neck pleading for a good home.

It looked as though it had been waiting for some time.

The journey took less than ten minutes. Stromvar Drive was spotless at one end, slightly more 'bohemian' at the other. Dali seemed to have forgotten her embarrassing encounter with Costello, too busy talking about the stress her staff were under. But Costello had no doubt it was tucked away at the back of her mind, a weapon of destruction that could lay dormant, to be armed when needed. That's exactly what she herself would do.

Dali's stream of consciousness was a rant about her anger and her passion for women and women's rights and their safety, and furious too that Lorna McGill, the young social worker, had been battered by an expensive legal team determined to blame the death of Bernadette Kissel's child on anybody but Bernadette Kissel.

Then it dawned on Costello that it was the same social worker they were talking about. Piecing together the strands of Dali's rant, she deduced that Lorna McGill had gone out to visit a five-week-old baby called Polly. And was determined she wasn't going to leave until she saw her. Polly's mum Orla wouldn't even open up until the guy from upstairs had come down and battered on the door. Dali described Orla as 'thick as mince', mahogany with fake tan and ridiculous black eyebrows. The excuses followed; first the 'wean' was asleep, then it was asleep at her mum's, then it was with a friend in the pub. Like it wasn't there at all. Once she had gained entry Lorna had carried out a quick check. No Polly. More alarmingly, no food, nothing to suggest that a baby had ever lived there. Costello thought of all the evidence lying around in the Chisholm's house as Dali ran through all the correct protocols the young social worker had followed, slightly defensive as if she was fed up of her team getting the shitty end of the stick. It was while Lorna was phoning Orla's mother that Orla said she was going to the loo and then climbed out the window.

Costello had to smirk at that. 'How was she to know?'

'Indeed,' said Dali, 'Lorna's a good kid, go easy on her. She's had it tough the last few weeks. And what motivation do they have now. They are too young, too inexperienced, too big a case load and not enough support. I mean it's the bloody lawyers and the bloody fiscals, all those arses who pass letters here and emails there and nobody ever makes a fucking decision about anything. All they are interested in is a blame hound. And this girl Lorna is good, she is very good and now we will lose her to the profession, and—' she started banging her fist on the dashboard – 'we cannot afford to let good staff like that go. We cannot allow that.' She sat back and took a deep breath. 'But how do you solve a problem like Orla Sheridan?'

'That sounds like a cue for a song.'

The flat was the small one, bottom right, one tiny living room with a kitchen off it, bathroom in the middle with an air extraction unit, and an even smaller bedroom at the back. Even at the front door it smelled of damp and dope.

Dali had left her plastic bags in the back seat of Costello's car, only taking a well-worn black diary with her. She waddled straight through to the living room, obviously familiar with the property.

Costello introduced herself to the young woman standing by the window, waiting their arrival. 'Lorna? DI Costello.'

'I'm sorry, do I know you?' She sniffed, her eyes red and sore from crying.

'I worked the Kissel case, Lorna. You might have seen me at court.'

Lorna looked worn out, defeated, ready to cry again. 'Well, I fucked that up and I think I fucked this up as well. She got away from me.'

Costello cast a look at Dali thinking that she might remonstrate at the language, but the older woman just patted her younger colleague on the shoulder.

'Well, you didn't fuck up the Kissel case, but you did let Orla escape out a window – trick 2A in the book. Chalk it up to experience. Costello may be a DI here but she's not beyond the odd fuck up herself,' Dali said cheerfully, 'and she is still standing so don't you worry about it. It wasn't your fault, not your fault at all. In this job, we never do anything right so we may as well settle for doing our best. We will always get roasted by people with testicles who never get off their fat backsides. It's shite.' Dali readjusted the huge navy blue duvet of a jacket, her armour against an unfair world. 'The big question is, have you ever seen this baby? Ever?'

Lorna shook her head, wretched. 'Never.'

'Never,' Dali repeated, glancing at Costello, making sure she got that.

'I think this might be Daniel Kissel all over again. Or am I seeing something that isn't there?'

'Innocent people don't climb out windows. And you've checked to see if the child has been here recently?' Dali wobbled her way round the sofa, her pen pointing, her head twisting to get sight of the worktops in the small kitchen area.

'I've checked the bedding, the food cupboards, the clothes, the fridge. There is no sign that Baby Polly has been here for a while. Or ever.'

'Good, you've done good,' said Costello, looking at Dali.

'Lorna thought there might be an issue going on here.' She raised an eyebrow at Costello from behind the sofa, a silent tic-tac, not to be talked about in front of the young social worker. 'Orla is what? 18? 19? Legged it through the back window while saying she was going to the loo.'

'While I just sat here and let her,' moaned Lorna.

'You'll learn. But we need to find her. And the baby, she's only five weeks old. And not Down's syndrome,' she added knowing the way that Costello's brain would jump.

'Five weeks?' confirmed Costello. Sholto was six weeks. Moses five. She realized Dali was looking at her, making sure she was joining the dots. 'I presume that you have checked relatives, friends? Anywhere the baby—'

'Polly.'

'Polly might legitimately be? And are they reliable?'

'I did. I have phoned everywhere, all the contact numbers I have. They all seemed to think that the baby is elsewhere. Should I phone Family Protection?'

'I already have, they are sending somebody out to do a report,' Lorna said.

Dali raised an eyebrow at Costello. 'Nice of them. But I think we will get DI Costello to do it instead. She can kick a few arses for us.'

'I would but I have my hands full with—'

'With what? A missing baby? Well, while you are looking for that one you might find ours. We might get a BOGOF. You know, buy one get one free.' Dali's look was slightly more threatening this time. 'There is deliberate manipulation here.'

'You're telling me?' said Costello, just so they understood each other.

'Sorry,' said Dali. 'But I want you to find Polly. Quickly.'

'Did she have a phone, Lorna?' asked Costello, reminding herself that she did have the power of a police officer, not a social worker and grudgingly saw Dali's point.

'Oh God, yes,' replied Lorna, the absurdity of the question making her forget her stress. 'An all-singing, all-dancing one. With them it's a bigger priority than feeding the kids. Hers was an iPhone 7, in a black and white diamanté case, skull and cross bones. I have the number, she never changed it. She also had an iPad, she was always taking photographs on that.'

'Of Polly?' asked Costello.

'Of herself.' Lorna scrolled down her own phone and pressed once, and held it out to show Costello. 'It's just ringing out.' She tried it again with the same result.

'OK, so ringing and traceable. Orla is not a priority but Polly is.' Costello took the phone from Lorna and moved over to the front window to call the station and leave a message that they needed a trace on that number and would somebody call her back. 'She said she was going to the loo?' asked Costello, making her way to the small square hall. Dali had to move round the sofa to let her past.

'And she did. Then she came in here to put a jumper on and then climbed out the bedroom window.' They walked through a cloud of cheap perfume into the tiny room at the back of the flat. All three of them stared at the peeling wallpaper and the mould growing up the corner under the window. It was a study in bright pink. A poster with six tangoed male strippers, each one wearing a tiny thong with a couple of socks jammed down the front, dominated the room but there was no cot, no crib, no nappies, no baby clothes, no bottle. Wherever Polly was, she wasn't expected back.

With a gloved hand, Costello lifted the window. The sash ran up easily, only the smallest of rumbles giving it away, easily masked by the closed door. It was low enough for Orla to slip through and drop out onto the bed of weeds beneath, across the back green and out. She had the choice of three or four different escape routes. Each would have taken her to a street not visible to Lorna in the living room at the front of the flat. But the weeds were flattened and broken by something more than a pair of feet. Costello looked around.

'Did you see her take anything with her?'

'Can't say, I just saw her close the door.'

'There was something sitting here?' She pointed to a distinct rectangle of clear floor between a box and a pile of dirty clothes. 'Every bit of floor in this room is covered with crap except this wee bit. What do you think? A small suitcase sitting upright? A big handbag?'

Lorna looked round the room. 'Well, she had a leopard patterned suitcase. You know, a small one with a pull handle? I noticed it when I came in, I thought she was taking her clothes to the laundry.'

'Do you know if anything in the wardrobe is missing?'

Dali looked at her. Then at the mess on the floor. And opened her arms – how would they know.

Lorna shook her head. 'No idea.'

'This is worse than my daughter's room and she is the

messiest person I know. What a tip. Orla could be housing twelve illegals under her dirty laundry and we wouldn't know.'

Lorna flicked a smile at Costello, Dali's sense of humour was well-known.

'Can you look for a handbag, a passport, a bank card? Anything like that?'

'I'll do it,' said Dali. 'I've been into Shareen's room and got out without any notifiable disease. Well not that I know of. I'll have a good look. Bloody teenagers.'

Costello handed her a pair of nitrile gloves.

'Are these for my health or your evidence?'

'Both,' answered Costello.

Lorna smiled as Dali squeezed past her into the hall to deposit her diary somewhere safe.

'What was she wearing when you last saw her?' Costello had her notebook out.

'Tiny skirt. Bare legs, flat black pumps and a black T-shirt. I think she put on a red jumper but I'm not sure.'

Costello nodded. 'And that, Lorna, what do you think that was?' Costello pointed to the small picture lying on the bed in bits, the frame separated from the glass, the glass away from the picture.

'It was hanging up there earlier. It was a picture of a stupid wee dog, like a postcard.' She pointed to the empty nail. 'Could she have knocked it off the wall as she made her way out?'

Costello showed her the metal claws on the back. 'Maybe, but she has prised these clips open. It's an odd thing to have in a room like this with her Ed Sheeran poster and the Highlanders with their pecs. This wee Westie is a bit twee. The only reason I can think of as to why somebody would remove the back of a picture during their getaway was to retrieve something hidden there.' She gauged the size of the indent. 'Money? Credit cards?'

'Sort of thing my granny likes,' said Lorna, looking closely at the picture. She turned it over. It had been cut from a calendar.

'She must have dropped that on the bed this morning if she slept in it last night.' Costello picked up all the layers of the picture, feeling the odd width. She tried to put it back together. With the backing replaced, the picture at the front was bevelled.

'Looks like there has indeed been something stuck in there. Look at the size of it, what do you think? Cash? Was she a prostitute? Drug dealer?'

Dali was standing at the door, her face grave. 'Neither that we know of, well not in any big way. But she had some cash stashed. And her baby is missing.'

The lift up to the yoga studio was on the exterior corner of the Blue Neptune, right at the back on the junction of Sevastopol Lane and Inkerman Street, a complex comprising a nightclub, bars, four restaurants, executive offices and penthouse apartments. The rental included access to the gym on the top floor and that was where the yoga studio was situated. Anderson could have accessed it by the main door of the Blue Neptune and walked through the marble foyer to a reception where he would have to explain himself, so he chose the lift with its direct access to the gym and the studio from Sevastopol Lane.

He stood in a little inshot, a marbled porch protected by a metal slide gate that was pulled back and locked at the moment. He pressed a button to call the lift. The door clicked open, and he entered directly into a lift filled with the scent of flowers. The green marbled walls and the carpet tiles on the floor were very clean. He imagined there was a well hidden camera, scrutinizing anybody who pressed that button before they were admitted. Nobody who looked like they needed a pee was ever going to get in here.

It played a sweet light tune, not the usual banal lift muzak, it sounded like an acoustic version of the Beatles? 'Blackbird'? The lift took him, silently and smoothly, right up to the sixth floor.

He wondered if Sally owned the gym, or managed it? Had she ever finished her degree? Or had her career been derailed, as her life had in many more subtle ways. He was curious, maybe more than curious, about what had become of her. He had been very sure of himself when he had told Costello that Sally and Andrew were still together, but he didn't *know* that. He only knew what was stated in the file at the last update. Anything could have happened to them since then. He didn't know what he was hoping for. So, he didn't hope for anything.

The doors opened and he was immediately overwhelmed to complete surrender by gentle greens and beguiling blues, the heady aromas of eucalyptus and lavender.

A young woman as slim and neat as BA cabin crew, brown hair pulled into a bun, sat behind a glass counter, on a rattan and blue cushioned chair, the counter an artistic mix of bamboo and glass. On the wall were similar bamboo shelves and tinted glass. The shelves were stacked with rolled turquoise and sunflower towels, ornamental vials of azure liquid and small wooden sticks that looked like instruments of torture.

'Can I help you?' Her smile was very friendly. She looked young and . . . Anderson struggled for the word . . . clean. Almost sterile. She was either very pretty and wore no make-up or was so good at putting on make-up, that it was enhancing but invisible. She didn't look like the usual beauty therapy bimbo, more like a nanny from a posh nanny academy.

'I'd like a word with Sally, Sally Logan, or Braithwaite.' His smile said, this is official business and you would really be better off not asking. His fingers flicked round his warrant card, upending it on the glass surface of the reception desk, ready to show it if needed.

'Can I tell her who is calling?' A saccharine smile as she lifted up the phone, then placed the handset back on its cradle.

'Don't worry. I think I recognize that voice. Hello, Colin.'

He recognized her voice. He knew it in an instant. Soft and low, with a slight upward inflection that hinted at invitation. Or was that his wishful thinking?

He turned to see her standing in the doorway of the office behind him.

And for a moment he drank in the sight of her. She was older, but unfathomably so. She was, in essence, exactly the same. He would have recognized her anywhere. Her dull golden hair was wound up loosely on the top of her head, as if she had scooped it up and stuck two long pins through it. Her face was a little more lined, her lips a little thinner. Her pale green eyes were now hidden behind round-framed glasses. She was dressed in a kind of Japanese kimono, open at the front, wrapped round her blue leggings and her loose T-shirt.

'Hello,' he said.

'I think this is where you are supposed to say that I haven't changed a bit.' She stepped forward, the kimono billowed out a little behind her. Even in her blue trainers, she was nearly as tall as he was.

'You haven't changed that much.' Their eyes met and held. 'Not that much at all, if truth be told,' he said, honestly.

She stepped forward, easily slipped into his arms and proffered a cheek for him to kiss.

His heart thumped as he caught a scent of lime, the perfume that Helena used to wear. It confused him and for the quickest beat, he closed his eyes and held that moment; a beautiful woman in his arms and the scent of lime. When he stood back he hoped she didn't notice the moistness of his eyes. Well, why not, they were old friends. Maybe more than that.

Then she stood back and looked him up and down, a slow blink of those green eyes behind the glass rims.

'I think I can guess why you are here. Have I worked my way to the top of the pile again?' She turned away and looked back over her shoulder. 'Do you want to come through?'

'You don't need to speak to me,' he said, not moving.

She wrinkled her nose, a tic that took him back twenty years. 'No, I don't need to, but I would like to.' She gestured that he should follow her into the office. 'Robyn, hold any calls.'

The office was a fair size, the same theme of pastel shades, saved from looking too cold by the warmth of the golden sand colour, and the matching swirls of muslin at the huge window that formed one wall of the office. The view of the Clyde snaking in the distance was impressive. Today the sky was low, grey and rolling but it was pleasantly warm in here.

Anderson walked up to the glass, and stood, aware of the draft of heated air coming up from a gap on the floor. 'What a view.'

'I like it. I have my desk looking out the window. Bet you don't get that at your job.' She had climbed up on her desk, folded her long legs underneath her, easily, sitting in the lotus position in supreme comfort.

'If I had, I wouldn't get any work done. I presume you know I'm a cop?'

'I have heard that down the grapevine. And I may have read

about you in the newspapers now and then.' Then her face changed, as if remembering why he was here. 'Do you want a seat?' she indicated the two pastel blue sofas behind the desk, huge cushions nestling in wicker frames. She swirled on the desk, so while she was facing him, she was also looking down on him. He could give her that. If she felt the need to be in control, to be at home, then so be it. He noticed the slim wedding band, the small solitaire engagement ring slipped over it. Did that mean she was still with Andrew?

Suddenly she was awkward, messing with her hair, a nervous biting at her lip. The tic of wrinkling her nose again.

'So how did you end up with all this? I am very impressed.' It was trite but it got the conversation moving.

'Not all this, I have the gym, the spa and the studio. That is about it. I really got into yoga, you know. All those years ago I wasn't really getting over it.' Her eyes flicked up to meet his, the consent to talk about 'it'. 'I went away for a while, travelling. I spent a few months in India, did all kinds of soul-searching and navel-gazing. And yoga.'

'Oh. We were wondering where you went.'

'We? We or you? Did you ever wonder where I went?' She learned forward, searching him for a response. He was unsure what was expected.

'Of course I did.' He was indignant, he meant it. 'I think we all wondered about you. God, when did I see you last?'

'I can tell you that. I can tell you that exactly. It was at a party, at the uni, there were cocktails and the bar staff were so pissed they were just sticking anything in the drinks. We all got very drunk and ended up in the park.' She coloured a little, some other little memories filtering through. Then she said quickly, 'And you ended up with Brenda. Was that the girl from the hockey team? Business studies?'

'Accountancy. We have two children.'

That made her face cloud over, a slight tensing in her long, tanned neck. She flicked the small chain that hung there, quickly as if in irritation. 'So, you and Brenda are still together?'

'Sort of.'

She laughed. 'What kind of answer is that? Surely you either are? Or you are not?'

'We are close but we live apart. It's a long story. And complicated.'

She smiled and nodded, content to leave it at that, as if Colin Anderson from uni should never have matured into somebody 'not complicated'. 'So what do you have? Girls or boys?'

'Youngest is a boy, a sloth who lies in his bed all day and . . . Well, I have no idea what he does apart from eat and sleep with occasional forays to school. But my daughter is a beautiful girl who is the most marvellous creature on the face of the planet. That is a scientific fact, I am not biased about that at all. She's 17. Some kind of talented mega being.'

Sally giggled. 'A daughter? How marvellous. And what makes her tick? Is she going to be a detective like her dad?'

'Bloody hope not. She's an artist, hoping to go to the art school in Glasgow.'

'She must be good. What is she doing?'

'What do you mean, what is she doing? Makes a lot of mess as far as I can see.'

'I mean, is she doing fine art or sculpture or design or . . .?'

'Painting, painting pictures, that is all I get told. And I see things going through on the credit card that make me wonder what she is actually painting. It looks like I am sponsoring enough paint for the Forth Road Bridge and three undercoats. Oh, I know, her latest thing is fluorescence. Fluorescence and Warhol.'

'We have fish downstairs that glow in the dark, in the big restaurant. You should bring her in to see it, it's very beautiful.'

We?

The Blue Neptune had one of the most expensive restaurants in Glasgow and he wanted to say that money was not a problem, he could afford to eat there, but chose not to. He wanted to take her in his arms and say it's OK and I can take care of all this.

He chose not to do that either.

That was not why he was here. And there was nothing that needed taken care of. Sally was doing fine, the same Sally. Except . . .

He was here to ask her to revisit the most awful day of her life.

She inclined her head, peering at him over the top of her glasses, a few strands of reddish gold hair toppled, a scent of lime drifted across to him. 'But you didn't come here to talk about fluorescent fish, Colin.'

DS Viktor Mulholland looked at his iWatch, swiping at the screen with his thumb while the phone was jammed between his right ear and his shoulder. He had been waiting for Social Work to answer their phone for thirty-three minutes. He had read all the bits of paper stuck on the blue-padded partition of the office and had rearranged his desk, counted his paper-clips, if Big Brother hadn't been monitoring his computer activity he would have been playing FreeCell.

He slunk down in his chair, a parody of death by boredom played on his handsome face.

DC Gordon Wyngate, swinging on his chair like a slow metronome, held up his hand from his position on the opposite desk. Somebody had answered. The phone had actually been picked up. He punched the air in sarcastic celebration then collapsed again. Wyngate listened for a moment to the voice on the end of the phone, his hand stroking the top of his head, then he slowly turned his swivel chair round until he faced the handsome features of his colleague slumped down at the desk opposite him, shaking his head. 'Yes, but we are not Child Protection. I can put you through if you want.' Wyngate stuck his tongue out at Mulholland and got a two-fingered salute in return.

They both pressed mute on their respective calls.

'That will give them a taste of their own medicine, God I am bored.'

'I have applied to get back to MIT. Did you get anywhere the last time you tried?' It was a conversation they had often had in the last few months. 'I had heard there was another big reshuffle, thought I might try my luck.'

Mulholland pulled a cynical face as he was informed yet once more that his call was very important to somebody but not important enough for someone to bloody answer it. He covered the receiver. 'Colin Anderson has a cold case post now, do you know that? Why is he still working anyway? If

I was him I'd be in Vegas having three blondes lapping Jack Daniels from my belly button while watching a box set of *Game Of Thrones.*'

'That's an image I didn't want in my head before lunchtime.' Wyngate checked the phone, still on hold. 'And if you get to MIT, and Anderson leaves, then guess who might take over cold case, and think of the pleasure they might feel as they swipe you from your true vocation, back to looking at cold cases by desk-bound file review.' He raised his eyebrows in a speculative way, the small plaques of scarring on his face, white and circular, made him look like an overanxious panda when he pulled faces like that.

And Mulholland's mind moved up a gear. Back to a log cabin at Inchgarten, crouched in the corner as a forest fire raged around him, holding onto two human beings he barely knew. Not able to get out, not able to get away, his injured leg failing him. Colin Anderson and Costello had put him in the safest place they had, they had locked him away out of danger and gone to face the unknown. And somebody Anderson loved had died. That was the job, he could live with that. But he wanted to work that again, he wanted to be on the front line. This secondment was a slow death by a thousand paper cuts. He looked at the phone number flashing up on his phone. And then did a double take.

He widened his eyes at his colleague, lifted the receiver and said, 'Of all the gin joints in all the bars in all the world, you had to walk into mine.' He allowed himself a smile, knowing that Wyngate had turned around wondering who the hell was calling. Mulholland leaned back in the seat and pushed himself into a little twirl of his own.

The voice at the other end was as caustic as ever. 'DS Mulholland? You are still a DS, aren't you? Not been demoted again?'

He smirked, Costello might be a pain in the arse, but she always attacked from the front, none of that political nicey nicey shite he was subject to now.

'Good to hear from you,' he said and with a bit of a shock he realized he actually meant it. 'And what can I do for you?' he asked in mock politeness.

'How long have you got?'

'I've been on hold to Social Work for twenty minutes so I think I might have all day.'

'What part of Social Work?'

'Well, I have now been passed to Child Protection, but these kids might be grown up and married by the time they answer this phone.'

'Child Protection?' she said out loud, watching Dali rummaging around in what passed for a dressing-table drawer, still looking for a passport or credit cards. 'Why was this call transferred through to you? Are you the office boy?'

'What do you want, Costello?'

'I am here with the head of a child protection unit. If you put a rush on this, I will get somebody to answer your call.'

'Deal.'

'OK, here's the whole story.' She told it, keeping the story of Orla, and Polly, short and sweet. 'I think she legged it out the window and went through the close. She might have been pulling a leopard-pattern hard plastic suitcase, a rigid one, carry-on baggage size. Might being the operative word. She might have called a taxi, that would have been about half eleven.'

She could hear him typing, he asked her to repeat the address. 'But she might not have called the taxi to this precise address, here or hereabouts?'

'Do you have CCTV there?'

'Maybe not on this street but you could check on the main road. Would you be a gentleman and do that for me too? And get a trace on that phone number, she's supposed to be not that bright so might still be texting her friends. We need to make sure that child is well and with who it is supposed to be with.'

'What do you mean by that?'

'No clear idea yet.'

'Is this a case for MIT?'

She said quietly, 'I think it might come to that. There's a lot about this I am not liking. We haven't found Baby Sholto yet either.'

'You involved with that? Any chance you might need some more feet on the ground?' He laughed to keep the longing out of his voice, knowing that she would be alert to his desperation, but he had to take the chance. He couldn't sit here with his career on hold.

'Feet yes, but you only have one good foot, so no, not you. Have a good day with the phone company and the CCTV. Get back to me ASAP.' The line went dead.

'Bitch.'

'So, Lorna? Give me some background on Wee Polly.' Costello was thinking of Baby Sholto and Little Moses and looking for any tentative connections to Polly.

'Well, we inherited Orla Sheridan from another department. She was a troubled teen, from a stable background, the sort that give their parents sleepless nights. She said that she didn't know she was pregnant until she was about eight months. Once the pregnancy was confirmed she was passed over to us,' Lorna explained.

'Eight months and she had no idea. You are joking.'

'If she had known, she would have already applied for a new flat, all kinds of benefits. She would have gone right to the top of the list so no, I don't think she knew she was until it was too late. She's not the brightest.' Lorna then added, 'But she knows the value of a dollar. You know the type.'

'And she could afford a brand new phone. Any idea where the money was coming from?'

'She wasn't a substance abuser beyond a bit of dope. And if she was a sex worker it wasn't a regular thing. It's what we a call a promiscuous profession that indulges in high-risk behaviours, those are the new buzz words. Covers a multitude of crap and criminality.'

'A small player but not professional, if you like. Just cash for favours, like the government,' Dali said shrugging, and Costello knew what she meant.

Lorna looked miserable. 'I shouldn't have let her walk out the room like that.'

'What were you supposed to do, rugby-tackle her? Lorna, I once held the lift door open for the man who mugged me, so don't worry about it. When he tried to get out the lift I sat on him so I got the last laugh.' Dali held up a stylish pair of skinny leg jeans. 'Size 8. They have been worn recently, pulled inside out and left here. Top of the pile.'

Lorna looked at her boss, not making any sense of it.

Costello started to sift through the clothes that Dali had already searched, nothing was elastic-waisted or loose fitting. She was a young fashionista, a size eight. The slim-fitting skirt was a size eight. She would have known the minute that she started to put on weight. Orla Sheridan had known that she was pregnant, Costello was sure of it, but had kept under the radar despite the financial benefits social services would have offered her. Was there financial benefit to be harvested in some other way?

'Where did she have the baby?'

'The Queen Elizabeth.' Lorna's eyes creased up at the corner. 'I think.'

Costello phoned in to check, not really surprised that there was no record of Orla Michaela Sheridan having given birth at that hospital, but their record-keeping could be notorious. She would run a full check later.

'OK, so has anybody, anywhere, actually seen Wee Polly?'

'I have . . .' Lorna began, then corrected herself. 'I have seen photographs of her.'

'Or of a baby?'

'Yes, a baby. But Wee Polly? I wouldn't know. I really wouldn't know.'

Valerie Abernethy walked into the huge, high-ceilinged hall of her flat. Her flat, not their flat any more. Her flat, it had been that way since Grieg had walked out, plucking his car keys from the small ebony bowl that still sat on the hall table next to the picture of Abby and the kids, taking his Audi and driving out of her life. She tossed the keys of her Porsche in the self-same bowl, just to show she didn't care. The mirror above, all six-feet high and four-feet wide, ornate in its guilt frame, looked back at her with somebody else's eyes. Black. Barren. Guilty. She dropped her small suitcase, her handbag and her laptop under the table, and kicked off her shoes, dropping three inches in height suddenly, going back to what she had become; small and dumpy.

She clapped her hands, the slap echoing round the empty space. That normally brought Alfred running. He was a strange little cat with funny bulging eyes that were too big for his face, his round tummy too short for his legs. Black and white, he looked like a penguin or a film director. It was his resemblance to Hitchcock that got him his name.

Alfred didn't appear. There was no loud mewling from the kitchen demanding food, which was his 'Mohammed must come to the mountain' act. There was no banging of the cat flap, which was his 'where have you been all day' act. There was no sprint down the hall with heavy paws that suggested the weight of a full-grown Bengal tiger. There was nothing at all.

Just silence.

She skliffed her way on her stockinged feet, through to the kitchen that seemed empty without the pad pad of the cat behind her and put the kettle on before opening the fridge and taking out a bottle of vodka. She poured herself a long measure and downed it in one, letting that little frisson float over her. Then poured herself another. She sipped this one more slowly, walking towards the window that looked over the back garden and leaned on it, staring down. One of the neighbours must have been out sweeping up loose leaves. It looked very tidy. From up here on the Royal Terrace, she could see right over the city, Auld Reekie. Edinburgh. A city built of water colours; muted and rather quiet, distinguished and a bit . . . well, sad. A city with her best days behind her, a city with her guts ripped out. Anybody enjoying themselves in Edinburgh city centre was either faking it or a tourist, or a tourist faking it. She didn't think that the city had any soul, no real soul, it was very beautiful but without spirit. Like a few women she had known.

Or maybe it was the subtle but prevailing east wind, so cold it caught her breath and ran away with it. Even a warm day in Edinburgh had a chill about it, the way a warm day in Glasgow could still have rain pouring from the heavens.

She looked out at the gathering clouds and then down at the back garden again to where the bins were, neatly lined up and numbered. Two owners had their names on the lids. A black bag sat on the lid of her bin, folded and curled round its contents. That would incur another complaining letter to the factor about the bins being kept untidy and encouraging rats. Valerie put the glass down on the marble worktop of the central island and picked up the keys to the communal back door. She didn't bother putting any shoes on, hurrying in her stocking feet, out her own door and into the hall, then to the back of the terrace where she was smacked by a blast of cold Edinburgh air. Through the small gate, the roughness of the small brick path bit into the skin of her feet, snagging her tights.

The package was small, cold, heavy. It gave slightly as she lifted it with both hands. She unwound a little of the bag, exposing the small face, the little pair of white feathery spectacles, his open eyes stared into nothing, pink button nose with moustache of crimson blood. She rewrapped the plastic shroud. Her heart chilled. She couldn't look but she couldn't pull her eyes away. His intestines had come out his tummy, a string of pink sausage on the bin lid.

She stood in her black LK Bennett suit, realizing she was saying goodbye to her best friend.

And they had driven away, leaving him on the road.

To be scooped up and put on the bin.

Alfred.

The door behind her opened. It was the nosy cow from the other ground-floor flat, a right Miss Jean Brodie, tight-arsed in a cream Arran knit and tweed trousers.

'Oh, you'll get the death of cold about you, dear. Oh, look at the mess of it, the poor wee thing.' She stretched out her wrinkly old hands, trying to fold the cat back into the bin bag, squeezing him all wrong, crunching him up like an unwanted jumper.

'No,' snapped Valerie, elbowing the woman away. Valerie seized her sad little bundle, slamming the back communal door behind her, locking the old bitch out. Valerie wanted to scream at the top of her voice. Nothing went right for her, absolutely fucking nothing and now her little cat had been killed. What harm had he done to anybody?

She placed the little bundle on the central island, a small pathetic parcel in such a big and bright room, downing her vodka in one, then pulled a stool over and sat at the island, refilling the glass, not bothering to close the bottle. She wiped her mouth with the back of her hand, ignoring Jean Brodie hammering on the outside door. Valerie sat and looked at the bundle of fur and blood and bone for a long time, stroking his fur and flattening it all back down, pulling out bits of gravel and dirt that didn't belong there.

Unsteady on her feet, she went to fetch the red blanket from the bedroom.

She wanted to text somebody and ask them to come over. Grieg would be away with his new wife. Abigail would be at home with her man and her son. Archie would be 'busy' in Glasgow, visiting the wife who was incarcerated for losing her mind. Valerie found that a bit funny, then bit her lip until she stopped crying. By then her lips were bleeding.

She picked the blanket from the bedspread, now as smooth as a millpond. He was a good wee cat Alfred, never scratching the furniture but leaving circular patterns of dark hair on the bedclothes, spirals like ebony snowflakes. There was very little sign that he had ever been here. She carried the blanket back through to the kitchen, negotiating her way through the open kitchen door and round the end of the breakfast bar, holding on to steady herself on the sharp corners.

After another slug from the bottle, she climbed back on the stool and opened the sad little parcel. Slowly and carefully she started to push the soft intestines back into her wee cat.

Costello had left the flat, walked down the close and out into the back court and now she was squatting, looking at the badly laid concrete slabs and noticing the linear patterns of little clumps of earth, about eighteen inches apart, that stopped a couple of feet away from the edge of the flower bed under the window. Then her phone pinged. One text was from Archie asking her if she was OK, so she deleted that immediately. The other was far more interesting. McCaffrey had done a thorough job and came up with two numbers, both pay-as-you-go, that James Chisholm had called regularly. One had twenty- to thirty-minute calls over the last few months, the other had only two- or three-minute calls. Both had stopped the day before Sholto was taken. McCaffrey was good but he had had no training with CID, never mind a murder team.

He was intelligent, had sense and didn't mind staying on to get the job done. She texted back thanks and told him she'd order a triangulation on the numbers. That cost a lot of money but she was saving them a fortune in man hours. Whatever it was, James Chisholm was up to his eyeballs in it.

She had just finished texting when her phone rang.

It was Mulholland on his mobile. 'Hi, taxi company called me back within five.'

'What magic do you possess to get that info so quickly?'

'Taxi companies always do. I threaten them with you.'

'And?'

'We've already got the driver. Billy McDonald, he had just come into the office for his lunch. I mentioned a vulnerable child, five weeks old, missing, and the address of Orla's flat. They think it was a pick up on Primrose Street.' He waggled the handset around. 'I have been looking at the map, it looks right. Big black hair? Red jumper? Teens?'

Costello raised an eyebrow, moving out from the building to see if the reception got a little better. 'Sounds right. Where did he take her?'

'To Glasgow Central.'

'Shit.'

'But she didn't get on a train.'

'Really?'

'I could really do with something more interesting than hanging around on this phone like a bell end.'

'Where did she go, Vik?' She heard him sigh, it was pathetic. 'Look, Vik, you know you are not fit to be operational, but I will do what I can. I think this is going to pan out to something bigger and if so, I will put a word in for you, but in all honesty, the way my luck is going, as soon as I flag it up, the case will be taken off me. I hear what you are saying but as yet I have no connection between these two cases I am working. But, I think somebody with a better mind than me has already joined the dots.' At that moment she looked into the back window of the flat, Lorna had moved to the window and was watching Costello carefully and behind her was Dali, watching Lorna.

Costello moved the phone closer to her ear, as if they could hear her through the glass of the old sash window.

'There was no baby in the cab.'

'I think I knew that.'

'She gets off at the taxi rank but she asked, specifically for the one on Hope Street, not at the main door, so I figure she's not getting on the train?'

'What about a low-level train?'

'No, he watched her as she dragged her case across Hope Street, heading west,' said Mulholland. 'And Wyngate says hello.'

'Say hello back,' said Costello, 'I hope you are both very happy together.'

'The driver confirmed there was a small suitcase, leopard skin pattern but it was not heavy, she moved it about with no effort if it stayed on the flat. We've asked for the CCTV, it'll be here anytime now. They will buzz it straight through to me, and Wyngate and I have offered to view it for you and help you in any way we can.'

'You are so generous. What did your boss say to that?'

'Mahon? I think his attitude is more secular, and we should all stick to our own jobs. He didn't say it in quite so many words though.'

'Well, if you really want to annoy him, find out who owns these numbers.' She reeled off the two mobile phone numbers that James Chisholm had called regularly. 'I know they are pay-as-you-go but do what you can.'

'In exchange for . . .?'

'I will do what I can.' And she continued her slow progress round the garden, glad of the protection from the wind afforded by the high walls of the tenement. She felt like she was walking in a fortress.

SIX

'What did she say? Any chance for us to get out this office and stretch our legs?' Wyngate, unaware of his self-hypnotic suggestion, stretched his legs under his desk.

'I think she said that we were excellent little police officers and should both be promoted.' Mulholland jotted down the numbers. 'You get them traced.' He looked at the CCTV that was being uploaded onto his screen. 'These images are good, aren't they?'

'That's the one benefit of working here, stuff works, all kinds of gadgets for looking through CCTV.'

Mulholland was looking closely at the screen, 'So this is Orla going west, in the direction of some offices, big hotels . . .'

'And some very lower-end hotels. Rent-by-the-hour hotels. Was she a sex worker?'

'Costello didn't say. We should really be leaving the experts to look at this, they will do it much quicker than we can.' But neither of them moved, both staring intently at the screen.

'Where is she heading?' Mulholland leaned forward, eyes searching the quartered screen as the images on each flickered and morphed, people walking jerkily from one frame into another.

'Let's see if we can pick her up on Hope Street, she's easy to spot. A pelmet of a skirt, long cardigan thing and big black hair. Look for a skinny bird who looks as if she is wearing a Davy Crocket hat.'

Mulholland turned to look at the map behind him. 'Better to track her and see where she goes. There is no point in taking shortcuts. Too many big hotels for her to nip into. Once we know, we can send Costello round to follow it up. Are you sure Costello didn't say she was on the game?'

'She didn't *say* that.'

'OK, should we put an official request in? What was the name of the social worker she did a runner from?'

Wyngate leaned over and checked his notes. 'McGill, Lorna McGill. That name rings a bell.'

Mulholland stretched back in his chair and cracked his neck. 'She was on the Kissel case, wasn't she? She looks about 12. She let that woman kill her kid and then lets this one out a window, and this one has a five-week-old baby that nobody can quite locate. Do we see a connection there? Apart from Lorna McGill being bloody useless at her job.'

Wyngate pulled a face, making his gormless face look more gormless than ever, if that was possible. 'I had never thought of that.'

It was perfectly possible that he had not.

'I am sure that has not passed by Costello's radar. And she was on the baby swap case last night.' Mulholland pointed his pen at Wyngate. 'Did you see that in the papers? Three small kids that have come to harm, or might have come to harm, all of them right circling around Costello.'

'Yeah, but surely the Waterside baby abduction is a mental health issue, not criminal. Kissel wasn't abduction, that was just evil.' Wyngate tapped on the screen. 'When was the last time Lorna McGill saw this kid? When we had our two the health visitor was never away from the place.'

'I don't think Costello said.'

They continued to watch the screen. 'I wonder what the matter with these people is?' mused Wyngate.

'Some women are not cut out to be mothers.'

'I meant the social workers, why can they not do their jobs properly?'

'Over-stretched and under-resourced, that is their issue. You could argue that if the police had enough resources there would be no crime. And I think . . . look at that, is that her?' Mulholland pointed at the screen with his pen. 'Right there.'

Sure enough, there was a teenager, looking like any other teenager, maybe hurrying a little more, the odd look behind her as if she suspected she was being pursued.

'Yip, cardigan longer than her skirt and a black beehive, that's her. Where does she go?'

Mulholland clicked and rotated the screen, his eyes darting from one frame to another. He was rather enjoying himself. 'She crosses Hope Street, goes along Argyle Street, walking away from the city centre, there she is going past the Radisson and then . . .'

'What?'

'She turns down Brown Street, I think, at Kentigern House, going down towards the river. Come on, come on.' His hand tapped impatiently as the digital imaging reloaded. 'And she turned off, cutting through to Inkerman Street, right where the Edwardian Building is.' Again he typed, calling up more images. 'Down that lane, Sevastopol Lane, I think that is, and we lose her. She doesn't come out the other side into Inkerman Street, the system doesn't cover the shortcut.'

Wyngate took a note of the address, planning to phone Control to get somebody to look around on foot, see what the local buildings had covered by their own security systems. Then he caught sight of another figure crossing the road. 'Good God, have a look at that?'

Mulholland looked. 'Jesus, how pregnant is she, about ten months?'

'Ten months pregnant with twins, a pair of pachyderms from the size of her.'

Mulholland went off to get a coffee leaving Wyngate to watch the slow lumbering progress of an unknown pregnant woman in a blue coat, until she too disappeared up Sevastopol Lane. She moved out of range of one camera to be picked up on the next, but this camera was high and the lens was covered in street grime. The speed was slow, making her movements jerky as she made her stop-start progress down the narrow walkway, one woman who was just about to have a baby. Following in the footsteps of a woman who had just had a child.

'She just disappears.'

'Who?' Mulholland banged the coffee down, thinking that he had missed something.

'Miss Bluecoat. She vanishes.'

'Don't be stupid.'

'Seriously, she vanishes into thin air. You had better give Costello a phone.'

'Oh no. You are not making me look stupid, people don't disappear. Get another angle or something. They must have gone somewhere.' Mulholland put his feet up on the desk and went back to sleep, while still on hold.

The minute she was back in the car, Dali had asked Costello to take her back to her city centre office. Costello wasn't too keen. She was more intent on making phone calls, and very intent that Dali should not hear. It hadn't passed her by that Lorna was not the only common denominator, Dali was more so. And Dali had power. And she had the knowledge of vulnerable women, their pregnancies and their children at her fingertips. As soon as Costello had been put on the Sholto case, here was Dali, sticking to her like glue and trying to overhear her every word.

Given their history, one false move and she'd be in front of a tribunal so she knew she was walking a line. At the end of the day, no matter the political correctness of the situation, Dali was a civilian not a police officer.

'OK, I'll drop you in a mo, I just need to get back to this.' She waved her phone.

'No problem, I'll get on with this paperwork.' She started to reach into the back of the Fiat to get her bags, no mean feat for such a large lady.

Costello got out the car and perched on the bumper, aware of the Fiat rocking a little as Dali moved around inside, arranging the bags, retrieved from the back seat onto her stomach to be rifled through. All Costello's messages were from Mulholland, the single call was from Anderson. There was no update on the Sholto case. Was it worth doing a media appeal and suffering the tsunami of nutters it would bring in? Had Orla sold her baby for money? Holding off for the highest bidder? Was that why she had kept her pregnancy from others? Had one other woman done the same, then given birth to Moses, a Downs baby, which necessitated a switch and then Sholto Chisholm came on their radar?

That degree of organization was frightening. But it made sense.

She phoned Mulholland first. He suggested, again, that they should get together as they had something she might want to see. She accused him of withholding evidence. He said nothing, letting his silence do his bargaining for him. She took a deep breath and asked him if what he knew informed them of what had happened to Orla Sheridan.

He admitted that it did not. Then told her what he had seen.

She ended the call. Nobody knew what happened to Orla. She went down a street and disappeared. The most watched society on the face of the planet, and a woman can disappear. There was another woman, very pregnant followed by a pregnant pause, Mulholland had laughed at his little joke. Two women.

She thought about paying them a visit and seeing for herself. Then if they were at it she could give them a slap. Might as well add physical assault to racism.

Costello turned back and opened the car door, Dali didn't seem to have got anywhere with her paperwork. Friends close and enemies closer. 'Do you really need to be back in your office or are you allowed out to play a little longer.'

Wyngate was watching the CCTV recorded from the camera at the end of Sevastopol Lane. He couldn't help but feel heartened by this. The behaviour of a pregnant woman in a blue coat was only mildly questionable but it was mysterious. Even watching her made him feel he was getting his career back. This was what he had joined the police service to do. He knew he wasn't tough like Costello, and that he didn't possess Anderson's sensitive intelligence or Mulholland's unbreakable self-confidence, but he had been well-trained in computer intel and he was very determined. Oh yes, Police Scotland had spent a fortune training him, then side-lined him in a job that was little more than telesales. He looked at the clock, wondering if Costello was going to come over and see for herself. Mulholland was moaning their old DI sounded as though she was still a sulky-faced bitch and pondered if Archie Walker, the fiscal, was still involved with her or if he had taken up a less traumatic pastime, like juggling tarantulas. Wyngate was slightly kinder about Costello, he had a respect for her, whereas he thought the Mulhollands of the world would always have it easy, with their casual charm and charismatic smiles.

He had enjoyed himself on the murder team, something he couldn't admit to himself until he was faced with the boring banality of the job he did now, a time before he had to tell people how to plot a timeline of a crime. Obvious stuff.

He was following Orla on the tape, half listening to his colleague moaning about why should they do this at all as it would only go upstairs and be taken from them.

'We get the ball in their half, then they score. Always the bloody same.'

Wyngate watched, marking the time, making notes on his pad in front of him, then typing the number of the next camera, asking for the footage. Slowly street by street he traced her journey, watching her as she walked with flat shoes and big hair. She was easy to follow. He glanced up at the map, and where she was likely to go. Into a shop or a café or a hotel, a bar, could be any of them down in that part of the city. He printed off the screen grab of her last sighting, lifting it from the printer his eyes still on the monitor. It had moved on, another minute, the camera caught sight of the very pregnant woman, with her waddling, shuffling walk. As he watched she put her hands in the small of her back then hoisted the strap of her shoulder bag up once more, and continued on her slow way. Wyngate empathized, recalling the hours he spent rubbing his wife's back. He had three wee kids, he knew about sleep deprivation from the second child, a charmingly rotund little beast who survived on three hours sleep in every twenty-four hours in ten-minute batches. He watched her waiting to cross Brown Street, still heading west. He switched the camera, typing in the code for the camera he knew would pick her up on the opposite side of the road, and saw her. To his surprise she was indeed turning to walk down Sevastopol Lane, not lost, she walked confidently. She knew exactly where she was going. The camera lost sight of her as she went deeper between Wright's Insurance and the Old Edwardian Building. There was nothing else down there, as far as Wyngate knew, it was just the old service lane between two buildings. He could see the big electronic bollard in place to allow deliveries but no flow of through traffic. He typed in the coding for the cameras on Inkerman Street, and watched, curious as to where she

was going, hoping that somebody was waiting for her in a
car, or in a taxi.

But there was no taxi there.

He watched, waiting, realizing that she hadn't appeared.

The first set of CCTV had been right.

He went back to the previous camera, checking the times,
speeding through the time lapses until half an hour had passed.

Still nothing.

Where did she go?

He ran the tape back and forth, looked at other screens, at
other angles. But she had disappeared off the face of Glasgow.
Then as he was watching, he noticed something odd. Three
seagulls suddenly took flight, not easy flight but a panicked
and hurried flap of wings. What could frighten a Glaswegian
seagull? Wyngate had always thought they were bulletproof.
He sat moving the image back and forth until he saw something on the upper edge of the film, in the air. Another seagull?
But it didn't appear to be moving. Wyngate held the point of
his pen to the small object hovering in the sky above the
building. He closed in on it as far as he could. Was it a drone?
He picked up the phone, phoning the three businesses in the
vicinity, finding out which, if any, had ordered a drone, and
he would bet it had a camera on it.

Wyngate brought Mulholland up to date, trying not to sound
smug as he pointed out the drone and replaying the section
of tape when the birds took flight. 11.27 a.m. precisely.

Mulholland raised an eyebrow. 'We are doing the work on
this, let's call Costello again.'

'I am doing the work on it. Did she say she was coming over?'

'Not in so many words but we could put her off. You call
her and tell her we are still looking.'

'No, you call her.'

'You do it.'

In the end they tossed a coin.

Costello had just finished a call that confirmed how little
movement there had been on the baby abduction when her
phone rang again, she mouthed an apology to Dali who
was still in the car, on her own mobile catching up on some

business herself. She listened to Wyngate carefully, phone in her right hand, the palm of her hand up to her left ear to block out the noise of the council truck that had chosen this very moment to pick up the rubbish. She had to ask him to repeat the bit about the loud noise, something that made the seagulls take fright.

'OK, OK. So, track down the film from the drone first,' Costello said, then added, 'sorry I know you are doing that already but I'm still here with Dali. I think I'll call Anderson.'

'Why? Do you think we can't move this forward on our own?' Wyngate's voice was a little tremulous.

'Just in case we need the back up of a DCI, I'd rather have one I can bully.'

Wyngate breathed out down the phone.

'Gordon, this is more than a daft girl leaving her kid in the pub and doing a runner. We had Sholto yesterday and Polly today. I can't make out the connection but I'm sure there is one. Get on with the drone film and have a good look at James Chisholm's phone records.'

'Mulholland is on that.'

'Good.' She cut the call then bent down and smiled at Dali through the car window. She waved back, she was still on her phone. Costello wondered who to, and maybe she had not been so clever in getting out of the car in the first place.

She dialled and waited.

Anderson was curt. 'What is it Costello. I am very busy.'

'Yes, so am I.' She reeled off the events of the day, ending with the mysterious disappearance of two women down Sevastopol Lane. 'That's the lane that runs between—'

'The Blue Neptune and the Old Edwardian.'

'How do you know that?'

'Why are you telling me?'

Costello was confused. 'I am telling you that because I want Mulholland and Wyngate back on board, on my team.'

The end of the line went quiet. 'I thought you were telling me because of where they were last seen.'

'Sevastopol Lane?' Costello's brain tried to backtrack, she had missed something but then she had it. His reaction had given him away, that slight defensive pause, the fact he hadn't volunteered it. 'Are you familiar with that location? The lane and Inkerman Street? Have you had a case there?'

'I am there right now.'

'The file you had under your arm at the water cooler?'

Silence on the phone. 'Just send me a picture of the girl that went missing.'

'Orla? We are not sure that she has gone missing, we just don't know where she is. It's Wee Polly who has gone missing.'

'Send me a picture of Orla anyway. If I am your DCI then that is an order.'

She refused to say goodbye, her turn to let the pressure behind her silence build up.

'I am offering to help but leave it with me. And don't nag at me.'

'OK,' she said, wondering what he was really trying to tell her.

Colin Anderson was thinking about Sally, how one event could shape an entire life. She hadn't rejected the idea of getting involved in the SafeLife campaign, saying she would mull it over but she'd need to talk to Andrew, but wouldn't it be great to catch up. She had picked the phone up there and then and asked her husband – 'Guess who is on his way?'

Andrew; the man who had won the heart of the best girl in the gang. Anderson hadn't realized he was so distracted until his third U-turn. He ripped the satnav from the dashboard and pulled the BMW into the yard of the Braithwaite's smallholding, set off a B road outside Blanefield. A wooden sign nailed to a tree had the word 'Milestone' painted on it, the 'e' had been elongated to create 'Millstone'. The sign was illustrated with the outline of a small owl. Colin Anderson drove the BMW slowly across the yard, manoeuvring his way round water-filled potholes and mounds of manure. There was no hard standing in the yard, so he drove as close to the half-demolished porch as he could, parking beside a battered, rusty jeep. He couldn't make out any proper front door, or garden. It was a mish mash of outbuildings, all in various states of dilapidation, all single story, all honed from the same beautiful grey stone. It looked as cold and unwelcoming as a bitter north wind.

He got out the car and looked around, seeing land, grass and more grass, but he could get a better sense of the layout now. The smallholding was built in a square and through the arch in the wall that faced him, he could see the cobbles of the courtyard, an old water trough and on the far side a vine was trying to grow along the top of the wall. The thick grey brown of the trunk showed how old the plant was, yet it had made little headway with the lack of sun and the coldness of the winter. And no matter how much time passed, it was never going to get much further. Colin Anderson knew how it felt.

The small house was heavy with the sense of past days, good times and old memories. The twisted ivy that crawled over the tree trunks, smothering them, was doing much better than the vine. That sweet smell of mulch and humus scented the still air, there was a backing track of flies buzzing and melodic birdsong from somewhere high in the trees, not visible to him.

He approached the old porch, a ramshackle hut of slatted wood, badly painted in white. The whole carcass was rotten and flaked, cracked open and cream-coloured mushrooms blossomed on the rumpled felt roof. The door lay at an angle, leaning on its top hinge. The glass panel in its upper half was smoky with dirt and condensation. The Braithwaites must be very sure that anybody pulling into the driveway would be either heard or seen. But even then, Anderson thought that Sally would have insisted on more security, after everything she had been through. Even for her peace of mind, there should be a gate, a lock, a door.

Five Rottweillers.

But he was proved correct as the door shuddered, the bottom catching on the concrete floor. As it slowly screeched its way open, Anderson had clear sight of the whitewashed wall of the main building. Hanging on the wall by its front wheels, was an old message bike. It made him think immediately of Sally riding around on her bike in Kelvingrove Park in Glasgow, the last week of the summer lectures at university. When they were young, and drunk. The bike had ended up in the fountain. They had *all* ended up in the fountain. He saw the frame of the man appear through the gap in the door, filling it. Andrew Braithwaite was still a bear of man, a gentle giant. Colin had liked him then, and he hoped he would like him now.

'Long time, no see. How are you? Sally told me you were on your way over.' Braithwaite held out both hands, open in a gesture of true friendliness. 'Bloody hell, you look *old*.' He laughed and punched Anderson on the upper arm.

'I think a good look in the mirror might sort that out, Andy.'

And they were right back in the zone again, back in the park, back in the day.

'Come on through,' Braithwaite said, gesturing that Anderson should follow him. 'Don't worry it's quite safe.' He tapped the side wall, sending a few flakes of plaster to the ground, and the bike rattled alarmingly on its hook. Braithwaite let out a low growl as he walked past it. 'We're not quite condemned to the hard hats yet.'

Anderson followed, stepping over a broken Dyson and a few odd wellington boots, into the warmth and patchy darkness of the long narrow kitchen. It looked awful, and smelled wonderful, somebody had been baking recently, the smell of cinnamon and scones filled the air.

'Take a seat.' Braithwaite removed his specs, folding them into the V-neck of his shirt.

Anderson sat down, comfortable in the domestic war of the functional and the filthy. He felt disloyal as he relaxed. Disloyal to Helena's super clean state-of-the-art white and black marble kitchen, or his own at home – a family kitchen with a bulging laundry basket and a fridge door covered with drawings by the kids. Pictures that had been there for years. Pictures too precious to be taken down and put somewhere safe. There was a huge, uneven wooden table, surrounded by ten or twelve wooden chairs, each of them sported a different coloured cushion fastened with little ties round each upright, the end dangling and frayed like they had been chewed by canine teeth or teased by feline claws.

The kitchen itself ran the whole length of this part of the smallholding, an Aga sat along the long wall, not the cosy, clean and comfy Aga of the detached bungalows down in the village of Blanefield. This was a working Aga, paint-scratched and peeling, the top plates burned the colour of stewed tea. In front of it, a small red rug lay twisted on a floor that was little more than a collection of cracked terracotta tiles, the colour of the parched earth of a long hot summer.

On the walls, open shelves covered the old brick walls and as he looked round, Anderson watched a ginger cat jump from the window sill, onto the bottom of the open sash window, skilfully balance itself on the narrow wood, then slip down the inner glass and meander over to see if anybody had filled up his food dish in his absence. He failed to hide his disappointment and looked at Braithwaite, mewling like violin being tuned.

'Bloody thing, always wanting fed. There's acres of woods out there full of small tasty things running around, but he wants a tin of tuna.'

'My dog prefers ice cream to dog food. But then so do I,' said Anderson. 'This is some place you have here. Are you doing it up?'

Braithwaite threw the empty can of tuna towards a swing bin, the lid resting on the rubbish underneath. 'I would like to say that was the case but we have been in here for a decade or more. Sally inherited the place and we have learned to live with it. We keep intending to do stuff, turning it into a small spa and exercise studio—' he absentmindedly rubbed his huge belly as he said this – 'but I think we might be better waiting until it all falls down around our ears and we are forced to do something.' He looked round, a gentle scrape of his honey-coloured beard, his eyes looking at the spidering patterns of damp ingress. 'Yeah, but it will be fabulous when we get the money together.'

Anderson was surprised by that. He had remembered Sally and Andy as a couple that money would never be a problem for, although he couldn't recall exactly why he had that impression.

'I've seen the set up at the Blue Neptune, that must be worth a bob or two.'

'Oh to see that you'd think we were bloody rolling in it. But that is Sally's problem; too bloody soft.'

'She runs the gym there.'

'And takes classes.' Braithwaite was rubbing his knee now, conscious of early rheumatic change. 'But she's so soft she runs it like a drop-in centre for fat people, doing classes for nothing and a one-hour class means they hang round for a couple of hours and then go downstairs for lunch.'

'I hope I didn't upset her.'

Braithwaite shook his head. 'It'd take more than you to upset her.'

Anderson caught a trace of resentment.

'Oh you know Sally. She's the real deal but she has no head for business. She fosters poorly kittens and kisses puppies, she's bloody useless.' The resentment rolled into affection, he shrugged as if to say, but what can you do?

'And you?'

'Well, I work at the hospital, do a couple of afternoons privately in my clinic at the Blue Neptune. It's not a great job and it pays the bills. Have you ever met a woman happy with her appearance? No, so there will always be work for me.'

'You're a plastic surgeon?'

'Well, I remove wrinkles and there's not a lot of money in that but you come to a point in life when all you want is peace, quiet and enough. And we have enough. We had more than enough when we were young enough to enjoy it. And we enjoyed it.' He smiled at Anderson including him in the memory. 'I wasn't surprised you ended up a cop.'

'No? I think it surprised me.'

'Oh you were always the level-headed one. The one warning us against being too loud and frightening the horses. Captain Sensible, that was Sally's nickname for you.'

Anderson had forgotten that, his brain letting it go as a memory he didn't want to retain. Was that what she had thought of him? Braithwaite stood back up and placed his hand on the side of the kettle. Then he leaned his back against the worktop. 'I know why you are here.'

'What do you know?'

'Everything. I know Sally was assaulted, I know that happened. I remember the day very clearly. I know she got pregnant as a result and I know that she lost the baby. By that I mean she miscarried it. She was going to keep it and have it adopted as soon as it was born but nature took a different route.'

Anderson nodded. Sally had alluded to as much when he had asked why she had changed her mind about the campaign. It would have highlighted another tragic consequence of her attack and, maybe, made the child an object of media speculation. The loss of anonymity was a door that once opened, could never be closed.

Braithwaite reached round and unhooked two mugs off the bottom of the shelf, selected a jar of tea leaves and a jar of coffee, holding them both out for Anderson to choose.

'Coffee please, splash of milk.'

Braithwaite set off, his bulk leaving the kitchen made the space seem bigger. He went through the arch and Colin heard the fridge freezer open and close, a chink of a milk jug and the room dimmed as he passed the dirty window on his return.

'This is a splash of milk, straight from a cow.' He sat down again, the chair creaked a little in protest. The cat left its plate of tuna, the milk now a more interesting prize.

'When did you two get together officially?' asked Anderson.

'After I convinced her you weren't her type. And after everything else. She had disappeared for a while, do you remember that?'

'I think I was head down in my finals by then. But she said she went to India.'

'Yes, meditating knee-deep in cow shit. Sacred cow shit, mind. We were never really together before that, more when she returned.'

'Oh, I thought you two were an item all the way through?'

Braithwaite laughed. 'No Colin, what you saw there was a young man struggling with his medical degree, head over heels in love with that beautiful English lit student. She was cleverer than me, wittier than me, more popular than me but I thought if I hung around long enough she might notice me. And ignore this blond dude that half the lassies fancied.'

'God, I wish I had known.'

'We never see ourselves as we are. Thank Christ. I'd get arrested for stalking nowadays. But then—' Braithwaite's voice dropped, he patted his knee for the cat to jump up – 'then it was just love. And it has been that way ever since.'

SEVEN

Mulholland had sent Wyngate to explain to their boss why they were working on a case that should have been based at Govan. Wyngate's basic vagueness could be useful, he'd refer Mahon onto Costello and so it would move up the food chain, leaving them alone to get on with it.

He was honing his investigative skill on the phone records of Roberta and James Chisholm, and deciding that James might have some questions to answer. And now he had a copy of the film from the drone, he had it all to himself. The drone had been ordered by Wrights Insurance which was the building on the south side of Sevastopol Lane. He had his phone open at Google maps, just to keep his references right. Wright's had wanted a survey of their own roof and as the drone swung out, it caught a bird's-eye view of the lane and the edge of the Old Edwardian, which was the building at the start of Sevastopol Lane on the north side. The drone gave them great quality images, all digital. He moved his seat, so that his sore leg rested more easily. He could be here for some time, as although the image itself was clear, it jiggled about, making it difficult to see exactly what was being looked at. At the start it was concrete, puddles, bits of pipe and patches of different roof coverings, felt slates, tiles and the odd casing for ventilation units. The roof then started to move from side to side, a little at first as if gaining momentum for a sweep, then growing in its parameters. The film was soundtracked by the monotonous birr of the drone's motor. It started moving in straight lines, sensing its way round the perimeter of the building and moving steadily so he could easily make out the elegant carvings on the balustrades. That would be the Old Edwardian. But only occasionally did it move far enough over the edge to see anything on the street below or the lane. After a few minutes of floating around the sides of the square, flaring in overshoot at each corner, it started the same manoeuvre but this time a slightly wider swing before it started a right-angled discourse at a lower altitude, getting close-ups of the outside edge. Then a roof garden flashed into sight and the drone jumped and jerked out the way, as if it had got a fright. Its operator had obviously realized how close it had come to crashing.

Mulholland leaned closer in, but the drone was going up Crimea Street, then turning down, making its way down Inkerman Street and then turned up the lane, reversing the route the two women had taken. He concentrated, waiting for the drone to do its survey, catching a teasing glimpse of Miss Bluecoat now and again. Then she came into view, not moving, standing very close to the brick wall, leaning on it. The drone bumped slightly, caught by a gust of wind, Mulholland waited, willing the drone to return to its bird's-eye view. When it did, he pulled his seat in for a closer look and dragged the curser back, replaying the last few seconds. It was definitely her, tucked close into the wall, as if she was getting her breath. The drone moved out slightly, then the wall came back into view.

She was gone.

Anderson found himself talking about his kids for the second time that day. Braithwaite might have got Sally but he, Colin Anderson, Captain Sensible, had ended up with a family, his son and his daughter and nobody could change that.

Braithwaite had invited him through to the living room, a cosy room down the narrow stone-floored passageway, past the extension of the old porch where the air was humid and musty. Green moss snaked and flowered its way up the windows. Somebody, Sally maybe, had thought about putting a curtain pole above the window and then given up, leaving the pole lying against the lower slope of the roof, where it looked totally at home, as if it was giving some support to the ceiling.

Anderson stepped over it, realizing that Braithwaite was talking about the mess the place was in and this bit needed this and that bit needed that. He was talking technically about damp proof courses, dry rot and how much it was all going to cost and Anderson found himself sympathizing, then he realized he could buy the whole place lock, stock and barrel. This room was small cosy, the air felt dry compared to other parts of the house. A low beam in the middle meant both men had to duck their heads as they carried their mugs of coffee towards the wood-burning stove, Anderson knew that this was where Braithwaite must have been when he heard the car; it felt warm and lived in. He settled himself into one of the seats at the fire as Braithwaite knelt down and opened the stove door, the flames immediately coming alive. He added two logs of wood from a very neat stack beside the fire and closed the door over and the flames died a little. Braithwaite looked as though he was preparing for a long sit in.

They had reminisced long into the night, first with coffee, then with whisky. Braithwaite becoming more open as the drink took hold. Anderson remembered to text Claire and say he was out late, maybe out all night.

Sally had changed when she came back and some steak and salad appeared. There was wine. On the outside Sally was the same, but there was something more human, flawed. Not just the sparkly life and soul of the party Sally, but a more vulnerable one. They were both very easy company.

Anderson could see that what Braithwaite had said was true. He had stopped 'fancying her'. They became true friends. Then lovers. Then they married.

Through the assault of the whisky and wine on his senses, the warmth of the log fire and the chill of the old armchair he was sitting on, Anderson couldn't tell if that was true. Was his own memory so different? He had thought Sally and Andrew were an item in their final year. If he'd known they weren't, he might have made a move. Well, he had made a move, hadn't he?

How much had Sally remembered?

How much had Sally told Andrew?

Andrew waited until Sally had gone out to feed 'the animals', before he asked, 'So why are you here? Something about a new campaign? You could have phoned, no need to come all the way out.'

Anderson remembered that Braithwaite was bright. He looked like a big cuddly bear, slow and lumbering, but he was sharp, sharp like a shark. So Anderson found himself telling Andrew about his colleague who was trying to track down a woman who went missing in the side street that runs up the side of the Blue Neptune. And vanished into thin air. How could that happen?

Braithwaite didn't seem to think the question odd but said that Sally was very particular about who goes in that lift, there was a good camera. Braithwaite told him to get Sally to show him the footage, it might help if it caught any of the lane in its field of vision.

'You don't know her, by any chance?' Anderson pulled out his phone and found the email with the update and he showed the picture of Orla Sheridan to Braithwaite. 'We were lucky that there was a drone going overhead and we can see her quite clearly. One minute she was there and the next minute she wasn't. And there was another woman, very pregnant.'

Braithwaite looked at the phone. And handed it back. 'The pregnant woman might be something to do with Sally, she runs prenatal classes, but not this girl. I haven't seen it in the papers?'

'No, we are keeping it quiet, one of those cases that she may or may not be missing. And if she is it will be our fault or that of Social Services. Not her's though.'

'No, never theirs. I lamped a drug addict last week. He had a four-inch stab wound in his abdomen, was going to walk out of A and E.'

'What, to die in the car park?'

'Yeah. If he had made it as far as the car park, I'm past giving a shit about that but three nurses got hurt trying to restrain him. He hit two of them and the third one injured her back slipping on the blood.' Braithwaite pulled an amused face, his eyes crinkling reminding Anderson how charming he was at uni. Not conventionally handsome but there was something about him that women admired, chiselled cheekbones, a nose slightly too large, a big gregarious smile. He would grow more handsome with every year that passed, his grey hair would look distinguished. Anderson just looked old, his forehead ever growing up to chase a receding hairline.

The smile was benign. He snuggled down in the chair. 'So just how curious were you to know what Sally had become. "Professionally"?' The question was asked with a raised eyebrow. 'Or personally.'

Costello sat lower in the driver's seat of her Fiat, her hands round the cup of tea she had bought at MacDonald's, and listened to the slow strains of Nina Simone on her CD player. She was worried. Her head felt like she had spent all day in a tumble dryer, tossing about ideas that came out in more of a jumble than before. It was well after eleven and she knew how far away sleep was.

She had Wyngate and Mulholland on one side, and McCaffrey on the other. Moving around her like a couple of giant planets were Anderson and Dali, pulling her into their orbit, not quite letting her do what she wanted to do. In the end, Dali, she was sure it was Dali, had offered to take them all out for a curry. It would be much easier to get them all round the table in a quiet office and decide on a course of definitive action. She had tried to call Anderson at various times that day. At first he wasn't answering but then he had turned his mobile off. On the day he was going out to see a woman he used to have feelings for. She could read him like a book, a Mills and Boon, a bad Mills and Boon. She had found herself talking to Dali, aware she wanted to keep something back, not knowing why she didn't quite trust her. But they had gone back to Dali's chaotic office, papers everywhere where the phones never stopped. And Dali had said that was a quiet day.

They talked about children, vulnerable children, and she found herself talking about Malcolm without mentioning his name, that disconnect, the feeling that the child was excluded from the family that was supposed to be caring for him. Dali had nodded, that was when they should take action, there was no point in waiting until the abuse got physical, by then the psychological damage had already been done. Physical scars heal, psychological ones don't.

Dali asked about Sholto's parents and whether that child had been an intrinsic part of the Chisholm family. Costello told her about the two numbers on James Chisholm's phone. One number had been called consistently, and that person had called back.

A woman, Angelika Kauscher.

Dali had just pulled a face that said bloody typical. Angelika had been upset, asking if Sholto had been found. Costello had smooth-talked her into admitting that she was James Chisholm's lover. She was Polish, working here as a waitress. She sounded very young, talking about James with filial reverence. And young enough to be scared into honesty when talking to a British police officer. According to Angelika, James and Roberta had been having some problems. James had been flashing his money about, his wife didn't understand him and all that crap. Angelika was surprised that Sholto had come along. James had not been happy about the pregnancy, he felt that he was now trapped financially. Costello said that Angelika might need to come in and make a statement to that effect but she would try and keep her out of it, as long as she said nothing to James.

'And the other number?' asked Dali.

Costello shook her head. 'That phone is on and it's in Glasgow – that's all we know.'

'When will you confront Chisholm?'

'When I need to, but I think it's all part of a bigger picture.'

'Why do women fall for that crap?' Dali then laughed. 'Christ knows, I did. My husband had two lovers on the go at one time and I still had no idea. No wonder he was too knackered to cut the grass.'

They had laughed. Costello told her about Archie without mentioning any names. Dali had said she wished she'd agreed to her mother's suggestion of an arranged marriage. Then the bad choices would have been somebody else's fault. Then Costello had drunk a cup of tea and picked the social worker's brain for the appeal for Sholto.

She had agreed with Costello's thoughts to be careful, just keep the focus on Moses. That was safest. She had then handed Costello her personal number. 'Call me if you need help, it needs careful handling. I know good people.'

The psychologist had advised against the parents doing a media appeal for the return of Sholto. There was a delicate line to walk. She had been advised against using strong-arm tactics, if the abductor hadn't responded to his face then should she ramp it up by showing the mother's distress over Sholto being taken? What if that scared who ever had him into harming him, or disposing of him? But maybe they could show more of little Moses, but that might provoke righteous headlines writ large on the moral high ground, how vulnerable is a five-week-old Down's syndrome baby? That was right up there with blonde orphans and golden retriever puppies. If they were going to do it, it had to be mother to mother. Moses was doing well at hospital but missing his mum, there had to be lots of reassurance, nothing threatening. While the real message was 'please make yourself known to the authorities so we can get the babies the right way round'.

Costello couldn't see it working. Emotional intelligence told her that the swap had been a case of a woman wanting a healthy baby, but the mechanics of the incident told her differently. There was a cold, hard, planned logic about this. Without her knowledge Roberta Chisholm had been stalked like prey, and had her young removed from her. A flash of some David Attenborough footage of lionesses and baby wildebeest crossed her mind. She had shuddered then and she shuddered again now, sitting in her own car. There was something feral about this, something very basic. Roberta's husband had been having an affair, those long nights he was out, he had not been working late. Then there was the matter of that other number, the mystery number that had much shorter phone calls. At least they weren't to Poland.

She had sipped tea while Dali picked her own brains about Orla. And where was Polly? The same place as Sholto? Costello had shown her the still of Orla, immediately recognizable, and then Miss Bluecoat, about to have a baby, had also disappeared into thin air. Dali had not known her, or she said she didn't.

Costello was a trained interrogator, she saw the flash in Dali's eyes as soon as she mentioned Sevastopol. When asked Dali had admitted she knew it was off Inkerman Street but denied that she had ever been there. And Dali then had moved the conversation on to the subject of the best curry houses in Glasgow and would the rest of her team like to come out and try one.

And now here she was sitting outside Malcolm's house, in her car, sipping another cup of tea, this time from McDonalds.

Over the meal, both Wyngate and Mulholland had come up with good stuff, shame that it showed they were talented at desk-bound information gathering and therefore proving Police Scotland's theory that they were better kept in an office and out of harm's way. She would help them out as much as she could. Sometimes cops needed to be on the ground and doing, not sitting reading and phoning. And whatever else she was up to, Dali recognized that; the need to do something and not sit back and wait until the irreversible happened.

And Mulholland was quick. She had mentioned Malcolm in passing and now Costello was sitting outside the house of Malcolm Haggerty aka Harry Fucking Styles, where he lived with his mother Abigail and his father George. The older half-sister, Mary-Anne or Mary-Jane or something like that, Mulholland could never recall double-barrelled first names, didn't seem to be living here anymore. The villa, in its highly desirable area, had belonged to Abigail's first husband, Oscar, and he had died in mysterious circumstances. That had perked their interest as they leaned in to rip the naan breads apart. He fell and hit his head when working in the garden. He had been a little dizzy and came in to sit down until he felt well enough to go back out again, feeling a bit groggy. The next day he had gone sailing, as per usual, and he had never returned. Mulholland had given them that potted history, gleamed from all the media clips online on his phone as any member of the public could. Mary-Anne or Jane had been about six at the time, Abigail had then remarried and had Malcolm presumably.

She burped loudly, glad that she was alone in the car. Dali had paid for the meal, she was so pleased that Wyngate had asked for a night off from babysitting and made the effort to come along. Mulholland had no bother telling Elvie as she would be at work anyway, stuck in a hospital listening to some surgeon being sarcastic to her. Dali had continued the conversation, interested in the pictures of Orla, but more interested in the picture of the woman now known as Miss Bluecoat. She had lifted the photographs up, looking at them sideways as if changing the angle would give her a better view of the pregnant woman's face. Professional interest? Professionally too interested? At one point Mulholland had cottoned on that she was gently interrogating the woman who was paying for their meal. He had then kicked Wyngate under the table when Wyngate had tried to change the conversation, hurting his own leg in the process.

Somebody, she couldn't recall who, probably Wyngate, had mentioned Grahamston, the old village underneath Glasgow. Maybe that was where the women had gone. And they had laughed. Dali had nodded her head and took a sip of her Kingfisher lager.

The evening had moved on as these informal occasions do, the conversation flowed. Wyngate as a younger officer, driving kiddy's electronic cars round a cash and carry as he waited for the paperwork to come through for a break in. It had been a police car, a New York cop car and he thought it might be the only chance he got. Dali said she would have loved that, but her arse would have got stuck. Mulholland told the story of telling drunks that if they were sick in the car, they would be made to eat it. They never did after that threat, they always asked to get out. Then the three of them looked at Costello, who paused, then she asked Dali about the horrors of her job. Dali laughed a hearty laugh and told them too many to mention. Kids, six of them of the same family, all under eight years old, being left in the house while the parents went to the pub and the eight-year-old making a very good job of looking after his siblings, two of them still in nappies. And that wasn't occasionally, for a couple of hours. It was all day, every day. It ran the gamete from that tragedy to trendy fucking women in the west end, still breastfeeding their ten-year-olds and the cops having to tell them 'not at the school gate' and the subsequent fallout of mothers' rights issues blowing up in their face, missing the point of the eight-year-old changing the nappies. They had enjoyed Dali's foul-mouthed rant about that, and she had looked at Costello waiting for her to contribute a story of her own, Mulholland had said something like, *So come on Costello, do your worst.*

She had sipped her water and asked Dali, as the silence at the table began to strain the happy atmosphere, why she was actually here, sitting with them. And what was it she wanted. Really wanted.

She knew that Mulholland and Wyngate had exchanged a glance, thinking that she had lost the plot.

Dali had taken another sip of her Kingfisher thinking about lying, saying something disingenuous or hiding behind confidentiality. She had looked round her and pushed her plate away slightly, dabbing her mouth with a napkin.

Off the record, this goes no further.

The way the other three lent in was comical.

Costello, you know the way you felt after you walked away from the Kissel case.

Oh yes I do.

It doesn't go far enough does it, we should have stepped in sooner and that wee boy would not have died that horrid death.

Costello now remembered how Dali had looked at Wyngate, the only one of them to have children that young. He had flinched; his mottled skin had gone a little red which was as close as he got to fury.

Then Dali had told her story. They had ordered more drinks, delaying their goodbyes, some tacit agreement that this wasn't to flow past them, this was happening right here and right now. Dali had got a fiscal involved after a woman she knew couldn't have a child, did just that. Diane Speirs? Dali had shaken her head. Diane had tried to say that it was a private adoption, but she wasn't so sure, the story didn't quite add up. And Dali had referred it up to Archie Walker and at that minute she had pointed to Costello, your Archie. Costello began to see the cogs in the wheels, not connected yet but somehow all trying to come together to make the machine work, and then they would see it all.

There was no way she could sleep after that.

Then after half past ten, Costello dropped Dali off at her large rambling house, with her five kids and no husband on the scene. A Merc stood on her driveway. She was a professional doing her job, and was harvesting them for information, as any concerned professional would.

Her parting shot was that she was at a conference in Edinburgh for the next two days, she had kept her hand on the door of the car as she explained, 'You might be interested in what our subject matter is. It's about the increase in the number of young girls coming through our maternity units, pregnant, receiving adequate care but then disappearing before we have sight of the child.'

'I think I see what you are getting at.'

'They are, well they tend, to be Roma. They have a very different culture, a healthy child is a thing of value, something that can be sold. Maybe we are not so far away from that culture ourselves but for different reasons. Everything in this life is a commodity, everything has a commercial value. So keep me posted, DI Costello.' That was delivered with her death stare.

Costello couldn't shake off the thought that she was having her strings pulled. But she wasn't sure by whom.

And now she was here doing her bit, watching out for something she knew in her bones was going to happen and she was going to use the wee bit of power she had to stop it, if she could.

She watched the upstairs lights of Malcolm's house go off, a curtain being pulled in an upstairs room, a small face at the window. Costello dropped her driver's window to see better, the face was joined by a hand, a wave. Then the window opened and a black trainer appeared, an ankle, a bit of trouser reached out, toe pointed to search for the flat roof of the bay window below. Then a light came on in the downstairs hall, the leg was retracted. Costello closed her window, kept her head looking straight forward, as though keeping her gaze on the house. She glanced at the clock, half eleven. She had parked on the other side of the road, but she could see the full view of the front of the house from here.

The front door opened, Malcolm's dad walked out, round the sightline of the monkey puzzle tree, right in her direction. He had known she was there.

Then she saw the patrol car pulling up behind her.

So not only did they know she was here, they were not happy about it.

As she got out the car, showing her warrant card, and after a quick check of her credentials, they asked her how the Waterside abduction was going and if her stake-out here was part of it.

'Not yet,' she answered vaguely. Their offer of backup was politely refused, their offer of violence to whoever had taken the kid was rejected because of the length of the queue. So that was how it was being perceived. Sholto had been taken and probably murdered already. The four-hour rule. She hoped Roberta had not got wind of that.

And she was trying desperately not to think, 'Why him? Why Sholto?'

She got back in her car and drove off slowly, slowing down when she thought of the Porsche she had caught sight of the previous night, but now it was nowhere to be seen.

She looked in the mirror, monkey puzzle right enough.

EIGHT

Thursday 12th October

At her desk, Valerie sat down and checked the time. Half seven, she was red-eyed from another sleepless night, exhausted from the concentration of driving to work as if she was sober, worn out, nerves pulled to the thread, thinking about the decisions she was about to make. Ruining somebody else's life, ruining her own. She looked at the files in front of her, three cases of child abuse. Did it ever stop? A man battered his daughter's face against the wall and then asked which finger she wanted him to cut off. And then cut off a different one. That file was thick, too thick. He shouldn't have been allowed out after the first time, after the story the first daughter told. What was the point of putting them in prison, if the only lesson they learned was how to avoid getting caught the next time?

And why were they allowed the keep having children if all they did was abuse them? She was angry. What was the point of doing the job if she made no difference at all? Maybe she was wrong in trying to save all those kids at risk. The courts moved slowly, many children slipped through. Too many abusers given a second chance. Maybe she should try to save one, or two. Or three, but do it herself and make sure that it was right.

Sometimes she fantasized about getting hold of an AK 47 and working her way through a list.

She had about an hour to make some tough decisions, she lied to herself. The decision had already been made. Everything in life had consequences. But she could not stand aside and do nothing. She had, she thought, given much of her life, her time, her marriage and her personal happiness to this career. And for what?

'"In My Defens God Me Defend",' she muttered as she

pulled out the beige file and ran through it again, the bile rising in her throat. She could destroy it. She could destroy the entire case, all the documentation. And just walk away. They would piece it all together eventually but by then it would be too late. She knew at first hand the perpetual chaos the fiscal's office worked in. She could cover her tracks easily enough, even drunk as she was now, she was still able for any of them. They were overworked and understaffed. They would search for the paperwork and not find it, have a second look through the computer system and then move onto something easier.

She turned to her computer. The disc was already in it, burning away, leaving no trace. As she sat there the algorithm was writing random data over all the sectors on the disc. It wouldn't come back to her, there must be no trace near her.

She did allow herself a smile at the thought of that social worker, with her big happy face telling her godfather about a case that he promptly passed to her, thinking it would interest her. And it had been with her for every minute of every day for the intervening couple of years. A woman who could not have a child, had had a child. A difficult thing to prove but the crux of the matter was that the baby she now possessed must have come from somewhere.

That case had moved along with Valerie Abernethy watching it every step of the way. Easy from her viewpoint in Edinburgh, while the woman in question lived down in Dumfries. She had the hard copy. She ran her fingertip over it, reading it again, anybody watching would think she was doing her job, diligently and well, when it fact she was ensuring that she had memorized everything she needed to know. Again, and again, feeling the panic arising inside her as she heard the disc whirr on and on. Rubbing out her old life like an advancing tide smoothing out footsteps in the sand.

She heard the door to the outer office open, a little squeak that could have been anything.

Or nothing.

Then footfalls coming towards her.

Heart thumping, she closed the file over, pretending to copy down an important detail on a Post-it note, thinking fast now. She folded the file papers, too big, too bulky, the photograph would not fit without being folded over, it would look odd.

She lifted her water bottle, popped off the cap and took a long gulp, letting the vodka run down her throat. She had been up most of the night, thinking about Alfred, missing him in her bed, his little warm body lying over her ankles on top of the duvet. But he had given her a way out, if the plan all worked out, they would want to know where she was going and why – maybe with the traumatic loss of the cat, the final straw after her marriage break-up and the rest of her trauma. They might draw their own conclusion and think that she had let her depression, her addiction and her loss get the better of her.

Which was exactly true.

But not the loss that she had let them believe it was.

She walked to the outer office, eyes down on the files she was carrying. She felt she was walking stiffly, trying to look natural and sober while doing something she did a hundred times a day. The outer office was strange, cold without the phones ringing and the background chit-chat at the hub of the water cooler. Strange shadows fell on the carpet tiles, there were sounds outside of Edinburgh wakening up. Metal shutters being raised, engines running. Quickly, she fed the sheets into the shredder, one at a time, trying not to look over her shoulder. When it came to the photograph she made a point of letting the shredded strands run through her fingers, mixing them up just a little more.

She returned to her office, leaving her door open as she sat down at her desk and began to type. Then stopped. Then started again. Then stopped. Suddenly she swore and swiped her briefcase from her desk with a single blow of her arm, sending it flying onto the carpet where it stood like a little tent in an abstract patchwork field of papers and files.

She dropped her head into her hands for a few moments and took a deep breath.

Then she took her water bottle, another flick, another mouthful of the vodka.

She saw her colleague come into the outer office and she

tried to close her office door with her foot but had left it too late. Now it would now look awkward and obvious. Bill Nelson smiled at her, said, *Hi. You are in early.* She lifted the phone handset, pretending she was on a call. He walked away, the smile cut from her face the minute he turned from her line of vision.

'It's Valerie Abernethy here,' she said to nobody.

All the while she was aware of Nelson, moving around in the outer office, looking at the small pile at the bottom of the shredder, daring himself to have a closer look.

Costello had come into the office early, she had put a note through the door of Mrs Armstrong to make sure Mrs Craig was up and out of her bed OK. They knew she sometimes had to do that when work called. So at seven in the morning she was sitting quietly with a cup of tea and some chocolate-covered cornflakes, and the side of a box of chocolate biscuits somebody had handed into the station at Christmas. They were out of date now so she had thrown them out, then pulled the box lid back out the bin, to be drawn on.

There was already a note on her desk, from some top brass she had never heard of. George Haggerty was complaining about harassment.

Good for him. She hadn't even started yet.

She took a drink of her tea, tired, wishing that small amount of caffeine in it would help to wake her up. She had been awake most of the night, thinking about Dali and Wee Polly, thinking how ineffectual a social worker may be in the chaos they had to work in, certainly in the office that served this area. It was always somebody else's job and they were never in that day, usually off sick. With stress.

But they were both so fed up with cleaning up the aftermath of domestic violence, when they would be better preventing it.

It had been a good night, a very good night. She had phoned Anderson again this morning, his phone still turned off. She had pressed her own to her lips and thought, wondering if he was spending the evening with Andrew Braithwaite or with Sally Braithwaite. It wouldn't be the first time Anderson's zip had taken him very close to trouble.

She sipped her tea to contemplate. One tantalizing piece of evidence they needed was that second pay-as-you-go number, a red light that sat at the back of her mind and niggled. James Chisholm was another man whose zip was going to get him into a lot of trouble. However his one saving grace was that no huge amounts of money had gone through any of the Chisholm's bank accounts, so she presumed, Sholto had not been 'sold' by either of his parents.

She picked up a blue pen and drew a line, on the lid of the biscuit packet. Baby Sholto, where was he? With some woman who had given birth to a Down's syndrome child? And where was she? Or was he taken for another reason? Baby Sholto, Little Moses, Wee Polly, the tiny trio. And they were all linked in some way.

But she couldn't see how.

Little Moses had appeared from nowhere. All the Down's syndrome births for the last three months in the Argyll and Clyde Health Board had all been tracked down and were all present, correct and accounted for including the one that Drew at the hospital had been worried about. Drew?

Andrew?

Friend of James? They played at the same tennis club. She googled Dr Andrew Braithwaite, and smiled as his image flashed up. Younger, slimmer but still him. She stood up and added him to the wall. Andy and Jimmy were up to their necks in this.

Little Moses' DNA had been taken, it wouldn't be long until the results were back and that might give them something, even a familial blueprint. *Have any female members of your family been pregnant recently?* And now Wee Polly, what was going on there? They had checked over with the dirty squad, they had their feelers out in case the babies were being taken for some paedophile ring. The intelligence said no. If this was a sophisticated abduction ring, they would know about it and Costello would be locked in a room being interviewed by overweight men who she would never get to know the name of.

Somebody who knew Roberta or James had taken Baby Sholto? And left Little Moses. That woman was not Angelika

Kauscher. The blue light of the other pay-as-you-go number was still flashing but it never moved from the Glasgow area.

Because of his Downs, Moses was not good enough. It made her angry to write it down, but he was . . . What? Faulty? A baby returned because he was faulty? Foetuses were killed all the time because they were 'faulty'. It was a little late to be moralistic about it. This was more like a business transaction? Just like Dali had hinted. Was Moses already bought and paid for. Then he had been found imperfect.

Who might know about that? Who else could she put that tentative theory in front of without being told to piss off?

She scrolled through her phone for a number she had never, never dialled, but maybe, this time they would be on the same page. Then she changed her mind and phoned Mulholland again asking how big an ask it would be to review that tape.

So, there must be a connection between Orla and Roberta. The only way that Costello could join those two was through their pregnancies or their babies. Except Orla had kept hers a secret. She needed Wyngate to run a deeper search, where Roberta and Orla crossed paths. Or Orla and James. Or Orla and Andrew.

They had no idea where Orla had given birth to Polly.

On the basis that Orla was now teetering on the brink of morphing into a missing person, Costello had sent Wyngate round to gain entry to Orla's flat before he came to work. He had measured the indents in the back of that card, the one with the picture of the Scotty dog. He had texted back, 165 by 87 mm, the size of a Bank of England fifty-pound note. A lot of them.

So was this a business transaction, and the baby had a price tag from the moment Orla took the money – the money she had hid behind the picture in the bedroom? Could she be that daft? Of course she could. But the wee bitch was running rings round them at the moment.

Somewhere in all this was the child abduction. She looked at her watch. The baby seat had gone to the forensic lab, it was primarily clean of baby sick so they were right. The baby, the seat, the blanket had all been ringers, and somewhere Baby Sholto was out there in his own seat and wrapped in his own blanket.

But it was organized and then . . . And then she remembered Anthony Laphan, the fertility consultant she had come across in the Grace Wilson case. His happy little clinic at Inchgarten had turned out to be no more than plenty of sex, relaxation and cannabis. The genesis of that had come, surely, from a need Laphan had seen in childless women in his NHS fertility clinics. Circumstances, tragic circumstances, had closed his private little enterprise down. She couldn't help the cold shiver that snaked its way up her spine, the memories were too close, too raw, but putting the horrors of Inchgarten to one side, had the cessation of that operation left a gap for something more sophisticated, more calculating and lethal?

She flicked through her phone for the number of that tumbledown wee cottage sitting on the side of Loch Lomond. But first of all she phoned Anderson, she owed him that. Any mention of Anthony Laphan would bring up old memories too traumatic for Anderson, and Costello didn't want him stumbling across it by accident in some banal report a few weeks down the line. Her boss's mental health was better, but he was not that much better.

Anderson's phone rang out for a long time.

'Yip Costello? Make it quick I have a hangover.'

'I was thinking about interviewing Daisy and Anthony Laphan, about infertility. What do you think?'

'You don't need to ask my permission. Phone them, see what they have to say.'

'Will you be happy with that?'

'They are not witnesses, you are just gathering background information. And I am busy.'

'Doing what? Nursing your hangover? Reigniting old flames?'

'Trying to establish a link between the rapes of Sally Logan and Gillian Witherspoon.'

Costello's tone changed immediately. 'You onto anything?'

'Nothing much apart from the obvious. The victims were

alone. It seems opportunist but both mention a noise they heard just before. I need to get Sally to remember that, tell me what kind of noise it was. Might be something or nothing. But it would be good to run it through a database.'

'Let me know if you come up with anything. You might need more than one pair of eyes.' She heard him mutter *thanks* and the phone cut off.

Anderson closed his phone and took another sip of water, waiting for the headache tablet to kick in. Infertility. Not something he had given much thought to until he had met the Laphans and then he had realized how devastating it must be to some people, not to be able to have children. He had always taken family for granted. And that was one area where Sally might be considered a non-achiever, her life had stalled. If the attack had brought Sally and Andrew together, maybe the lack of family would pull them apart.

And was he hoping for that? He hoped he was not.

He felt guilty that he had talked in omissions, not wanting Braithwaite to see that there was a chink in his marriage. Why? In case Braithwaite thought he was going to rekindle something with Sally. Was he in danger of rekindling something with Sally? He had dreamt about that one night, that night with the drink in the park.

And now he was thinking of Andrew Braithwaite and the way he had shown him the photos of his lovely wife. Sally on the top of Kilimanjaro, framed in silver, freckled, suntanned, big floppy hat and her long brown legs, lithe with muscles, descending into rolled up socks and walking boots. She held two walking poles; one sticking in the ground, the other held high, pointing to the top of the mountain. It was a lovely picture, and he was aware that Braithwaite was bragging to him. *I got her, you didn't.*

It was all a shrine to her, nothing about him, about Andrew. Nothing at all.

Was that adoration? Or control?

Costello hoped Anthony Laphan didn't hold any grudges. Anderson and the team had only been there to solve a murder, it wasn't them who had brought the flames and the death with them. Those evil little imposters had already been there, in full sight, hiding under the banal cover of normality.

Daisy answered the phone, her voice as cheery as ever. She greeted Costello like a long-lost friend, leaving Costello feeling guilty and a little fraudulent.

'How are you, pet?'

'I am fine, I am doing fine. It's Anthony I need to speak to.'

'He's in his caravan up at the new site. We are rebuilding you know after . . . well after everything.'

Costello knew better than to ask for a mobile number, there was no chance of getting a signal up there.

Daisy said, 'Give me your number I'll get him to call you.'

Anthony called back ten minutes later and when she realized she had scribbled four pages of notes, she decided to record the rest of the conversation. Now she was listening to it again, adding bits in, jotting his words down in between lines, getting as much detail as possible so she could type it coherently later.

Anthony Laphan had qualified in medicine at university, and his speciality eventually, had been infertility. He understood the difficulties that childless couples found themselves in and he explained the way the family as a unit is reinforced in the media, and the unbearable stress that could bring to bear to those who found themselves unable to reproduce. She already knew that the adoption process took a long time but according to Laphan it could take four years to adopt a young child due to the lack of supply of babies. Costello underlined that. Laphan had added that according to the law, even if the baby has been fostered, by the state, the natural mother was always allowed another chance. And who would take on a baby, with a full heart and with all that emotional turmoil, just to have the child taken away.

Then Costello thought of Bernadette Kissel and snorted.

And it was babies, young babies, who were in demand. People didn't want older kids already damaged through years in the system, or the children of substance abusers. People didn't want that amount of hassle.

She pressed play, ready to scribble the next bit, something

she hadn't thought of. 'They want a blank page they can mould, they don't want somebody else's problems. They want a baby they can mould to their lifestyle, they want a DNA profile of intelligence or physicality that matches theirs so the child will grow in their image. People do want to leave something of their own. And there is a huge shortage of babies due to the laws of surrogacy and sperm donation. Even a kid born because of sperm donation now has a right to know its father. So what happens when it all goes wrong, when the kid grows up and has no money and then decides to come after the donor for support? Or the marriage breaks up and Mum goes after the donor for maintenance?'

According to Laphan, the students who used to wank into a tube for a bit of beer money have gone to work in Tesco's instead.

'The market has tumbled. Much of the sperm now is imported from Denmark, but its parentage, if you like, is still unknown. The legal means of gaining a child are becoming more and more limited and surrogacy, that is expenses paid and nothing more, is perfectly legal. Babies do sell well round the world, so forty or fifty grand in Glasgow would not be surprising. It would be a lucrative enterprise.' He then sketched out what he called the typical customer: a woman who delays starting a family due to the progression of her career, then she realizes too late that there might be fertility issues. She works until her early thirties then has two years of trying and failing, another two or three years trying a few IVF cycles and by then she's forty. She's probably got money. She's got everything in life except the one thing she really wants. But she will have the money to pay for that.

By now Costello was scribbling furiously. Transgender people do not qualify for IVF, men in a new childless relationship do not qualify for IVF if he has had a child in his first relationship. 'So the pool of people who want a baby – a baby not a child – is growing and the amount of babies coming onto the market is shrinking. When you have demand and a limited supply, the price goes up.'

Costello pressed rewind and listened to that again.

*   *   *

Dali phoned from a break in her course, from the sound of running water and the roar of hand dryers in the background, she was phoning from the toilets. 'Hitler wasn't wrong,' said Dali after Costello had given her the gist of Laphan's conversation.

'Oh I think he was.'

'I'm a persecuted minority so I am allowed to say that.'

She heard a door open and close, it was quiet now on the end of the phone. 'Babies to order. Say I was fair-haired and tall, blue-eyed, and slim. And white. Yeah, I know, but imagine I was infertile. My bloke looks like . . . an Aryan god.'

'Lucky you.'

'Well, genetics are what they are. And I want a bright child from healthy parents. I'd look at somebody like you and Anderson to produce a child because you echo my fair-haired, tall, intelligent requirements.'

'That's a horrible thought,' said Costello with such ferocity that she heard Dali give her belly laugh at the other end.

'No, that is genetics.' Dali thought for a little bit. 'Say you know a student or an actress, somebody bright but skint, somebody who wants to earn money while getting on with something else, then they find out they are pregnant. They might want to think about selling the baby, and somewhere is a list of parents who are waiting. It's like playing Happy Families, you just need to get a match. A bright, healthy baby that will have some semblance to his new parents because the parents resemble the natural parents. It's not rocket science.'

'But you can't suddenly appear with a baby? Surely folk know they take a few months to cook.'

Costello heard Dali's earrings clink against the phone. 'Think it through a wee bit more. They might know the baby was coming from about two months, even one month in to the pregnancy. They have seven or eight months to set the story. Or let it be known that they are pursuing adoption.'

'But they need a history, a birth certificate.'

'If it's in a private clinic, who is to know. Travelling folk don't, the Roma don't – they never have a birth certificate or a national insurance number. But say two women go in to a clinic; one pregnant, one not. Two woman come out; one with a baby, one without. The chances of a normal person needing a transplant or getting their familial DNA checked is not high. And it can be explained, it doesn't make it illegal. Is it even immoral? And,' she was on a roll now, 'nobody ever says anything, do they? Not if there's been problems, you know, conceiving. People wait to be told and accept the good news. So does this Laphan bloke think we have a mail order business where a central broker takes money organizing the girls? Then the new parents register a birth that never happened or announce the arrival of their adopted baby. So this person would need to be skilled an obstetrician or midwife maybe? But maybe not, young healthy women give birth to healthy babies. Maybe not as difficult as we think. It's been going on for a thousand years before we invited birthing pools. Probably learn it from You Tube these days.'

'But these kids aren't borne from mothers who are bright – Orla Sheridan would struggle to fill in the form for Mensa.'

'That might be what the broker tells the prospective parents. The parents don't know the mothers, do they? They could be told anything. They are not going to try and return the child when it fails to get into Oxbridge.' Dali nodded her head, her earring rattling again on the handset. 'Oh, I think he's right, this Laphan bloke. Do you suspect him of having a hand in this?'

'No, not them. It's not their style. Do you really think there's somebody out there and I just need to google Babies R Us.'

'Oh no, I am sure it's a more subtle process than that. The agency who looks after the unwanted pregnancies needs to talk to the agency that deals with infertility. It could be as sweet as that. I was reading in the paper about the Down's syndrome child that was left.' Dali sounded angry.

'Little Moses.'

'Can you find a record of him being born in a hospital?'

'No, we are still looking but no.'

'Well, that's your answer, isn't it? And there is a simple blood test for issues of the twenty-third chromosome now, so why didn't they do that?'

Mulholland stopped his car at the side of Central Station and turned down towards Brown Street, not a part of the city he knew well. He knew the Barracuda Bar that occupied part of the lower floor of the Blue Neptune from his days before he knew Elvie. Days when he liked, well, when he liked the kind of woman who hung about places like the Barracuda Bar. Expensive. Vacuous. It was the place to be seen, with its celebrity hang out, the giant aquarium. The Admiral, one of Glasgow's most exclusive restaurants upstairs. He had eaten there once, trying to impress some girl, a model who had a weird name. She had ordered a lot and ate none of it, doing little more than picking at the salad garnish. If he took Elvie there, she would need to stop for a sandwich on the way home. The food there was pretty, but small and expensive. Not like the curry the previous night when he and Wyngate had stuffed their faces and taken home a doggy bag each. Mulholland had eaten a breakfast of cold bhajis dipped in mayonnaise, a treat because Elvie was on an early start and wouldn't find out. He drove round, pulling the Audi into the lane beyond the Barracuda, stopping suddenly at the bollard. He reversed and bumped the car onto the pavement as close in as he could, the Wrights Insurance was on his left, the Old Edwardian and the Blue Neptune to his right, both five or six stories high, both refurbed all the way through from their original cara-pace, old tobacco warehouses probably in this part of the city. He looked to the name of the lane, Sevastopol. The Blue Neptune covered the whole block apart from the quarter taken up by the Old Edwardian. In all twenty-seven businesses had registered this address as their legitimate premises.

'What do we do now?' asked Wyngate.

'We have a copy of the film on the phone, let's follow that, find out where they went.'

They got out the car, leaving a note under the windscreen wiper and began to walk down the lane, pausing where, according to the film, the girls had last been seen. There were two doors in the side wall of the Old Edwardian, both looked iron rusted and graffiteed over. There was only one opening on the side wall of the Blue Neptune and that housed the inshot and the door to the lift up to the gym and the studio, but was too far down the lane.

Orla and Miss Bluecoat went somewhere. Mulholland

looked at the iron bollard; it must have made a hell of clatter when it fell. Had that noise frightened the birds? Did that mean a car had come through but they had not seen it? Not possible.

Wyngate was already walking ahead, scanning the older parts of the wall, checking the graffiti and the old metal, recessed doors with litter and rat droppings piling up behind them. He was standing in the middle, his bony little head twisting this way and that as he tried to see where else the girls might have gone.

The lane was narrow enough for a delivery lorry to scrape past if the bollard was down. Solid brick walls on both sides except an empty strip of land between the Blue Neptune and the Old Edwardian not more than twenty feet square. A low wall ran two-feet high from the end of the Edwardian to the start of the Blue Neptune, the wall supported old iron railings, spiked on the top, covered, as Wyngate found out, by anti-vandal grease. As he withdrew his hand and inspected the mess, he heard the noise of two security cameras on the Wrights Insurance building twist on their spindles to catch him with their black see-all lenses.

'If that camera is motion activated . . .?'

Five minutes later Mulholland was being his charming self to the receptionist in Wrights Insurance, showing his warrant card and explaining that they would like to view the security footage. She steadfastly refused to look at Wyngate's disfiguring skin pigmentation and when she did, her smile got stuck on her face for a couple of moments.

The security man, Kinnear, however was ex job. He knew Mahon vaguely, having got drunk with him on more than a few occasions, which they were learning was the way that most people got to know Mahon. But Kinnear was good; he took them up for a coffee and rolled through the security tapes with them. If Wyngate had been impressed at what they had at Central, it was nothing compared to what the insurance company had.

Mulholland reeled off the time they were looking for, 11.27 a.m., and Kinnear added ten minutes onto the front, then some

Jaffa cakes appeared. All this comfy office, good coffee and Jaffa cakes. Who needed a pension?

'You know, it's always been rumoured there's a way into Grahamston from here,' said Kinnear, 'if you think of the way the city was built, you know on top of the old city, then this area around Inkerman Street is the western border of the old city. There's supposed to be roads and shops and all sorts down there.'

'But is any of that fact? Grahamston is just a myth,' said Mulholland.

Kinnear smiled. 'It appears on Victorian maps, nothing before that, as if they had just made up the idea to amuse themselves, but they might, just might, have been mapping something that had been secret up to that point. It's a wide enough rumour so some of it has to be true. And there's history here of folk disappearing.'

'Really.'

'A hundred years ago, I mean. The Old Edwardian is called old for a reason. It has a long history so maybe it does have something to do with where your lady has gone. There she is.'

They watched her as she came down the lane, long legs, big hair. As the camera swung away, and back, she vanished.

'Can we see the bit in between?'

'No, the camera does a sweep. It's a finite space down there. We watch the two ends of the lane, there's nowhere in between for people to go, they can't . . .'

'Can't what? Appear and disappear?' Mulholland was watching the tape. 'The same thing happens with Miss Bluecoat.' He said this just as she walked into the film as the camera swung left. She was not there when it swung right again.

Then Kinnear pulled out a scrolled-up map, an architect's drawing of the area, showing the position of the camera, the lane and the distance of the Old Edwardian, the Blue Neptune and Wrights Insurance. 'There are a lot of pub cellars under the lane. There's an underground car park on the far side. These basements have basements and there's rumours of underground tunnels going through to Central Station and Grahamston. We have had a bit of bother with urban explorers trying to get down there.'

'We?' asked Mulholland for clarification.

'Sorry, the police. But as for access from the lane? There are a couple of doors on this building but the insurance insists they are welded closed and have metal shutters, I can vouch for them myself. But, in this part of town, there are stories – very old stories, mind you – of doors being fixed so they open from the inside, letting muggers come out of nowhere. But they have been welded shut years ago.'

'Black Donalds?' muttered Wyngate.

'Pardon?'

'The Victorians called them Black Donalds, those doors. So folk can appear from the dark and mug you? Did you not pay attention in school?' said Wyngate and scoffed another Jaffa cake.

They scrolled back, watching the different angles, following Miss Bluecoat as she walked straight down the lane, pausing slightly for some reason, checking that she had something in her pocket, or checking her phone. And then she was gone. They let the film roll on for a few minutes, nobody appeared. They set it to go forwards every five minutes. Twenty minutes later they saw a woman walk up, her baby in a buggy, long coat, almost jogging in her loose trousers. They watched in fascinated silence as she drove the buggy into the alcove, then reappeared with her baby in her arms and stepped forward again, presumably to go up in the lift.

Back out on the lane they stood exactly where both girls were last seen, one at 11.27, one at 11.45 a.m. They both stared at the blank wall, looking at the cobbles under their feet. Any metal slab that might indicate a way down. Mulholland had a bad feeling that Wyngate was thinking about the Grahamston option as a serious contender.

'Whit ar youse up tae? And can ah have some?'

Wyngate smiled at the man shuffling along, plain brown paper wrapped round his can.

Mulholland tried to pull him away. 'He's pissed. Leave him.'

'You live down here?'

'Me?' The guy looked astounded. He wasn't as old as they

first thought. 'Nae, but they gie me a dig oot to piss off. Tae posh, tae git me oot eer.'

Mulholland looked at Wyngate.

'He means they gave him money to go away,' Wyngate translated.

'And were you down here yesterday . . .?'

'Maybees? You looking fur her?'

'Who?' asked Mulholland.

'The bird, Alice. They are all fuckin' Alice.'

'Alice?'

'Aye, ahm telling yeh, she was like there wan minute and then like she wisnae there at ah . . . like she just disappeared through a hole in the ground.'

'And how much had you had to drink at that point, Mr . . .?'

'Schwarzenegger.'

'Mr Schwarzenegger, Arnold?'

'Nae Billy. Billy Schwarzenegger, Arnie's ma brother.'

'Indeed. So, Alice?'

'She went through a hole in the wall, like Alice doon the ferret hole.'

'He's a waster, come on.' Mulholland was keen to get away.

'And how was she, Alice?'

'Fucking knackered.'

'Why?'

'Fucking oot tae here?' He pushed his can in front of his body, indicating pregnancy.

'Precise waster though,' agreed Mulholland.

'Through a hole though? Or down a hole?' asked Wyngate.

Their happy informer looked confused. The confusion vanished at the sight of a crisp new tenner. 'Through. Sideways. Like this . . .' He shimmied to the side with the skill of a show dancer.

'Just like the other one. The whore.'

'The whore?'

'Aye her wi the stupit hair.' He belched loudly and held a single dirty finger up to his lips. 'They've gone.' He looked around him, eyes flitting from side to side. 'To Grahamstoon. And Ah'll tell you whit?'

'What?'

'They never come back from there. No, not ever.' He put a grubby hand out for another tenner.

Mulholland pulled Wyngate away. 'That's shite.'

'Where's Grahamston?' asked Wyngate.

'The auld city, unner yer feets.' He looked round to check. 'Awe the way doon frae there tae here.' He pointed the toe of his battered trainers. 'Aye right here.'

Wyngate got excited. 'Surely that's the answer.'

'One problem.' This time Mulholland pulled him away.

'Yeah.'

'Like I said, Grahamston doesn't exist.'

NINE

The man with the crew cut and the bad scar down the side of his cheek looked like a Bond villain. He was pleasant enough as he led Costello up the carpeted stairs, deep-pile, claret red, immaculate. The pile going in opposite ways on each tread. On the walls of the stairway were framed photographs of trucks, departmental heads, two chief constables, all to showcase the legitimate part of the business. She might be a hard-nosed little cow up to her waxed armpits in organized crime, but Libby Hamilton appeared to have friends in high places.

Libby was one of the most powerful women in Scotland. She'd give the love child of Nicola Sturgeon and Angela Merkel a good run for their money. There was the size of her desk, the two male heavies doubling as secretaries, both with battle-scarred, angry faces sitting outside, even the female at the front desk looked as though she could go a few rounds with Henry Cooper.

And Libby was good. It was easy to take over a business with a little bit of carrot if you could back it up with a lot of stick. Refusal to be bought out for a reasonable fee resulted in something being burned down and then worth nothing. After that, any offer was likely to be accepted. Costello had no idea how the organized crime unit felt about it, there was no doubt the family were running huge amounts of drugs around the country. But she felt it in her bones, rather than knew, that Libby was more useful to the control of illegal substances, than legitimate forces of law and order. Remove her family from the equation and there would be a vacuum, that the Russians, or the Chinese would fill. As far as she knew, there had never been any real attempt to remove Libby's family from power. Those that tried were found floating in the Clyde, if they were found at all. Nobody knew how many more were helping to hold up concrete pillars or had provided some sustenance for pigs.

It was far from ideal but the drugs on the street were cleaner than they used to be.

And there was a lot to be said for knowing the enemy.

Mr Scarface opened the door to the office and stood to one side, the cloud of his pungent scent drifted and dispersed to be replaced by another, more vomit-inducing stink.

The top of the huge oak desk was like any other company director's, monitor, keyboard, mobile phone neatly beside a gold pen, the landline telephone resting on a stand. But the woman in the corner was unrecognizable from the suited and booted young successful woman about town, which had been Costello's last impression of Libby. This was a fleece-wearing, hair scraped back, exhausted human being, holding another smaller human being by the ankles while she scraped away at its bottom with a cloth.

'Bugger,' she said, turning to see Costello. 'Oh hello, can you hand me one of those wee wipes?'

'Aye.'

Libby took the fresh wipe, having to hand Costello the one smeared with foul smelling brown lumps. But she did it with a guilty smile. 'Sorry, there's a bin and a sink over there. I never have enough hands for this. I mean, how are you supposed to manage?'

Costello opened the tab on the plastic bag lying next to the bin and added the latest offering to what seemed a large collection. She taped it back up.

'Congratulations, I hadn't heard.' Costello took a large squirt of Molten Brown's hand cream and had a good rub in, it gave her nose something else to concentrate on.

'My baby was born in better circumstances than I was.'

'Yes, I remember. I was there. One of my first crime scenes.'

'Your first murder scene.'

'Yes, it was,' Costello said.

'I heard later that you got into trouble for holding her hand, my mum's hand.'

'I probably did. Terrible what happened to her.'

'But I survived, thanks to you.'

'Thanks to the surgeons at the hospital,' she corrected.

The small person seemed intent on escaping before Libby could secure another nappy on it. Once she had, she set it free on the floor, the chubby baby rolled over, got up on all fours and started lumbering around the carpet like a drunk, over-weight puppy.

'Do you think that's bad for him?' Libby asked. 'I mean I work on the principle that it builds a healthy immune system, you know, exposing himself to anything that happens to be stuck on that carpet.' She sat behind the desk, cleaning her hands with sanitizer, twice, then caught Costello's eye. 'What do you want?'

Now it came to it, Costello didn't know how to start; it was the baby who was putting her off.

'If I wanted you dead in a canal, Costello, you would be but I acknowledge we have history so you get a bit of leeway. If you want somebody dead in a canal, just let me know.' Libby smiled as she pressed the button. Then Mr Scarface came in. 'Could you take that out and put it down the waste chute. God help any dosser asleep at the bottom of it.'

She waited until the door was closed. 'He stinks. I pay him enough money so he can buy very expensive aftershave, shame he also bought a bucket to put it on with.' She sat back in her seat a little, looking like any tired mother of a tot. Then looked directly at Costello.

'I was just wondering if you knew of any activity, any paedophile activity, that's picked up recently in the area and—'

'No. I wouldn't allow it. Next question.'

'It's extreme. I am concerned that very young children, babies, are being abducted.'

'Abducted? Or sold.' Libby swung round in her seat a little.

Costello noticed the lack of surprise. 'I am not sure.'

'If it was peado issues, in this city I would know. And there isn't. Not in the way you mean. Those bastards watch videos, but those were not filmed here. Have you spoken to O'Hare, your pathologist friend?'

'Why?'

'You should.'

Costello was acutely aware of the small one making his

ungainly way around her feet. She was also becoming cognisant
that Libby knew more about the situation than she did.

'People think that the city is safe with all the surveillance
present in the corners of the city where the lost and vulnerable
gather. They stop thinking about it but it's business as usual,
it's easy to pick on the vulnerable. In the past they were taken
into the shadows and abused, now they are taken out of view
and abused. Nobody is more at risk than a pregnant runaway
or a prostitute. They can be persuaded to see their baby as a
way out.'

'Baby brokering?' Costello's brain was already joining
the dots, knowing that Libby never gave a straight answer to
anything.

'I am not saying anything.' Libby licked her thin red lips.
'That's not so difficult. I spend my life dealing with people
who wouldn't blink an eye at that and worse. You do too. But
see how my office is nicer, I get paid more.' She smiled at
her son. 'Why not let women sell children that do not exist
because nobody knows they have been born. Travelling families
have been doing it for years.'

Costello had heard that before. 'In this Big Brother society?
Nobody knows that these kids are born?' Then she thought
about Paige Riley. Nobody close to her had even noticed that
she had gone missing.

'Nobody. Where there is a will to do something, it can be
done. Anybody involved in criminality knows that. It's all
doable. More doable because unimaginative cops never think
it could be done. It actually makes it easier, all that hidden in
plain sight. Just think what they did back in the old days.
Pregnant women left town to have a child, then came back
minus the kid. Easy if nobody knows about the pregnancy in
the first place.' She reached down and pulled open a drawer,
then slid out a photograph. 'Do you know that girl?'

Costello looked at the picture; a girl, sitting on a railing
somewhere, smiling, early twenties. 'She was a drama student,
well, actress.'

'As opposed to a hostess?'

They exchanged a smile that went nowhere.

'And have you seen this, yesterday's paper?' Libby licked

her forefinger and flicked over a few pages. 'Look at this girl here.' she showed Costello the article. 'Sex worker, another one found dead beside a skip in a back alley out in Anderston.'

'Yes, I heard about it. But I am working out in Domestic Abuse now not in Major Incident so it passed me by.' Costello guessed she knew what was coming.

'She went up there with a punter and whatever transaction passed between them ended with him grabbing her head and battering it against the edge of a skip. She died later in hospital.'

'I know.'

'For what? The forty quid she had in her hand for five minutes? She was left dying, collapsing slowly in her own piss and shit, his spunk still running out the side of her mouth. If she had been able to phone somebody, she would be alive. But he had stamped on her phone.'

'You should be a cop, Libby, come and join us on the domestic violence unit.'

'Prevention is better than cure, you know that.'

'Are you saying you are out there looking after prostitutes? Libby, really, did you have some kind-hearted vigilantes out there, watching her?'

'Not to . . . not on my watch.'

She had been about to say 'not to one of my girls' then confirmed it by adding, 'This however was one of my girls.' She pointed to the girl on the railing. 'She was a resting actress, worked as a hostess in one of my clubs.'

Costello quoted, 'And anything that happens beyond that introduction was a deal brokered between the two of them and a totally private matter. Kind of standard phrase for people who are little more than pimps.'

'Indeed.' She looked at the picture again. 'She was murdered last year.'

Costello looked at the picture again, trying for recognition and failed. Even without a name, the face should have meant something. Was she so disconnected, so focussed at domestic abuse that she was missing a bigger picture.

'These might help you more.' And Libby handed her a thick file of photographs, glossy 12 by 10s, from the coding on the bottom, the date and time stamp the police logo at the top, these were obviously the scene of crime photographs.

'How did you get your hands on these?'

'Never mind, just look.'

'Libby, it's a criminal offence for you to have these. Do they have a leak at the MIT?'

'Oh, stop it,' she laughed, incredulous at Costello's innocence. 'Everybody has a price, Costello, even you.'

'No, I don't.'

'Yes, you do.' She pulled the photographs back. 'You won't report this, you will ruin an honest young man's career.'

Costello remembered the pictures on the wall as she came up the stairs. Maybe she was not the only one who'd sat here and asked for help.

'My jungle, my rules,' she said, tapping the picture, 'and this is not acceptable. She had just had a baby, you know, there was no sign of it. Anywhere.'

'A missing baby.'

'Well, the baby wasn't where it should have been.'

'It wasn't my case,' said Costello, quietly, knowing how inadequate it sounded.

'Maybe it should be now. You should talk to her friend.'

'Who.'

Libby ignored the question. 'She had been talking about changing her job, and that she had come across something more lucrative, much more lucrative.'

'What, cutting out the middle man, sorry woman, and keeping all the money for herself?'

Libby smiled. 'Well, she didn't get that far. She got killed instead. When are you seeing your pathologist next? Maybe you should talk to him.'

'I will, can I keep these?' Costello asked mischievously but Libby put the pictures in her desk drawer. 'Those photographs are Police Scotland property.'

'What photographs?' asked Libby with a face that wouldn't melt butter. 'And while you are about it, can you find out what bastard did that to her and then let me know.'

'I will find out what happened to her, the rest goes to higher power than mine.'

'I am a higher power than you.' Libby stood up and looked out the window, and was quiet for a few moments. The baby crawling on the floor started mouthing a bubble-blowing tune. 'I grew up without my mother. I don't know . . . how had she looked? Alive? Tell me, can you still see her, in your mind's eye.'

'Yes, I do. Clear as day,' Costello answered honestly.

'We are not so different.' Then she was her animated self again. 'Here's the number of somebody to speak to. Call her Suzy and she'll be happy to talk to you. Watch yourself going down the stairs, they get slippery when wet.'

Valerie Abernethy was drunk, but she was a functioning drunk so nobody really noticed, or if they did notice they didn't care. The lies were about to start now, she could do the right thing or the wrong thing. Archie had advised her that she had to do the right thing for her and not for anybody else. It was her life. OK, so she had totally misled him as to what the issue was, but the end result was the same. Since her dad died, she had become to rely on Archie. Funny how life seemed when there was no backbone to it, no Dad, no Mum. Valerie had woken up the day after her dad's death to realize that she was now the responsible generation. She had been drunk most of that day.

Archie never saw it. He never saw anything bad in his god-daughter and she gave him a false impression of how happy she was. Archie thought he knew how much Grieg had hurt her yet he had nothing to do with the black state of her mind.

Was it a common thing in the world today to shape or ruin a life by the pressing of one button? When Fat Boy had been deployed, its mission to wreak havoc on the population of Hiroshima, did the person who pressed the button have any last-minute little doubts, at the final point when all the talking and decision-making that had gone on before, came down to the pressing of one button?

One look in the papers told her that on Facebook one status, or comment, like a photo could spark off cyberbullying that could lead to suicide. One click could start a petition that could bring down a government. Another click could start a war.

There was a message on her phone. Her heart quickened when she read it. This was what she had been waiting seven months for.

She would be happy. She quickly typed a reply and pressed send, feeling weirdly free of the stress ball that had been gathering in her stomach over the last few weeks.

She closed the phone and put it into her bag. She went upstairs into her bathroom and looked at her face. No evidence of her fall last night. She took a few mouthfuls of vodka from the bottle she kept in the cabinet. Her face betrayed nothing. No evidence of her problem, the grey ghost that stalked her. The hidden little friend, the beguiling little companion that told her everything would be OK. And how much delusion was possible. How much self-delusion.

She turned sideways and stuck her stomach out. Is that how she would look if she was pregnant?

She'd stop drinking then. She'd have a reason to.

She drank because she was unhappy, if she was happy she wouldn't drink.

She was the master of self-delusion her entire life. God, her entire life was a delusion – she was here in her six-hundred-thousand pound flat, with her Porsche and her Christian Louboutins. She was a feared prosecutor in court. In reality, she was a single woman who was so devastated at the death of her cat, she had got pissed and passed out on the kitchen floor. Looking closer in the bathroom mirror, she could see her make-up was doing a good job of hiding the bruise on the side of her face, but that too, that face, was a delusion. She had two different faces, one for each world. She had thought that her law degree would be enough in her professional world and that her marriage was enough person-ally. Both had failed her. Grieg had had an affair with a girl called Tania, Tara, Toni, something like that. She was eight years younger than Valerie. But Valerie had had her affair first, with a cheap bottle of vodka.

Now she didn't even have Alfred to tell her worries to.

She had tried to save her marriage, saying she would stop drinking and would try an IVF programme but that was a non-starter right from the get go. Her private gynae had sat in that posh office. She could remember the feel of the polished wood of the chair arm under her hands, her fingers were coiling and uncoiling. She knew what he was going to say before he said it, and why he had suggested, pointedly, that she might want to attend her appointment on her own.

You've got to stop the drinking.

With all the Bernadette Kissel's in the world, he had sat there in his posh office and told *her* that she was unfit to be a mother.

'You aren't suitable for the programme?' Grieg had asked, as she was holding onto the worktop for support. He had asked her to seek help. Her hesitation had been a moment too long. And, though her recollection wasn't too good – she had been drunk at the time – she was sure that was the moment he had walked into the bedroom and started packing for the first time.

And, she thought, looking at the water as it ran down the sink, that was the last time he had packed.

She turned the tap off and went to pack a suitcase of her own.

Eddie McFadden was settling down to his favourite evening of the week. Thursday nights were for chilling. She was away at the bingo and if he was in luck, she would be out before he came in from work. Then he would nip out the house for special fish and chips with curry sauce, the pea and ham soup that the wife had left him would go to the dog – although sometimes the dog turned his nose up at it. Eddie would scoff his high cholesterol but delicious supper with a hot cup of tea and a whole box of Jaffa cakes. He would spend the night at the computer looking through his photographs, the ones he had taken the weekend before, at his regular haunt, the RSPB reserve at Lochwinnoch. The weather hadn't been good last time but he had spent a good hour moving from hide to hide. Although these days he was finding the reeds and the water more interesting than the birds although he always had a soft spot for the swans, majestic, beautiful and bloody vicious.

He boiled the kettle again and filled his cup, put an old episode of *On The Buses* on the TV and settled down, loading the photographs from the memory card onto the hard drive.

He clicked through them one by one, deleting all those out of focus or misfires.

It wasn't unusual for the images to catch something that he himself had not seen. The old adage was true, the camera never lies. When he first saw the ghostly shape in the water, at first he thought it was a dead swan, white and undulating below the surface, caught in the reeds as the slight waves buffered it. Then he thought it was a shadow on the lens on the water or a bright reflection of the moon. Then he noticed its extreme white colour, blanched, devoid of all tone, floating around and seeming to shimmer between the frames. It was difficult to make out any real shape. He brushed his salty hands down his cardigan and looked again. Plastic bag? They were so bad for the birds, it made him furious, Castle Semple and the loch were not in the city centre, they were not places that attracted other people's garbage. This was a nature reserve, people had to know the place was here and drive out or get the train out. People came here because they loved nature or because they canoed or rowed. The kind of people that should respect the place.

He sighed and swore under his breath. Last year there had been boys down there with airguns, taking pot shots at the swans. He'd bloody drown them if he ever caught them. He was a big guy, he could still handle himself.

He clicked on a few frames. The white ghost in the water took on a definite shape and form, bigger than a swan, much bigger. He had the semi-submerged tree trunk to scale it. Was it two swans, wrapped together in death as they were in life? As he focussed he thought he could make out a waist, shoulders. It faded as it sank deeper onto the water like two wings or two arms, or was it all a trick of his mind. But the last photograph confirmed it. He spread his fingers on the screen. He had a good camera, the larger image lost no resolution. He could see wisps of ebony hair across the stark ivory of her cheek, like a doll thrown away in a fit of temper. He looked closer at the detail. Not a doll, not a doll at all.

Anderson wanted some peace and quiet. He had been sitting in his kitchen with a strong cup of black coffee and a pile of

toast ladled with butter. On the island in front of him he had
the pictures of Gillian Witherspoon and Sally Logan as she
was then. He had been studying them for a while, a blank A4
notebook on the worktop beside him, the virgin white page
was now full of scribbles.

He had phoned Gerry Stewart. Gillian's widower seemed
happy to hear from him. And had answered his single question
with hesitation, and then said, Thank God you asked.

Gillian had been having her shoulder operated on when she
died. The pain from the ligamentous injury that she had
sustained during her assault.

And the more he flicked through the pictures, the more
similarities he saw. He was running his fingers over the pale
features of Sally, standing against a white wall, wearing a
light-blue paper gown, the camera catching the depth and the
scale of her injuries against a flat rule. He wondered if he
could talk to her about the noise and . . .

He shut the file as the kitchen door flew open.

'Dad, are you going out on a date? Tonight again?' Claire
was insistent, as if she wanted the house to herself. He shouldn't
have stayed out last night. He was overcome with a huge
sense of guilt, with no idea why. Should he have told Claire
to go out to Brenda's and spend the night there as he wouldn't
be home?

But he wouldn't have changed last night at all. It had been
such a long time since he had talked like that, drank like that.
He had left the car, forgotten and abandoned outside in the
mud. He had fallen asleep easily on the sofa at the Braithwaite's
house in front of the log fire that itself was tiring and failing.
He had woken up to the smell of bacon sizzling in a pan, the
pain that he had thought was angina turned out to be the cat
lying on his chest. He had a brisk wash in freezing cold water
in the bathroom, bare floorboards and curling wallpaper. He
had slipped his anorak on, not wanting to presume that the
bacon was for him, then had followed the quiet, low-ceilinged
hall back to the kitchen where the smell intensified to a mouth-
watering degree. The kitchen was empty, three rashers of bacon
lay on the frying pan, a cut roll beside it already buttered, a
mug, coffee in the coffee maker. Braithwaite was outside, in

the drizzle, anorak on, having a coffee and his bacon roll, his bum perched on the old fence that must have bordered the flower garden at some time. He turned around and gestured to the bacon.

Five minutes later, Anderson too was outside, feeling the light rain on his face. He was ripping apart the bacon roll like he hadn't eaten for a fortnight, and he knew why pathologists and crime scene officers loved bacon rolls after being at the grisly crime scene. They had a comforting aroma.

He had come home to have a shower and get changed before going late into work and was slightly miffed that nobody seemed to have missed him. Nobody asked where he had been, he could have been in bloody Casualty for all they knew. Or cared.

Then Sally had phoned. He couldn't say that he wasn't flattered about the way that conversation had gone. But it wasn't right, they were not the same two people now that they had been then. Not at all.

So he had gone to work and not concentrated on anything.

It was half eight now and he was lying down on the settee of the big house, trying not to think why the Marmite was out even though Claire hated it, or why Claire might want him to go back out again.

Instead he decided to lie down on the big sofa and have a think about the case. Costello had sent him an email with Laphan's thoughts on the issue of baby brokering, and his thoughts in a nutshell were that it could be entirely possible and extremely profitable.

Once he had sat down at his desk he had put all his memories of Helena and Sally behind him, and then spent an unfruitful two hours listening to his colleagues in the office, reading over the plans for the new poster girl for the SafeLife campaign, tinkering with it and making suggestions on how they might be able to sell this to Sally. She hadn't said yes, but she hadn't said no.

And it was an excuse to see her again.

He had still been in the office when Costello phoned to update him on her visit to Libby Hamilton and that she was following a solid lead. He had been surprised, an email and a phone call. Was it force of habit, a habit that she had not acted on for the previous few months? Or was she taunting him, making him jealous as she ran around, out in the big world doing detective work, then phoning him with leads and asking him what he thought. Or had she sensed that he was jealous of the curry they had all been out for. He was jealous of the meeting she had set up with a prostitute called Suzy.

He was jealous of her.

Libby and Dali had arrived at the same conclusion, one was a woman of utter integrity and the other wrote her own rules. They had both hinted there was baby brokering going on. That was illegal. But more worrying was the abduction of other children.

And Mulholland's story intrigued him, a pregnant woman in a blue coat had walked down the lane and disappeared. He closed his eyes and imagined the lane with walls on either side. Two doors in the wall of the Old Edwardian, then that wee patch of dirt. There was no back door, no entry to the building or the office building on the lane apart from the lift. He had an invitation to view the security film from the lift but thought it prudent to send Mulholland and Wyngate. They had checked out Wrights Insurance. Did she get picked up in a car? Not with the bollard up. There had been no noise of a motorbike or scooter. There were no outside iron stairs up the building. What about downwards, any basements? He wondered if that had been checked, the floor of the yard? A trapdoor of some sort? He was being fanciful but they had learned a lesson one night on a hill above that long, slow drag known as the Rest and Be Thankful. There could be anything underground.

Curious, he pulled out his phone and typed in the word Grahamston.

The fictional village that lay under Glasgow. It had never really existed surely. The rumours were that it had been abandoned in the 1870s. It was supposed to be buried under the concourse of Glasgow Central Station and to spread westward. And it was a fiction. A mere fiction that had grown up over the years, nothing but whispers and conjecture that had blossomed to fact.

The lane was less than two blocks away from the western edge of where Grahamston was purported to be, go one block further south and there was the river. The river still had old tunnels underneath, right in the heart of the city. The rotundas, now restaurants, were used for turning horse-drawn vehicles back in the day, allowing them to shuttle back and forth.

OK, so he allowed himself that hypothesis. What was going on that warranted a pregnant woman to hide there? The concealment of the birth of a baby.

'Hello.' The door opened, a pleasant-looking blonde smiled.

Costello walked into a flat, decorated in every shade of grey, very trendy with a circular settee that nobody could sit in. She couldn't help herself but look at Suzy's arms, no track marks. She was clean, she looked healthy. Libby's punters did not like girls infected with the needle. It was bad for business.

The recent TV adaptation of *The Handmaid's Tale* was on the television. Suzy clicked it to silence as she sat down.

'Suzy?'

'I know who you are and I know why you are here.'

'I would like to think that you are talking to me without duress.' Costello sat down. 'And that you are free to say what you need to say.'

'I am, I knew Janet or Sonja as she was known professionally. I knew her quite well in the early days, two years back, we both started out in . . .'

'Business together?' Costello offered

'Some of the girls do a bit of extra work, to help with their grants, you know. Some men coming into the nightclub want young, bright company, especially if they come from overseas.'

'I get the picture,' said Costello, 'but to my mind you are no better than the girl who ended up with her head bashed in against the side of the skip. You live a risky life.'

'I am a hostess not a prostitute.'

'You live a risky life,' Costello repeated.

'Janet and I, we were hostessing together at the Red Door, do you know it?'

'I know it as a knocking shop.'

'We can earn a lot of money, and I do declare it for tax before you start on that.'

'I wasn't going to.' Costello wondered about the society they lived in. OK to sleep with men for money, not OK to exclude it from the self-assessment tax return.

'It's not illegal to work as a hostess,' Suzy said primly.

'So I keep hearing. What about Janet?'

'Janet was there as well, she resented the fact that we had to give some of our earnings over as rent to the . . .'

'Management?' offered Costello.

'Indeed, and she decided to go out on her own, make more money and the next thing I heard she was working at another nightclub.'

'What club?'

'Something like The Pond.'

'The Pond, is that anything to do with the Blue Neptune?'

'Yes, it's a small cocktail bar at the back. It's quite exclusive.' She looked at Costello, wondering how somebody like her knew about it.

'I've arrested a few guys in the toilets,' lied Costello in answer to the unasked question.

'Well, Janet was working there until the bosses found out and then she was asked to move on. Then I heard she was pregnant and I thought, well, that will be her, you know, out the game.'

'Not hostessing or . . .'

'Or just get rid of the baby.'

'Occupational hazard in the world of hostessing?' asked Costello, trying to keep the sarcasm from her tone.

'Maybe.' Suzy wriggled forward on the couch. 'But she said to me that it was the best thing that had ever happened to her. And that she was going to earn a fortune.'

Costello felt her heart jump, and resisted the urge to rush the next question. 'What? Did she say how?'

'Not specifically but I think she was talking about . . . well, somebody wanted a baby and . . . well she said why not. She mentioned thousands of pounds, thousands and thousands of pounds.' Her envy was obvious.

'Selling it?' Costello tried to keep her voice calm.

'She didn't say exactly, but I think so. She was off work for a while. Then I heard she had been found dead in a bedsit.' Suddenly Suzy looked young and vulnerable.

'Why did you not come forward?'

'Libby said I was to wait until you came to me.'

'Has anybody ever approached you to carry a child?'

Suzy recoiled in horror. 'That's disgusting.'

It had taken Costello forty minutes to track down the port-mortem reports she was looking for, O'Hare had been helpful but distant, as if he was too tired to be bothered with it all. But as she gave him more details he admitted he did recall the case, for one good reason. His colleague's comments over lunch that she had just done an autopsy on a woman who seemed to have given birth, lost the baby, then stitched herself up.

'And that's not something you hear every day.'

Costello made an involuntary squeaking noise. 'So we are looking for a medically trained contortionist with little maternal instinct?'

'I don't know, there was a rush put on it by the fiscal, so somebody has walked this road before you. Good luck.'

And that had sparked her interest. If there was a fiscal out there suspecting criminality, then her life could get much easier. She flicked through the report sitting in her office, late, accompanied by a packet of Liquorice Allsorts. Janet Gibson had decided her name was not sexy enough, so she became Sonja. She noted the stomach contents listed as they had been at the time of the post-mortem: Devon Crab, deep fried seaweed and tofu curd. Not the average Glaswegian fayre. Devon crab was expensive stuff. She presumed the pathologist had tested to try to ascertain where the deceased had eaten their last meal. The food was largely undigested, so she had died a short time after, which might explain why this report had been scanned in at the front of the file.

She clicked on to a colour picture of Janet lying on the slab, looking rather thin-faced and a bit piqued at being dead. The next click brought up the same picture that Libby had in her drawer.

Costello scanned the report, picking out bits and scribbling them down. Janet had not been an active sex worker. She was well nourished, not a drug abuser, her death had slid past the pathologist as Janet had given birth recently, and fatality from post-birth embolism was not unheard of. The red flag for Costello, and maybe the mysterious fiscal, was the lack of a baby. There was a suggestion it had been stillborn but only because it was absent, which was an arse for elbow way of looking at it.

Janet was ripe for the taking; bright, overworked at uni and had no close family. She had nobody at all. And, noted in bold, the door of her bedsit had been locked from the inside so the attending police officer had deduced suicide or natural death.

Costello wasn't aware that cause of death was now in their remit but she believed in 'live and learn'.

Even the length of the post-mortem report was cursory. Costello started clicking through the images, the good clean images of the crime scene that she had seen earlier. Janet was in bed, dead. It was a PC Maria Delany who was first on the scene, a quick check showed she was a constable on the south side. A new graduate who seemed to have taken a lot of it on herself.

There was a sense of presumption in the report that Costello didn't like. Janet was not a prostitute, the pathologist twice reported that it was unlikely Janet was a sex worker yet there was a derogatory tone to the language that didn't belong in any murder report. Except there was no sign she was murdered.

The report went back to the fiscal, V. Abernethy. And it ended there.

She clicked back through the images of the room, a typical Southside lower end of the student market bedsit. A thin, badly stained beige carpet covered three quarters of the floor, leaving a wide strip of blue curled lino along the wall at a kitchen unit. A small flat-screen TV, a brightly patterned rug, a jug of water beside her bed and her iPod still sat in its black cradle with the green light on, showing it was powered up when the photograph was taken. Costello felt her heart sink, these little things, her iPod had still been alive when she had not.

Above the bed was a calendar with May showing a golden retriever puppy looking impossibly cute. She noted the date of the death. Sixth of May 2016. Only last year but she had no memory of it. The wall had recently been painted in a futile attempt to cover the bright yellow wallpaper with its large black flowers, with light cream paint but the pattern underneath was already showing through.

The room said a lot about her. Not a pleasant room. Delany's report showed she was thinking death from natural causes straight away. A dangerous think for a young cop to think and a stupid thing to write down. But Costello knew the type. Delany had been qualified a fortnight, looked her seniors straight in the eye and pronounced a natural death *obviously*. Because she had wanted to get off duty.

Costello had had it rammed into her as a PC, that there was only one chance at the evidence. She found herself looking at the big window in the photographs, a modern window in an old bedsit flat one floor up. By law, it had to open far enough to let an adult out in the event of a fire.

Or if you needed an exit after locking the door from the inside.

She clicked on through the pictures. The camera had moved to the exterior of the room now, showing the narrow landing where the cord carpet beneath a pair of visible boots was worn to a thread.

Then there was the body, Janet lying in her bed, staring at the ceiling as if she was thinking about getting up, just contemplating the day and wondering if she could have another five minutes before the alarm went.

If Janet had been a student at the university there would be friends, tutors, counsellors that would spend the rest of their lives wondering if there was something that they should have said, or done. Questions that will not have been asked. Or answered. While Delany had been happy to stand outside looking at her watch.

There was a photograph of the crime scene manager, his face visible as he came up the stairs, phone clamped to the side of his head. There was the outline of a clipboard held in someone else's arm, marking the arrival times and the identities of those attending the scene.

The body had been found by the landlord after concerns raised by the guy in the next room. Adele 21 had been playing continuously all night. So he had chapped the door, but Janet had not responded. The neighbour only knew her to say hello to on the stairs. Janet had kept herself to herself as was the way of bedsit land. And it was not unusual for her to play music late into the night but this was louder and later than usual, and she had been very quiet recently. So much so he thought that she might have been away, so did the landlord. Somebody had been careful enough to write that – away. Away to have her child?

The landlord had been called, he had a master key and together they found her body.

Costello looked at the images, willing Janet to tell her something. She had a growth of dark root at the top of her head, Costello knew pregnant women stopped putting peroxide on their hair. She saw a few books stacked under her bedside light, *Der Antichrist: Fluch auf das Christentum*. Neitzsche. She wore red and white pyjamas, cheap nylon with the words, *I want it all* over the top. Costello examined the date on the puppy calendar again. Dates marked off with a cross in a thick black pen, the day before she died was marked with an asterix. Was that her due date?

So where was the baby? Foundlings were front page news these days; people do not have psychotic breaks quietly. And, she read the small footnote, Janet had no food in that bedsit. She hadn't been living there.

She flicked back to the name of the fiscal who had requested the reports. V. Abernethy? She googled her and stared for a long time at the picture of the young, dark-haired lawyer. And the pretty silver butterfly necklace that hung round her long, feminine throat.

Then she googled five of the most expensive restaurants to see which ones served Devon Crab. At least the answer to that cheered her up.

TEN

' I haven't seen you around for a while.' The uniform on the outer tape smiled. 'Good to see you wrapped up, DI Costello. It's going to be a cold one.'

She should have known the cop on the tape but she drew a blank so she just muttered something into the scarf round her mouth. It was one o'clock in the morning, she needed to take a moment to settle herself so she stopped walking, pretending to be taking in the air and the sight of the water. To those already at the locus, it might appear as though the approaching detective was getting her bearings. She knew the scene was in good hands. O'Hare, the pathologist's car was already in the car park. He would be keen to get the situation sorted out, time always a critical factor for a body, especially one in water. Her brain was trying to unscramble that fact. What was a body doing out here? Was it Orla?

But this young man was looking at her, encouraging her. She must look like she enjoyed her job, even at one o'clock in the morning.

She lifted the tape and tucked underneath, his outstretched arm showing her the way down the path which was obvious even in this darkness. On the other side, she hesitated, thinking that she should say something to this man, something about the case. What did he know? Who was the body? Who found them? But he had let the tape drop and he had walked away.

She walked on, digging her fists deeper into her anorak pockets, and retracted her neck into the deep collar of her scarf. There was a cold bite in the air this morning, the breeze was light but carried a nasty chill. She went on along the path in the darkness, some of it duckboarded, other parts just a less muddy track through the deeper mud. The path wound round a hedgehog house, past reed beds, before leaving the water's edge to veer much closer to the wall under the railway line. Her progress was faltering but steady, towards the little crowd and the lights. Some people were pointing things out to the pathologist, others looking past him and at her, waiting. Maybe it was their first body. Lochwinnoch was not known as a murder capital of Western Europe. Well, it hadn't been until now.

She saw O'Hare point back up towards her, then a uniform came back in a hurry, almost jogging, speaking down his radio as he approached.

'There's a young woman in the water. She matches the description of a girl you have been looking for. Down there, keep to the right side of the path. She's still in the water.'

Costello stopped and watched him go past, wondering about a young man like that, so occupied within himself that the tragic event in the water had left him so untouched. The world had moved on, for somebody else the world had stopped.

Poor kid, whoever they were. They had been looking for Orla unofficially, but there was no way she was a missing person.

This was a lonely place to die, but lovely compared to the vomit-stained streets that witnessed most murders in Glasgow. Costello ran through a few scenarios in her head. This was a bird sanctuary, there would have been nobody here once darkness fell, between half six and half seven last night. Night out here in the country tends to take its time, it falls like an incoming tide, slowly and embracing. It wasn't like in the city when the clouds gather, the buildings cut out any spreading light.

This place would have been quiet and abandoned. She knew it was a bird-watching paradise on this side of the water and a water sports centre on the other side. If anybody was going to park up to drug deal or for illicit sex, they would drive over there. This side of the water was deserted. It was for birders and photographers. There was a car park followed by a long walk, not a drive, right to the water as there was on the other side of the loch. Which suggested she either floated across or was walked here, then killed. Dead bodies are heavy, a dead weight in fact. She had no idea if a body of water like this had a current, if it had waves or if the wind had been strong enough to move the body across.

Costello could see more as the path widened out. She could see two crime scene guys and three uniformed constables. O'Hare was half hidden by the rise of the land, or he was standing knee deep in water. Their feet in inches of mud, they moved in slow-motion.

As she was nearing the inner tape she looked at the sky again, it was as dull and grey as the muddy gravel path in front of her. Had they checked the weather, ordered a tent? She was in her water-logged cradle and both being manoeuvred into a plastic bag. Then the cradle was pulled clear of the water to allow the contents to settle. The bag was cut in the upper corner, then the cradle was tilted slightly so the water emptied, leaving any debris and evidence behind with the body. It was a skilled job and she didn't want to interrupt them.

Costello approached down the middle of the path, walking through the puddles as an act of defiance. They needed to get that tent up here, once the crime scene lights arrived, the place would light up like a stage show and the commuters on the early train would get a fright.

'White female, early twenties from the look of her,' offered O'Hare.

'And how did she die?' asked Costello, taking the shoe covers that were offered to her by the crime scene manager.

'I don't know but can you send somebody over there to block off the car park.' He pointed across the water, then turned to Costello. 'And you need to speak to that man there. He's soaking wet.'

Costello looked down. All she could see was the nacreous tangle of arms and a vast beehive of matted black hair. She was very young. And very dead.

O'Hare, the pathologist, opened the bag up a little to let her have a better look. The body was the colour of a ghost, deadly white and the skin of her face had lifted slightly, with her huge dark eyebrows totally unaffected by the water and the process of death. It gave the lower half of her face the look of being slightly out of focus, as if she was still under the water, the shimmer blurring her lower features.

'I think she was dead before she was put in the water, if that helps.'

'Don't suppose there is a phone in her pocket, no ID, nothing as useful as that?'

'No, nothing. It's her appearance that alerted us.' The SOCO pointed to the remnants of the hair ring on top of her head, the 'drug dealer's doughnut' as it was known colloquially.

'And those are similar, if identical to the clothes she was wearing when she went out the window. I know it's not protocol but let's get Lorna to do an early ID. But it's Orla Michaela Sheridan. I'd swear to it.'

She turned to Eddie who was sitting watching it all, dripping on a tree trunk near the big wall that supported the high railway line, he was wrapped in a blue blanket. A young cop sat next to him, they could have been sitting there talking about the fishing. Eddie could confirm that the body had been there early the previous evening. *Had there been other people about?* He reeled off the names of two other guys that he knew had been taking pictures too. They might have caught something.

'She was further out though,' said Eddie to nobody in particular.

'Further out?'

'Yes. In the picture she's further out, under that trunk, way out there. But when I got back here, she had floated right in. I didn't realize what it was and reached out to see, and fell in.'

'And you still have these pictures?'

'Oh yes. Loads of them.'

She turned to the young cop. 'Maybe you can go home with Eddie here and collect the pictures.'

The young cop nodded.

'Do you know these waters well?'

'Not well, but yes . . .' He was still shaking, either from the cold or from the shock.

'Is there a current? Could she have floated across?'

'At this time of year, yes. Not enough water current but there is a strong prevailing wind, hence the windsurfing.'

'I think you should take this gentleman home before he gets

pneumonia. And maybe get the other pictures?'

Orla was out of the water now, nestling in her plastic crate, with her blanket of plastic body bag. She looked relieved, death had removed the cares and stresses of life. Costello had heard it many times, how the victim looked at peace – usually only to be shattered by the court case and horrific forensic detail of the act that had put them in the mortuary in the first place.

The photographer's flash kept going, the video camera taking it all in. She heard O'Hare shout. 'Hey hey.' And he directed both cameras to the girl's flank, to her hip, to the bruised flesh. He actually stepped over the body and lifted up the edge of her sodden cardigan so they could get a better view.

'What is it?'

'Look at that, there's a concise, distinct pattern in the hypostasis. Can you read that?'

'It's a series of squiggles? Can you get that cleaned up for me and let me have an image,' asked Costello.

The pathologist nodded. 'As soon as.'

'So she was lying on her side, when she died?'

'And was left there for a good few hours, I would say. There's something ingrained in that mark, looks like dirty oil or something, something not washed off by the water.'

'Not bruising from the loch?'

'Doubt it. Look at the lettering.'

'I can't make it out.'

'You should eat more carrots.' And he turned away, getting back to work, pointing at the circular bruise on her thigh so the photographer could capture good clear images.

Costello had another glance round the scene, looking at the clouds and the dark. If they were all awake, she saw no reason why other folk should be getting a good night's sleep. And she needed to stay here and pick O'Hare's brains about Janet before she let him go. She pulled her phone out; she was going to test Mulholland's resolve to get back on the team.

Mulholland was glad to be woken up, he was never a good sleeper anyway. He stopped at the all-night truck stop, and sipping a hot tea, he looked at maps on his satnav, examining the various routes from the lane at the Blue Neptune to the loch side out at Lochwinnoch. He was going to spend the night driving around, looking at skips and ditches, rubbish piles and tipping sites. In fact he was looking for anywhere somebody would dump a plastic carry-on suitcase. In a hurry.

Hard plastic. Leopard skin.

He looked at the journey he would be going on at this time of night and had second thoughts. He wasn't a coward but he wasn't stupid either. In this car, his little Audi, he looked soft and as if he might have a bob or two. He looked like a target and there was no point in adding to the crime stats. He called the wimpiest guy he knew, just to make himself seem brave.

Wyngate too, was glad to get out the house, one of his children had been sick during the night so he was already awake and watching Netflix with a stinky kid snoring on the settee beside him, a plastic tub at his feet in case the wee guy decided to throw up again.

Both Wyngate and Mulholland had been incarcerated for too long and were relishing the opportunity of getting out. Mulholland was ignoring the question of the legality of the search, but they were looking for something that had technically, been dumped.

They had found one of the missing girls, dead. They had no idea who, or where, Miss Bluecoat was and there were now real fears for her safety.

The suitcase could be a vital piece of evidence. There would be huge kudos if they found it, a needle in a haystack it might be but they had experience and could read the situation. On this first night they would need to think like the killer, and do what they thought he would do. Thinking along the same lines, Costello had already ordered a torch sweep of the water at the other side of the loch, the suitcase would be near the shore if it had been thrown in there. The water was not deep, and he had agreed with her, it would have already drawn attention from the dog walkers and the canoeists.

They would give this their best shot in the time they had. The killer wouldn't have dumped it in the middle of Glasgow, too much CCTV, too many people ready to pull a good-looking suitcase out of a skip. It would take a very steady nerve to drive slowly with a body in the back. Wyngate suggested, and Mulholland agreed that the killer would have got on the motorway out the city as quickly as possible, and then looked for a dump site.

Once out on the A737, the dual carriageway was high on the surrounding land, it would be quiet at that time of night, presuming that they would move the body at night. They were presuming a lot, but they didn't have a lot to go on. Once they neared the turn off for Linwood they realized how high the road was, how steep the embankment. They drove slowly along the verge on the inside lane, catching sight of the odd mattress dumped over the side. They stopped, bumped up the verge as close as the metal barrier would allow them and got out the car. Torched up, they walked in different directions. Two hours, cold feet, three mattresses, a few kitchen units, five microwaves and one dead dog later, Mulholland saw a spotty surface that gleamed a little too shiny in the glare of the torch. He phoned Wyngate to join him before he went any further, but the pulsing of his heart was telling him he was right.

It was partially buried under a whole lot of damp, white-veined wood. They photographed it on their phones, then pulled their nitrile gloves on and got to work, wrestling the suitcase from under the wood that had been roughly piled over it. They worked in silence, dragged it up the embankment and then along to the car, Mulholland holding the handle at the side so as not to disturb any fingerprints that might have been left on the handgrip, the suitcase trundled obediently behind him like a young puppy.

They decided to open it up in the back of the car and have a look, but not to remove any items from it. The locks sprung open with very little persuasion from a small spanner. Dirty clothes, summer clothes, Mulholland noted, a smaller bag like a little plastic rucksack, black with red flowers, the sort of things that a wee girl might take to school. He shone his torch into the small bag; passport, phone with battery going flat, a few euros, a folded set of A4 papers, the print out of a boarding pass and an e ticket for a flight to Alicante that had already left from Glasgow. He counted the euros, twenty.

'I think somebody had relieved her of her sterling. Sure she wasn't stupid enough to go with twenty euros.'

'In any case, she was leaving the country, going on a little holiday. Didn't bloody make it though, did she?'

'That's a bit extreme, just to get away from her social worker.'

'But they were on the lookout for Wee Polly, and she couldn't produce that baby. She runs.'

'To Malaga?'

'She's young and stupid.' Mulholland looked along the motorway. 'She can't go to her parents, they think she still has the baby. She goes to the broker who has . . . bought the baby?' he suggested.

'And they give her money to leave the country?'

'Costello said she thought Orla had money, well cash, and had taken it with her out the window, she goes up Sevastapol Lane to meet whoever, and they run her to the airport.'

'Which we have just driven past . . .' Wyngate realized.

'They kill her and take the money. She has already told folk she's away on holiday, nobody misses her.'

'Or they kill her there and drive her out here. You wouldn't want her panicking when you drive past the airport exit.'

Costello was dog tired. She had gained an hour's kip in the office to be woken up by the cleaners coming in at seven. So she sneaked out for a roll on sausage for breakfast, not taking it back to the station but sitting at the window of the Tea Traders Cafe thinking. James Chisholm had trouble keeping away from the ladies. They were still to establish contact from the second pay-as-you-go. She was getting pissed off with it.

She phoned James to inform him that there had been a huge response to the appeal for information and there was a team dedicated to working through that intel so the scripted appeal was on the back burner for the moment. She didn't tell him that most of them were from timewasters, or the genuinely deluded. One woman came on the phone crying, saying that 'Moses' was her son. He had Downs and had been missing for thirty years. Thank God the cop on the other end of the phone had the good sense to take her name and number and would action a welfare check. Not one of the calls related to

Moses, not one call. So his mother either wouldn't get in touch, or couldn't.

'And while we are at it, who are these two numbers on your phone?' She read them out and she heard him move and a door close over, out of Roberta's earshot no doubt.

'Friends, private friends, nothing to do with the case,' he said.

She replied that Angelika had said that but what about the other number.

'Nothing to do with the case,' he said again.

'My decision, not yours, pal.'

He thanked her with only mild sarcasm and the phone went down.

It was getting on for half eight now, a decent time to phone a fiscal on her direct number. It was answered very quickly, the voice sharp and cold. Words slightly clipped, too carefully pronounced. It would have fooled most people, but not the daughter of an alcoholic.

Valerie Abernethy, the Porsche-driving fiscal, seemed to believe that police officers who phoned her early in the morning were a species to be ignored. She had told Costello to get hold of the file on Sonja Gibson in the usual way. Costello explained that she had done that and was now looking for some explanation as to the request the fiscal's office in Edinburgh had submitted.

That had stopped the fiscal in her tracks.

'Would you prefer that I ask Archie Walker to make an official request?'

The response was a snide, 'That would be easier for you as you know him so well. Why are you bothering me?'

That left Costello speechless.

Valerie said the case was still under review, said goodbye and hung up.

It had been a stupid thing to do, but she had wanted to hear that voice, to fill in the gaps in her picture of this woman. But she had slipped up, Costello had only referred to the Gibson death in Glasgow south side and repeated the case number. Valerie had called her Sonja – her professional name.

Interesting.

But two stupid things in a row? She may as well and called

Archie.

Five minutes later, she shut her phone and decided to switch it off for a couple of minutes.

Just to digest what Archie had said. Valerie Abernethy was his goddaughter.

Goddaughter. She had asked him why the fuck had he not said. He had replied in that superior way he had, that he didn't know anybody was asking. And Costello had felt defensive and was rude, very rude.

Then Archie had said, 'Funny you should ask but her boss in Edinburgh, Bill Nelson, had been worried about her.' No bloody wonder, pissed at her desk in the morning but she thought it more prudent not to say – even as she was talking she recalled her at the restaurant with Archie, Valerie had pushed the wine glass away and drunk water, the loose-fitting clothes, or shapeless. Was she pregnant?

Had she been but wasn't now, if she was drinking again?

Now she was off the phone she felt guilty.

And slightly stupid. She had pissed off two fiscals, one of them a witness. She had known that he was godfather to the daughter of his friends who had died a couple of years ago. But she doubted she had ever heard him say Valerie, or if he had, she had not registered it. She would have to apologize to them both. Eventually. But Archie had hinted that Valerie was troubled about something, so troubled she was pissed at her desk at half eight in the morning.

While she was there she decided to phone Dali and tell her about the body they had found overnight. There was silence on the end of the phone. Costello thought she hadn't heard. So she repeated it.

'I heard you.' A sniff, like she was holding back tears.

'Sorry, Dali, but I think it's Orla.'

'What now?' She was indeed crying. 'We have to do something, Costello.'

'And you have to leave it to us.'

Mulholland had strict instructions from Costello to be charming to Lorna McGill, a woman ten years younger than himself, and to show her the body of the girl she had let climb out the window. Orla's mum, still in a state of shock, had initially resisted showing her daughter's body to a potential witness but she understood the logic of it. Somebody was recruiting these girls, and they had to suspect everybody. All Sheila Sheridan wanted to know was who had killed her daughter.

Two coffees and a bacon roll later, he slid into the seat beside Lorna, introduced himself and shook her hand. Despite his tiredness, he felt alive and more alert than he had since he was discharged from the hospital after the last attempt to pin his broken leg.

She looked very relieved to see him.

'Can I have a word with you? I don't want you to record this anywhere, certainly not in any official notes.'

'Am I in trouble?' Her wide eyes blinked slowly. She was nervous, but that needn't be a sign of guilt.

'No, not at all, why do you think that?'

'Because I visited her at her house, I wanted to know where Polly was. I've been asked to pass the file to my supervisor and finalize my report.'

'Leave them to us. How old is Polly?'

'Five weeks.' Lorna nodded.

'We'd like you to identify the body.'

'What here? Now?' Lorna looked round nervously, 'I thought Sheila would identify her, she is her mother. Is that not normal, to get the next of kin?'

'You saw her last,' said Mulholland, 'it might help us out.' He got up and didn't let her argue any further. He led her to a door that looked thick and well locked. He typed in a number on the keypad, there was a whirring noise. Mulholland didn't speak to Lorna, making her hurry to keep up with him as he walked along a corridor, turned left, turned right, showed his ID twice and was buzzed through. They had organized that the mortuary technician would be opening the handle and pulling the gurney out before Lorna would realize where she was. The gurney's legs extended automatically as it left its cold hidey hole in the wall.

Lorna took a step back, Mulholland felt her hand brush the side of his own arm, whether it was accidental, or an instinctive reach for support, he didn't know.

They watched as the assistant unzipped the bag and opened the sheet. The assistant, a taciturn dark-haired woman with her hair pulled back under a cap, paused at the other side of the body and then freed up Orla's arms, leaving them on top of the sheet so the body looked, as they all did in that pose, as if they were asleep.

Lorna said nothing, although her mouth was moving, words would not come. She stretched her arm out to touch the sheet that lay in folds round the contours of Orla's body. A gentle touch, fingertips, making contact and no more. She withdrew her hand. 'Sorry, she looks so young.' She sniffed back tears. 'She always looked older, with the make-up, and the clothes and . . . everything . . . She looks like a wee kid now.'

'She was very young, Miss McGill. You had a professional association with this young lady?' asked Mulholland.

'Yes, only a few months.'

'And she had a baby five weeks ago? And you have no idea where that baby is?'

'No idea, I have never set eyes on Polly.' Her eyes were fixed on Orla's face. Tears rolling freely.

'Was she planning to go anywhere?' he prompted.

'She had booked a holiday somewhere, or so she said. She was a . . . well, a liar, a fantasist. She used to tell me all kinds of crap. She was getting a record contract, she'd met a millionaire, she was writing to somebody on death row, she was moving to the country and buying a pony, all kinds of rubbish.'

'Did you note down the rubbish anywhere, in any write-ups of your visits?' he asked hopefully.

She shook her head. 'I dismissed it as her crap. Maybe I shook have taken her more seriously.'

'Hindsight is always 20 20. Was she a sex worker?'

'Not on our system.'

'If she was working in that field,' he phrased the question carefully, 'do you know where that might be? Anywhere she mentioned?'

Lorna McGill closed her eyes, thinking. 'There were a few

places she mentioned. God, I can't remember, I am sorry.'

'Emma has something that might help.'

Emma, the assistant, picked up a small handheld UV light and scanned it down the skin of Orla's arm, showing blotches, subcutaneous contusions and café au lait patches under the intense light that were invisible to the naked eye. At the base of the thumb, she stopped, and turned the victim's left hand over so they could see the small tattoo like drawing, the outline of a spikey pattern.

'What is that?' Lorna asked.

'You can probably make it out better if you come around here.' Emma twisted the dead girl's shoulder to pull the hand away from the onlookers. Mulholland walked a reluctant Lorna round the body, staying behind her so they had the same viewpoint. The image was composed of blurred lines of a single colour, like a spikey flower.

'We think it's a nightclub stamp.'

'It is. I've been there. It's the Rockpool, it's a starfish,' said Lorna.

'Where the hell did she get the money to drink in a place like that?' asked Mulholland. 'Rich sugar daddy?'

'She'd need one in there.' Lorna had calmed a little. 'I was only there once, staff do. We didn't go back, it was too expensive. If you want a drink in the Blue Neptune you are better going to The Pond. Was she there before she died?'

'The day before she died.'

Lorna shook her head. 'How could she afford that?'

Costello had just walked back into her office at Govan when her mobile went, a call redirected from her desk number.

'DI Costello?'

'Speaking.' She nipped behind a set of double doors into a quiet corridor.

'I believe you are trying to track me down and I want you to understand that I have a private acquaintance with James Chisholm and that I am not connected, in any way, with the abduction of his child.'

'Thank you for calling. Can I ask the nature of your relationship with him?' Costello heard something else behind this woman's tone. Her speech rhythm wasn't right. As if she was reading a script, and was tense about doing it.

'Private, we weren't having an affair.' This sounded more natural.

'Was he just a friend then?'

'Yes, we would meet for coffee and chat. He was happy with Roberta but the baby just wouldn't stop crying. He was out of his depth and wanted somebody to talk to. Nothing more than that, I hope you understand.'

'Yes, of course. Can I ask your name?' Costello was super polite.

'It's Valerie. Valerie Abernethy.'

'Thank you, Valerie. Thank you for calling.' And the line went dead.

'Are you fuck Valerie Abernethy. You're sober for a start.'

She called Wyngate and asked him to get back to her with the location of what had become known as pay-as-you-go two, when it had phoned her Govan station number.

She made up her mind, did an about turn and ten minutes later she was knocking on the door of a beautiful three-story house on Kirklee Terrace. There was a clatter of footsteps, a rush of somebody coming down the stairs and then a shout of 'Dad, it's only David'.

'Oh no, it's not,' Costello said, then the door opened. 'Hi Claire, I need to speak to your dad right now.'

Colin was sitting in the kitchen, scrolling through a file on his laptop, a strong coffee beside him.

'Is this a social call?' he asked. 'Oh, of course not, it's Friday the thirteenth. My unlucky day. Do you want a cuppa?'

'Are you having one, another one?'

'No. I am going out for a meal tonight, with the Braithwaites no less.'

'That's great.'

'You are not invited.'

'But the timing is great. Now listen. Andrew Braithwaite. What does he do for a living?'

'He's a plastic surgeon, isn't he?'

'Nearly. He does Botox and fillers and stuff at the Blue Neptune for all the perfumed purple Pilates people, but that wasn't what he did when he specialized.'

'Don't tell me, he was a bloody obstetrician. Well, fuck me.'

'Well, no thanks but listen there's more. We need to be careful, Valerie Abernethy is involved in this in some way. Edinburgh fiscal and Archie's godchild. And somebody that knows her, knows about James Chisholm and the fact we were looking for that other pay-as-you-go. And that phone has not left Glasgow, even when Valerie was at her desk in Edinburgh and talking to me from her mobile in Glasgow. Clever, eh?'

'I am totally lost.'

'Good. We have to make a move, the clock is ticking if Miss Bluecoat is involved in this. Does Sally still have the hots for you?'

'What kind of question is that?'

'Just that I have a plan. I fancy you as bait. Well, she'll fancy you as bait. It's Friday the thirteenth, what could go wrong.'

Claire walked into the kitchen as he was about to call her and ask her if she wanted a cup of tea. And he needed to explain to her what was going to happen tonight, so she knew and she wouldn't worry.

'Tell me, is this another date, Dad?'

That was before he had even opened his mouth. Had she clocked the first wearing of a good shirt Brenda had bought him last Christmas? 'No, this is work.'

His daughter, her long hair gleaming, her face carefully made-up looked older than she had looked at the beginning of the week. She pulled a strand of hair slowly through her lips, a gesture that made her look a little like a porn star. 'Then why are you wearing your good clobber? Is she nice?'

'Like I said, it's work.'

'Really.' She now twiddled with the entwined lock of hair, absentmindedly, her eyes watching him carefully. 'Nothing to do with why you didn't come home the other night.'

'Maybe. It's work.' It wasn't like Claire to question him like this. There was something behind that intense stare. 'Have you spoken to your mum? She could hardly speak to me on the phone yesterday. Or the day before.'

Claire looked away, then dropped the lock of hair and started to examine her nails. 'She texted me this morning.'

'And . . .' Anderson pulled two mugs out, glad to have his back to her. This conversation was going to get difficult. And she was avoiding the question as much as he was avoiding eye contact.

'Have you and her had a fight?'

'No, nothing like that.'

'Nothing like what?'

'You know, how you have had . . . you know . . . girlfriends apart from Mum.'

From that affirmation of his infidelity, he snatched at the only moral high ground he had. 'One girlfriend.' How could he have called her that? 'Helena. You liked her.'

'Dad, I thought she was great. I really miss her. I think I might miss her all my life.'

Join the club, thought Anderson, saying nothing.

'How would you feel if Mum found somebody else?'

He was glad he was still looking away, unscrewing the top of the tea caddy. He hoped his voice would not betray him as he replied, 'Why, has she?'

'Yes.'

'Oh. And do you like him?'

'Yes. David and I went out for a curry with him last week.'

David and I?

'He was great. Peter really likes him. He's cool.'

Peter?

'We had to invite the stupid boy obviously after we got him off his Xbox. We went to Pizza Express. Rodge and Peter got on really well, we couldn't get Peter to shut up.'

Rodge?

Peter, his wee blond rascal who had turned into a sloth, couldn't say two words to his dad on the phone but apparently could chatter away to his mum's bloody boyfriend. He wanted to ask why Brenda had not mentioned it herself, but that was unfair on Claire.

'Are you going out tonight, Dad?' she repeated.

'Yes I am.

'So can Dave come round? Does he need to spend the night or are you coming home?'

'You can do what you want,' he said, knowing that she would anyway.

'Can I get a Chinese on the credit card?'

At least she still asked permission. 'Yes.'

'Can we have wine?'

'No, you can have a can of beer each and that's all.'

'Why? Why can't I have some wine? You are going out to enjoy yourself, why can't I?'

It was too much, what he called the 'Me Me Me' genera-tion of teenagers. He pulled the copy of the *Daily Record* off the worktop and skimmed it across towards her. It landed, right in front of her, a long-distance picture that was hazy in detail, of a body being pulled from water. Indistinct, but it was still easy to make out a human form, probably female. The hair hung down, long and black, just like Claire's. She was naked, lifeless. It was a stark picture.

'This is what I am doing tonight. I am working on that.' He couldn't keep his anger from his voice. 'If you think I am out enjoying myself then you need to sit down and have a wee chat with yourself.'

'Dad?'

But he had walked out, up to the ensuite in his room where he locked the door and took the small coil of wires out from their plastic bag. He clipped the tiny microphone under his shirt collar, another one was fitted to the side of his watch, the transmitter attached on the inside of his waistband, the discreet tiny button where he could easily switch it on, which he would do as soon as he entered the Blue Neptune. Not knowing exactly what he was walking into but comforted that Wyngate would be six floors above him, able to hear every word.

Gordon Wyngate sat on top of the roof having a sip of coffee from his flask. His hard hat protecting his head from the slight drizzle as he watched the cobbled lane between the Blue Neptune and the Wrights Insurance building, both having roof mounted security cameras There was a similar camera, this time a standard CCTV, focussed on the entrance and exit at the car park on Brown Street, and another on the small private car park that the Braithwaites used. The cameras were giving him a live feed onto a split screen and they had all entrances and exits covered. His earpiece put him in constant contact with Vik Mulholland. Once everybody was in their final position, they would be in a van at the end of the lane, near the door to the yoga studio. For now he had turned it low, fed up with the childlike bickering between Mulholland and Costello. He had enough of that at home. And he was sure, if anything happened, it would happen soon.

It was when Anderson was talking over dinner to the Braithwaites that things might get interesting. He knew two fiscals had been busy pulling legal strings. They had no real evidence and this was the only way they saw to get any. Costello had been raving about the health and safety Nazis, offering to sign any disclaimer – on Anderson's behalf.

A few folk had wandered up and down the lane going in both directions, a white transit had almost driven right into the bollard, then was trying to reverse out. Wyngate had turned up the volume on Mulholland's feed to hear his response. 'Absolute plonker.'

'I think that is our van. For later,' he heard Costello say, she was breathing hard, walking quickly, they were on the move at last.

'Who the hell is driving that?'

'No idea.'

'Bob Noakes,' volunteered Wyngate.

'Plonker.'

'Oh, this is nice,' said Wyngate, down his mouthpiece. 'Another car followed him, they are both now trying to get out the lane. They don't know about the bollard or they can't see it. Nice car but blind driver.'

'What kind of car?'

'A really fancy Porsche with an engine that could power a hurricane bomber from the sound of it.'

'Nice motor,' he heard Mulholland say, envious.

The Porsche reversed slightly away from the bollard and then took a right, circling round looking for another way in.

'OK, it's having a good look. It's not going away.'

'Or maybe he is lost?'

'She, I saw her driving past the car park.'

'You get her number,' asked Mulholland. 'She's my kind of woman.'

Wyngate read out the reg, VA2661, easily picked out on the still camera.

'A big car and a pulse and you are anybody's,' an unidentified disembodied voice sounded from somewhere. Wyngate could hear a snort of laughter. He was enjoying himself, this was what he missed. The inane chatter, the build-up of tension, the uncertainty of how the night's events would unfold. The sense that Anderson was walking into the lion's den and . . .

'She's female, and of child-bearing age so I'll look her up,' Mulholland said.

Wyngate smiled, stretched his legs out from his vantage point. He had enjoyed his shift on the roof. Glasgow looked very different from here. People never looked up, it wasn't the natural way of humans. He had read that in a book once, the contour of the eye socket and the prominence of the eyebrow made it very difficult to look upwards. Then he thought about the young women walking around down there with huge eyebrows plastered and thickened with pencil and glue. He was wondering what he would do if his daughter, all of a few months old, turned out like that. He thought his life was simple with two sons, but now he realized all the difficulties involved in bringing up a girl.

Then his earpiece crackled into life.

'Wingnut? She's only a friggin fiscal.'

'Yes we know. Let her be, just keep an eye on her,' Costello snapped down her mouthpiece. 'It's Valerie Abernethy. She's a friend of Archie.'

She told him about Janet Gibson's post-mortem. 'I have asked O'Hare to formally review it. Valerie had steamrollered, maybe even intimidated, that wee Welsh pathologist to . . . well . . . not being as thorough as she might have wanted to be. The deceased had given birth to a baby we can't locate.'

'Or she, as a fiscal, has obtained it as evidence, building it up as a case and didn't want any arsehole detective jumping on it. Maybe there was a connection with the Glasgow fiscal's office that might prejudice something?' argued Mulholland.

'Possible, in which case it serves her right for not sharing with us. We do need to make sure she's not getting herself into something she can't get out of.'

'That girl, Janet, had her last meal right here at the Admiral restaurant in the Blue Neptune, food she didn't live long enough to digest. Devon Crab, Tofu and Seaweed. It's expensive. Few restaurants in Glasgow stock it. It didn't take me long to find one that did. Why do you think we are here? With Valerie driving round trying to find a place to park, so she doesn't know about the metal bollard. Well, that proves whatever happens, it's going to happen here. We are going to have a good look round, you got that Wyngate?'

'Yip. Be careful.'

'If we are going in there then we need to get dressed up.'

'We are not, so we don't. I have my baton with me.'

Mulholland realized she was serious and tried to ignore the frisson that ran through him. 'What is going on in there? Exactly?'

'I haven't a bloody clue but Colin and I have a plan.'

'Good.'

Silence.

'Are you going to tell me?'

'Nope.'

'If anybody sees us, what are we supposed to be doing? This is Friday night.'

'Just don't look like a cop for God's sake, shouldn't be an issue for you with your bad attitude and brittle bones.'

He thought it was the nicest thing she had ever said to him. 'Well you don't need to dress up either, as you look like a bad-tempered good-time girl.'

They doubled back from the car, moving quickly through the crowds, not talking, at times they didn't even look as if they were together. The town was busy, they walked on. Costello hoping that in their loose clothes, they simply looked like a couple who were looking around a city centre. They crossed at Central Station, taking the same route that Orla had taken. Crossing the road, nipping across Brown Street and through the bollard, then up Sevastopol Lane. The wind got up, rustling the old crisp packets and sent an empty 7-Up can rattling over the cobbles.

Costello checked the utility belt that was under her loose jacket, making sure it was secure, then she double-checked it. They were on the trail of Orla and Miss Bluecoat.

'The Rockpool? Is that place clean?'

'I've checked with the drug squad and they do not have it on their radar,' Mulholland said. 'I've been there and it's a smart place, they don't even allow designer drugs in the door. You are more likely to run into the Lord Advocate than a footballer.'

'So they have good security, and if, as you say, the Lord Advocate is a member I'm sure they will have no problem letting us view the footage, whether they want us to or not. We might see who Orla talked to, who she left with. Or where Miss Bluecoat went.' They walked on a little, falling silent as two women went passed, talking about a meal they had eaten in the Blue Neptune. The single mention of garlic bread had Costello's mouth watering. 'I want to know who killed her like that, cruel. Nasty. O'Hare found a single blade wound up through her ribs, to her shoulder blade. It went right through her heart.'

They walked on in silence again. Costello's phone went. Not recognizing the number she rejected the call. She was busy.

'What about the marks on her leg? Any leads there?'

She pulled out her phone. 'That is the image stamped on her thigh, can you make it out?'

He stopped and looked at her phone. 'CG then something?'

'I think O'Hare recognized it straight away. It's the old Glasgow Corporation, the old city council. She was lying on an old stank or manhole cover, a drain, something like that. For some period of time after she died.'

'A drain cover in a city the size of Glasgow? We got lucky with the suitcase, we will not get that lucky with the drain cover.'

'You didn't get lucky. You were clever, and we will be clever about this as well. She came here, we know she did. She was dead before she went in that water. Maybe she was killed here, she would have bled out, a lot. Don't underestimate this.' She stopped again. 'So they were standing here and then they disappeared. Just this old yard, do they pull this fence apart? What did the drunk guy say? Went "down" the way?' She looked under her feet, cobbles, nothing else.

'No, he said they went sideways. He was definite about that.'

'One thing we have learned on this case is not to accept anything at face value. If you were standing here, thinking about getting pregnant women in and out that building and never being seen, I would purposefully set up that CCTV to show what I would want everyone to see – that they did not go in the lift and get up that way.'

Mulholland creased his eyes, his nose wrinkled like he was sniffing for a clue. 'So, are we not liking the perfumed Pilates people?'

'No, I don't think we do. I was looking at their website. At the entrance at the parking place they have for prams and buggies. They do a lot of pregnancy Pilates and baby massage. How easy would it be to get a picture of a healthy baby, their blanket, their pram and go and buy a duplicate set?' She tapped the ground with her foot. The metal grid clinked and clunked against its concrete frame. 'After looking at the amount of stuff Mothercare shift I think they should be reported to the monopolies commission. They had those specific items on special offer. If we have to go through that list we will, but somehow I don't think we have to.' She stepped back looking through the fence that surrounded the yard, then closely at the hinges of the gates, the hinges that attached to the wall. 'You do this side, I'll do that side.' She looked back along the solid wall at the side of the Blue Neptune and then the Old Edwardian building standing resolutely on the corner, thinking that Orla came down the lane from the direction of the train station. The first thirty, forty feet were the red sandstone Old Edwardian with its corner location. There were two old doors embedded in the wall, painted over, one with a metal grid, the other simply recessed. They both looked old and clearly hadn't been opened for years.

There had been a nasty murder of a prostitute down here many years ago, the place had been a no-go area then. It had been earmarked for development. What had happened to that? Why had the distal part of the block been demolished to allow the building of this super smart complex of high-end restaurants and offices while the lower end was kept like this? She stood back again, and looked up, in the darkness she could make out the top of the building bathed in dim lights of the city, it was ornate and beautiful stonework that could only be dreamed of nowadays.

'Hey, Costello, come and see this.' Mulholland was crouching down, looking at the wall at ground level. 'Look at that. Is that a lever?'

'A foot pedal?'

'I think it's one of those old cons, a Black Donald. Wyngate know about them. Some lassie comes up here with a punter, about to give him a blow job and then the girl sticks her foot, that door opens and two big guys come out of nowhere to relieve him of any cash, anything of value. Means nothing here and now, in daylight sobriety, but at three in the morning when you are pissed out your head, well what are you going to tell the police? Somebody came out a wall and robbed me and then went back in again.'

'Back on the day, this was covered by a flap, you can just see the screws for the hinge.' He was on his knees now, peering at it with the torch on his mobile phone.

'I'll take your word for it,' she said, looking at the sticky patches of stale urine. 'Instead of somebody coming out, can it be used as a way in? If they opened it up and timed it right, so the cameras were swinging away.'

Mulholland fell silent, thoughtful. 'She was on the phone, Orla? On the film, she took out her phone.'

'And Miss Bluecoat leaned against the wall and fiddled with something. Could have been her phone.'

'So shall we try it?'

'No, you try it. I'll stand back and keep well out of trouble.'

'I have a bad leg.'

'Oh, I thought you were fit for active service? Press it, you tosser.'

He placed his toe gently on it as Costello looked up and down the street, as if she was keeping look out. She looked down when she heard a small click, so quiet they couldn't locate where it came from. A taxi at the rank sounded its horn and broke their concentration. They lost the location of the sound. Costello now got out her torch and shone it over the concrete of the lane, nothing on the wall, the metal gates still locked, the door still in place, nothing had moved.

'We're missing something, do it again.'

'Can't, it's already in the down position. It must release on some kind of tension or timer.'

'Clever.'

'Victorian. If you don't know where you have to look, you will never see it.'

'Can we speak to some of the old coppers who used to work down here, they will remember this. They might be able to shed light on it, if as you say, it was used to mug people.' He had taken the torch from her and started shining the beam closely to the wall, with no intention of going anywhere until he had found the answer to this.

'Stop,' said Costello, sharper than she intended. 'Look at that.' She pointed to the old black door, metal painted and covered in graffiti, dirt drifted up against the bottom of it. It looked as though it hadn't been open for ages. There was now a line of clean black paint round the border.

'That wasn't like that earlier.'

'Well I never, I think it is a Black Donald.' Mulholland leaned closer and looked, placing a single finger on the door, pushing it ever so gently.

And it opened.

Parts of the Blue Neptune were so exclusive, nobody really knew what went on there. Anderson knew about the fluorescent fish and the exclusive roof terrace, but he had no first-hand experience of either. He had looked into the rental of the office spaces and they all seemed legitimate. An office for travel injection and inoculations now that the NHS didn't do them. A small pension company, a very exclusive estate agent. And two lawyers, including Helena Farrell's lawyer, the short one with the weird haircut; the one that couldn't spell, or pronounce her own name.

But Anderson was very interested in what was going on up at the rooms on the same floor as the gym and the perfumed Pilates people as they had become known. There had been a name of the Pilates list that caught their interest: Roberta McIver, or Chisholm as they knew her. He couldn't find anything listed for what was going on on the floor above. He wanted to have a look around, the kind of look around that might not be welcome. He had accepted Andrew and Sally's invitation to dinner and to drinks.

He had to keep his mind on that and not think about his wife and the new man that had so enchanted his children. Without telling him. How many times had they met? Had he really been so wrapped up in his own world that he had not noticed? Of course he bloody had.

He stood outside, checking the time, looking at the door of the Rockpool. That was a small club up on the first floor, with a door on street level that had two very well dressed, very big men posed outside it, plus a small blonde female, to take the sting out the fact they might be in need of bouncers.

She gave him a look. He wasn't dressed appropriately to go in there. He made a point of looking at his watch again. Then saw the double swing doors for the Blue Neptune foyer, bars to the left and right. The right one was the Sky Blue for a more student crowd with money, to the left was the Navy Blue, where all the staff were dressed as sailors, the female waitresses in short skirts and neat little white hats with gold anchors on them. It bordered on naff without actually getting there. In between was a man in a frock coat standing at a highly carved lectern, behind him the marble doors of the Admiral restaurant itself.

He went up and asked if there was a table booked. The name was Anderson.

'No,' said the maître d' smiling, 'I think the table is booked under the name Braithwaite. Welcome. We will sit you at their regular table, one of the best in the house.'

And Anderson wondered if they did own a slice of this

place. Was that why they lived the way they did? Had they sunk every penny into this or had they slipped too deep into debt that they didn't have a choice? Looking back at their university days, Sally and Andrew had always had money. Family money. What had happened to all that?

And what did they do now that they were asset rich and cash poor?

Earn money in any way they could. Was Costello right, were they selling children?

Then murdering their mothers?

Wyngate checked his watch, now sitting out on the van with Tom Stafford and Bob Noakes, big cops who knew how to handle themselves. Wyngate knew from bitter experience that he wasn't built for the rough and tumble. He had been injured twice badly on duty and he wasn't taking any more risks. Not that he was being allowed to.

He had a simple remit now, to sit in the van and listen to what was going on. And not touch any buttons on the recording device. Costello and Mulholland were going up the lane to see what was going on, investigating the mystery of the disappearing women.

Anderson was cashing in on his friendship with the Braithwaites to see what he could find out, they might know something. There was definitely something going on in that beautiful building, and he was to keep a watching brief on the off chance that they might see the girl in the blue coat. They had a slight side view of her face, the only image they had, now blown up and clarified, in case they saw her.

Or a baby that might be only a few hours old.

Costello had to ask. 'What kind of mind came up with a Black Donald?'

'Somebody with a passion for theft and hide and seek. I think the name comes from an old word for the devil. How old is this place?'

'The Old Edwardian? 1880? 1890? They loved mechanical tricks like that in the old days.'

They both stepped through the door onto an old concrete

platform bordered by rails of blackened painted metal. The top rail worn to dull metal with age, the paint weathered away.

Mulholland shone the torch. 'It's an old stairway, down to an ancient drinks cellar, I presume.' The stairway turned immediately to their right, then turned back on itself and continued twisting down into the darkness below. But three steps down and underfoot the steps were repaired and restored from their years of wear.

'I am leaving this door open. We agree that before we go ahead and cut off our escape route, we go in to see what is happening down there and then we report back. OK? We do not rediscover the ancient underground city that lives beneath us. Agreed?'

Mulholland nodded, glad that she had made that decision and he wasn't being left to look a wuss. They walked down the steps, keeping close together and turned the stairs heading down another layer, the air was cold but not stale. There was very little light now they had exited the relative shelter of the recessed stairwell. Costello shone her torch around catching a bumper, a black car, a few crazed white lines marked out on the concrete.

'It's a bloody car park. Where are we, under the Blue Neptune or the Old Edwardian?'

'Both.'

They stepped forward, rounding the end of an internal wall. It got a little lighter. 'Look over there.' Her torch drifted across the empty space to the wall on the opposite side, the gap in it that ran the full height of the basement, slightly wider than the width of a car. The gap was covered by thick black railings. Beyond that they could make out the boundary wall on the far side, topped by a series of small rails at ground level on the pavement side, so near the roof from the inside, four or five inches high.

They walked up to the railings which turned out to be two gates held closed, tight and strong, by a thick chain.

Mulholland looked through to the car park beyond. 'This must be good cheap storage for classic cars. Dry, cold, no bugger knows about it. That old Rover there must be worth a few bob.'

'How did these cars get down here?' Costello looked into the light across a central way to the car park, her torch sitting between the rails. On the other side, the concrete was better maintained, the markings a bright yellow paint, a typical city centre underground car park. 'It's the Crimea Street car park. There's a ramp that brings you under the road over in that corner.'

'Wouldn't know, I've never been able to afford to park there.'

Costello ignored him. 'So Orla could have come down here and got in a car and been taken anywhere? That does not help. If we know when, the CCTV would pick her up as she left the car park.'

'Or the CCTV from the exit of the car park might give us some clue as to how her body got out to Lochwinnoch. I presume somebody on this side can get those railings to open. If they had a key. There are drag scrapes here in the concrete.'

'Have you looked at these cars? Those at the back haven't been moved for years. And those two cars over here?' Costello pointed to a couple of new Fords on their side of the railings, two different colours of grey metallic paint. 'They have the same reg number.'

'Well spotted. We might make a cop of you yet. That is an alibi in the making.' He looked around her. 'You got a signal on your mobile?'

'Nothing.'

'Me neither.'

'We don't have enough to get a search warrant. Yet,' added Costello, 'but the Braithwaites park in that private car park on the other side of Inkerman Street, not down here. I am thinking that I'd like to find a manhole cover. O'Hare said there was oil in the impression on Orla's thigh, it must be from here surely.'

'But how do we get into the building? Whatever is going on is going on up there.'

'They appear to have no need for this space, which is what they want people to think. But somebody uses it for other purposes, like taking away the bodies of dead girls.'

They stood at the railings, looking through and both ducking at the sudden increase in volume of traffic noise above their head, a rumble that stopped then started again as the lights changed above from green to red to green again. Costello had her head right at the railings when the place was suddenly awash with bright light. It was a normal underground car park, bright yellow grid marks on the ground, the sign saying that it was a one-way system. The cars looked fresh and undusted, just vehicles that would come and go here every day, the commuter delight of city centre parking.

'We have triggered a sensor,' said Costello, nudging Mulholland then pointing towards the Porsche Panamera parked neatly in the corner. 'She is here, somewhere.'

They could see the end of the barrier from here and the keypad on a yellow metal pole, bashed and battered by cars that had misjudged the narrow gap.

Costello thought out loud. 'Our answers are not here, they are over there. Mathilda is processing the oil on Orla's thigh, it was deep in the skin, old, dirty engine oil perhaps?' She kicked at something with her toe before following Mulholland. This was a graveyard of old cars. From this viewpoint, he could see a small set of narrow concrete stairs in the rear corner. Mulholland walked over as Costello kept her torch light focussed on him as he climbed the steps.

'There's a small keypad here, a metal door and . . .' A noise alerted them. He fled down the stairs and they both darted for cover, Costello behind an old car with four flat tyres and Mulholland behind a concrete pillar.

They heard a click of light heels across the concrete. The heels stopped, started again and stopped.

The noise echoed round the hard walls. Then there was a hard click, which Costello prayed to God was not the Black Donald door closing over. She crouched down and peered out, Valerie Abernethy had no idea where she was supposed to go. As Costello watched, the fiscal looked at her phone and noticed the lack of signal. She was looking around her, her face looking a little fearful.

Costello moved slightly, her nose alerting her to something familiar. Looking at her hand, she saw it was covered in sticky grimy oil. It was on the knees of her trousers as well. And she realized that she recognized the smell, she was kneeling in a mixture of old oil and dried blood, her nostrils were full of it now.

She looked up to the car, the pattern of disturbance on the dust on the side panel, then the side panel of the car behind her. A black Volvo had a single clear palm print on the dark paint.

Then the car park was plunged in a darkness that was total and absolute.

ELEVEN

The meal had been lovely, a tiny steak cooked in some fine wine sauce that Colin could not pronounce. It was so delicately flavoured it made his eyes water, as did the price of it. Million-pound house or not, he was glad he was not footing the bill. Sally had sparkled in a black jumper, delicately fluffy, and black velvet trousers that skimmed over her slim hips and long legs. Her golden hair bounced as she told funny stories of her travels around the world.

It was as if the intervening twenty years had not happened. Andrew sat back and watched Sally and Colin, offering the odd comment, punching in with a few one liners. They laughed. And laughed. Sally drank three or four glasses of Pinot Grigio, Colin only one. Andrew had mentioned that he was on call and didn't stray from sparkling water.

Anderson excused himself and nipped to the toilet, checking that the wire was working just as Andrew checked his pager and said he needed to make a phone call.

Noakes' voice cracked back that they were hearing it all fine and what kind of sarcastic bastard was he, describing the food when they were sitting in the van with a flask of tea and one cheese sandwich between the three of them. Wyngate told him that Costello and Mulholland hadn't returned yet, so they must have found something. The constable's last words 'be careful'. It had been quiet on the line for a moment and then he had replied, 'You don't need to tell me that.'

And he didn't. They had been here before and here they were again, watching each other's backs.

When he went back out to the restaurant, Andrew's chair was empty and tucked back into the table. Sally was flirtatiously apologetic. 'He'll be on the phone for ages.'

'I know that feeling,' said Colin. 'What does he do exactly?'

'Andrew? He rents a room here and does Botox and fillers, light cosmetic work and he works in A and E, he's registered with an agency. Nothing permanent.'

She was quieter then. He didn't know if it was fear, a realization that this meal might not be entirely recreational or something more akin to the frisson of sitting mildly pissed, next to an ex-lover, and the husband now in absentia.

Colin wanted to get her talking, so he brought up a few names from their past. The chit-chat went on, over coffee, gossiping about people they had known at uni, postulating what had become of those they had lost touch with.

Once the coffee was over, she asked him if he wanted a brandy, her eyes flicked left and right, wary of the members of staff eavesdropping, as they floated around in that silent, ethereal way waiters do in posh establishments. She lifted her glass, the light glistening off the crystal of the glass and glinting in the blue of her eyes.

'It's nice to have you back in my life. There are a few advantages to renting space here. I get free access to the roof terrace. Let's go up there and look over the city. It's lovely on a clear night like this.'

'Can I trust you?' he asked, smiling.

'Nope.'

Costello had already switched her torch off, Mulholland did the same. They wanted – needed – to see where Valerie went and from the look of her, she was waiting for somebody to give her instructions. It had crossed her mind that she wasn't sure how to get out.

They both stayed hidden, listening to Valerie's footfall, three steps to the right, three to the left. Waiting. Apart from calling out, 'Is there anyone there?' and the occasional 'Hello?' she was quiet.

Costello wondered if they should make themselves known, Mulholland would follow her lead, but she wanted to see, or hear what was going to happen.

Then a small light shone in the corner of the car park, up to their left, under the Blue Neptune. Costello hit the deck, aware now what she was kneeling in. She heard a voice, too quiet to recognize. Valerie's answer was, 'Oh thank God, I thought you had forgotten.'

And they walked off, two sets of footsteps heading towards the small steps in the corner and the source of the light, which went out but not before Costello had crawled out to catch a glimpse.

Mulholland switched his torch back on and jogged over to Costello who was trying to get up without touching the cars on either side of her.

'Look at this, blood, handprints on the car. We have something of evidential value. Let's get out. We need to tell the boys to track Valerie.'

'And whoever that was with her, they didn't come out the shadow of that door, I didn't get a look at him.'

'I did. He was at the hospital with Moses, that was Andrew Braithwaite. No surprise there.'

'OK, we need to get out of here now.' Mulholland was shaking. 'Wyngate can't hear us down here.'

'Nobody can.' Costello sniffed at her fingers. 'That's definitely blood. Orla's blood. I bet nobody heard her either.'

The roof terrace was deserted. Colin was comforted to know that his colleagues were there in the traffic and the lights below, listening to him. Somebody had his back. Sally had brought the bottle of brandy, and he had carried both their glasses right up to the railing and the small wall beyond. Anderson rested the glasses there and made a point of walking the length of the rail, peering over the edge. Sevastopol Lane was empty, only a couple strolling down to the river. 'Are you still hearing me?' he whispered.

The lights on a transit van below flashed twice. Weird but still comforting, even though they were six flights below him.

Sally approached him, swirling the glass, the brandy rising and falling in gentle waves. 'There is much I have not told you, Colin. Things I think you need to know.'

'There's a *lot* you have not told me. But I am starting to figure it out, slowly. All is not roses in the garden, is it?'

'Oh,' was all she said, and closed her eyes, tears starting to fall. 'You know?'

'I know some of it.' He was deliberately vague, forcing her to talk first.

She placed her glass on the wall and laid her head on his shoulders. It seemed so natural to put his arms round her, glad that he was being kept on the right course by the three hairy apes sitting down below in the van, listening to every word.

'Maybe better to talk now, before Andrew comes back.'

That hit a nerve. She pulled back and swallowed hard, backhanding a few stray hairs from her face as she turned to lean on the rail, looking out over the river, the bridges lit up. It was cold, but very still.

'I'm a cop. I can help you, Sally. I know you, you can't be comfortable with all this.'

She sniffled, on the edge of tears. 'Do you ever think about all these people? Out there, living their lives.'

'Yes, I do. They all have a story to tell. Every last one of them. That's why I love my job. It's endlessly fascinating. "The evil that men do" etc. Hopefully the good I do will live on after I have been interred.'

'And you get their stories? The great and the good, the evil and the ugly? The innocent and the guilty?'

'And which one are you, innocent or guilty?'

'Depends what of?' She picked up her glass, took a mouthful in desperation. The flirtation had gone.

'When my mum died – was dying – in hospital there was a woman in the bed opposite. Nobody visited her. She was in there for three weeks, nobody came near. She wasn't old, well not young but not old old. And she died. She was folded up and taken away, curtain round the bed. I wonder if anybody went to the funeral.'

'That's sad. How did she get like that, so lonely?' He heard her take a deep breath. 'You know I was raped.' She said quietly, then repeated, 'I was raped. It's a long time since I said that, then you came along. And before you ask, I had no idea who by. But there were a lot of complications afterwards, that might be something that you are not aware of.'

'Complications?' Anderson persisted. 'I know you lost the baby.'

Sally looked away. 'I got a bad infection. But I didn't lose the baby.'

'OK.' His voice was comforting, engaging with her tragedy. She was a victim now.

She pulled away from him, trailing a fingertip along the balustrade. Colin put his hand under his jacket collar and felt for the coil of wire that ran from the microphone secreted on the underside of his lapel. This was not for public consumption. He forced himself to let go the wire, leaving it in place. That kind of thinking could get him killed.

'I let it go around the uni that I didn't want to talk about it. I had an infection and I was kind of happy about that as there was a chance that we, you, the police might be able to catch him if that bastard was attending a clinic somewhere. That came to nothing. Days passed, I was getting all kinds of treatment for broken ribs and the damage to my shoulder. I took a long, long time to heal and the infection had appeared to respond to treatment, massive antibiotics. But it hadn't, it had only worked its way further in as time passed. Then Andrew and I got married and tried to have a family. Nothing happened, and then it dawned on me why. There was damage. A lot of damage.' Another tear.

'And the rest of the story? The big bit you missed out there.'

'Is that the bit you are interested in? Professionally.'

'And personally. What happened to you back then has shaped your entire life. But you didn't let it destroy you.'

'I found out I was pregnant.' Her eyes creased over. 'And that wasn't as easy as it sounds. First test was negative, I thought I was OK. Then it was all too late, well, too late for me.'

'Did you go away to have the baby?'

She turned to stare at him, lower lip trembling. 'You seem very sure that I didn't get rid of it. I could be telling you anything, any lie that makes me look better.'

'Because I know you, Sally. You couldn't do that. Way too soft-centred. It wasn't your choice or your fault. But I bet you figured it wasn't the fault of the baby either. That must have been a very tough call.'

'You must be a very good policeman. You are very good at reading people.'

'Not really, you forget that I know you.'

'You knew me a long time ago.'

'People don't change that much.'

'Maybe you are right. I needed to have that child. And all of a sudden my life was public property. Everybody telling me to do this or do that. It was amazing the bloody experts that crawled out the woodwork to support me. But yes, you are right, you do know me well, detective chief inspector. I couldn't get past thinking that life was life. I still think it is. In that position, I would still make the same choices. I am sure I still would.'

He rubbed her arm, trying to comfort her and keep her talking.

'There was a presumption that I would have an abortion but I wanted to keep it. You never know until you hold that baby in front of you what that can feel like. I wanted to have that feeling, I wanted to hold my baby daughter. I have never felt it since. Won't get the chance now, will I?'

Colin leaned back on the rail. 'I know exactly what you mean. That amazing feeling when I first held Claire. Thrilled, scared, and a feeling of overwhelming love. I was terrified that something would go wrong, that she would get hurt, get ill. Brenda was so pragmatic, "This is a healthy baby she will be fine". I was panicking at every cough, at any sign that something was not right. I'd cut my right arm off to give her a happy life.'

'And I bet nothing has changed.'

'It's worse now. I have to let go of her, see her ride off in to the horizon with some man who can't even climb the stairs properly. It's bloody terrifying. Turtles have the right idea. Lay your eggs and then go for a swim. No sleepless nights, no Chinese meals, no driving lessons.'

'And I bet you would do it all again in an instant.'

'I would. Can't imagine what it was like for you. There must have been people around to give you support.'

'My parents said they would support my decision. At first. Then Mum took me to one side and said that they couldn't, in reality, have the "wee bastard" running around, reminding them every day of what had happened to me. My dad couldn't take it. That was why I pulled out of your campaign. I was in danger of not knowing my own mind. And that was more frightening than anything else. I had to get away.'

'To India?'

'For a bit, yes. But then I came back. I had my daughter.'

'Oh.'

'And then.' She took a deep breath, closing her eyes. 'I think I need another brandy.'

'And I sold her.'

Colin nearly dropped his brandy glass. 'Sorry?'

'This is the part when you realize that soft-centred Sally is a hard-nosed bitch.'

'I'd never think that.'

'I thought that everybody else was getting something out of it. Why not me? I didn't want to abort it and I knew a couple who were desperate for a child.' Sally rubbed the side of her face with the palm of her hand. The tears made her cheek glisten. 'Talk about the suffering of strangers. I thought Oscar and Abby had everything they could want in life. They were a perfect couple, but behind closed doors . . . That woman had tried everything to have a family, was almost suicidal with it. It became all consuming. Abby did get pregnant eventually on her fifth round of IVF. God, they had remortgaged the house by then – and then the baby died during birth. It got caught in the birth canal. They tried to pull it out, tried pushing it back to do a section. Forty minutes. And Abby got so damaged there was more surgery. And she was prepared to go through all that again. Imagine? She was distraught, of course, couldn't even talk about it. The worst bit was going back to the house afterwards, everybody's expectations of their child, the nursery all ready. Pink. They knew it was a girl. So I said they could have, could buy, the baby I was carrying. And my world went into meltdown.'

'That wasn't legal.'

'That's crap. There was nobody else involved, they were friends and I just said . . . My baby was going to become the possession of the court. Abby wanted a baby as soon as possible. So she took the baby, and she gave me money to get back to uni and get my life back. Some good came out of it.'

'It was illegal.'

'The rape was illegal but the moral outrage caused by the thought of me selling the baby was worse. This is a weird world we live in. What you need to understand was that I was in danger of losing everything, I had been raped, scarred, everything and I didn't want to add murder to that. I didn't want the baby to float away. I wanted to be sure it would be loved and wanted.' She slapped at the air like a child, mentally pushing him away.

'Everybody was still telling me to abort, time was moving on. The agencies who counselled me were patronizing. My mum and dad had made their opinion clear. They couldn't live with the memory of what happened to me on that day. So I came back once I had had the baby. Andrew paid for me to be in a private clinic in London, I had it there under Abby's name.' She started to cry, deep sobbing from the root of her being.

The cop in Anderson wanted to take her down to the station for further questioning, but he was a human being, and she was distressed so that was not going to happen. Not yet.

'Shall we go downstairs now? It's cold up here, you are getting too upset.'

She shook her head. 'I need to tell you it all.'

As long as they were getting this on tape, it was his call.

It seemed like a long time but was probably a matter of ten minutes or less as they tried to quell their panic, reassuring each other with both kindness and caustic comments. The door they had come in was closed firmly and a quick search round with their torches showed there was no easy way out of there. So they came back down the old stairwell, crossed the central way following in Valerie's footsteps to the very narrow clean stairs and the brand new door at the top, sitting smugly closed with a keypad at the side. Mulholland was for pressing the button and getting someone to let them out. Costello argued that it wasn't in the interest of anybody who knew how to open the door to actually do it for them.

It wasn't as if they'd be in here forever. Wyngate and Noakes sitting outside knew exactly where they were and would come looking eventually. There had been a chain of suspicion about that door being a Black Donald, it was Wyngate who had voiced his suspicion about it.

But the act of sitting here underground meant that Costello wasn't outside. And their plan necessitated her being on the outside. She had her part to play or the whole thing would go tits up, so they walked over to the railings that separated this old car dump from the modern car park on the other side. It was now shrouded in the same darkness that showed night had fallen outside. They stood and looked at the railing, there was a foot gap at the top about ten feet from the ground. The gap between each railing was too narrow for them to slip through but there was a horizontal bar five feet from the ground and another one along the top. It was Mulholland who pointed out that the one on the top was decorated with nasty sharp spikes. They looked at each other.

'Who's going first?'

'Well, you should punt me up as I'm a female and you're a male and that's the way of the world.'

'Alright, so that's why you're always banging on about equal rights for women and the fact my bad leg should keep me tied to a desk job. I'm going to play the disabled card here and suggest that you punt me up.'

'You're the one that goes to the gym and lifts weights on his day off so why don't you do it now and get paid for it.'

'I'm not lifting you anywhere, I could break my leg again.'

'I refer to my earlier point about you only being fit for a desk job, but in fact I'm your superior officer so I'm telling you to get down on all fours.'

Mulholland looked at the grimy oily concrete underfoot and said, 'You've got to be joking.'

In the end the need to get out won over the need to score points. Costello took off her bulky jacket and put it on the ground and made a cushion for Mulholland to kneel on, then she put the handle of her baton between her teeth and pulled herself up on to the rail getting one foot on the crossbar. Mulholland then got to his feet and handed her the jacket which she threw up so that it cushioned the sharp end of the spikes at the top. Mulholland, standing at his full height, let her stand on his outstretched hand as she placed the baton between the spikes, and holding it in both hands she pushed and pulled herself up and over, rolling on landing, her baton clattering across the concrete. Mulholland being much taller, could stand on the boot of an old Ford Granada and pull himself on to the middle railing. He then did the same trick as Costello, ripping her jacket even further. Once he had his feet on the crossbar on the modern side of the car park, he threw her jacket down to her and then he froze.

'For a while it went well. It helped that Andrew had trained as an obstetrician in the past.'

'I'm sure it did.'

'He knew what to do. Nobody was at risk. I don't want you to think that we ever put anybody at risk. But we knew child-less couples who wanted a child. We knew women, girls really, who were pregnant and happy to give the baby away, knowing where it was going to go.'

'Could be an emotional minefield,' counselled Anderson, hoping to God, they were getting all this out in the van.

'Not really. The girls were fine knowing the child was going to a good family where it would be loved. And they knew that from early on so it was more like surrogacy, that bond never had time to grow. We took the DNA, checked for abnormal-ities . . .' She faltered, remembering Little Moses on the front of the newspaper. 'I don't know what he did with her, how that child slipped through.' Sally looked weary now, worn down by her tears. She reached out for a hanky and blew her nose loudly. 'I really don't know what he did with her, the girl who had the Down's baby.'

'Who's he?' asked Anderson softly.

'Andrew. And her name was Adele, like the singer. Well, that's what she told us. She said that she wanted to be a singer, and God you should have seen her, she could hardly string two sentences together, not daft but brash and . . . awkward. And,' she took a deep breath, 'I think that was the one where I noticed it was all starting to change. Before, Andrew had

only taken level-headed intelligent women that understood
the discretion required. Adele was a rebel, didn't understand the
meaning of the word discretion. Well, I do know why he
did it, we had somebody offering us a lot of money for her
child. Over a hundred thousand pounds.'

'Jesus. But you can't just bank money like that.'

'You can if you own a place like this. Money laundering
is easy when you have a place to clean it.' She pointed out
as if he was simple.

'What happened to Adele?'

'I don't know. But he did something to her. Adele came here,
had the child. Moses. The media gave him a name – his mother
never did. She wanted to sell it. The other woman wanted it.
Downs or not. The dad didn't. Andrew said he would sort it
out and I think he did. He said the new parents changed their
mind and accepted the baby once they saw him. He said Adele
was happy to take the money. She was going to use it to have
some plastic surgery to get her nose fixed, and get singing
lessons, and she was going to go on the X Factor and win it.
She knew the money wasn't going to last for ever but she was
going to do some modelling in the meantime.'

'Have you heard from her?' he asked, knowing the answer.

'No. But she was so young—' she shrugged – 'early twenties. Old enough to know better than have dreams like that.'

'How did she know to come to you?'

'I think she came here to see Andrew about her nose. It had
been badly broken and she wanted his opinion on getting it
straightened. And she was pregnant, but Andrew side-lined her
into having the child. She was little more than a kid herself if
I am honest. She was the kind who'd treat a baby like a doll,
you know – wrap a ribbon round its head and get its ears pierced
but not change the nappies often enough. She stayed up in that
flat, watching music videos and Andrew monitored the growth
of the kid,' Sally said, talking almost absentmindedly. 'But it
was only later I found out just how far Andrew had drifted from
what we had started out to do. That baby was born with Downs.
I think he swapped it for Roberta Chisholm's boy.'

Anderson twitched a little at that. He thought about that
eyewitness, her evidence pointed to slim Sally, not a bulky

guy like Andrew. And Sally was the one with access to the car seats; she had access to it all. Was he being played?

'It wasn't rocket science.'

And Anderson remembered the inshot outside the perfumed lift, the safe parking place to leave buggies. Easily seen and traced. God, he would have their addresses on file up in the gym. She did also.

'And where is Adele?'

'I don't know. I had the feeling she was not somebody who was going to go away. And then she went away.'

'Do you think she has come to harm?'

'I fear for her. I know what Andrew can be like.'

Costello had seen it many times in victims; one simple act that would ensure their safety. And they can't do it. A psychological block of weird self-preservation simply calls a halt to all logical process. Mulholland's brain was being very dogmatic in its approach, if he jumped from that height of five feet or even if he slithered down the railings, his leg would snap like a twig. No amount of cajoling or persuasion could convince him that he had two legs and he could land on the other. Time was passing, Costello needed to get out and get out through the car park barrier, run down Crimea Street and take a left and she would be at the front door of the Blue Neptune. As soon as she was free of the six floors of building above her head, she could radio the team to come and rescue Mulholland. When she explained that to him, his ambition overruled his fear and the fact Costello had said twice that she would never let him forget it. She bent over and formed a cradle with her hands, allowing Mulholland, who was chivalrous enough to hang his weight through his arms, to place one knee on Costello's back, the other foot in her cupped hands and then lowered himself gently to the ground. Where he stumbled and cursed, sprawled on the concrete floor. They looked at each other.

'I can't get up. Seriously I can't. My leg!'

Costello stared at the mess of the palms of her hands, covered in grime, old engine oil and probably Orla's blood and knelt down, cleaning her hands by wiping them slowly and deliberately, down the front of Mulholland's designer jacket as he lay pale faced and gasping.

'I'll be back for you.' She jogged away, ignoring the obscenities he was shouting after her.

Sally stood back from the rail, her eyes red and swollen with tears. She looked all around the roof terrace, taking in the rattan furniture, tied up and forgotten, covered with pigeon shit. 'I didn't know how we got from that to this. But I guess it's all going to change now.'

'I think you should come down to the station and make a statement. We have a lot to sort out, we need to know where the babies are. We need to know about Sholto and get him back where he belongs. And I don't doubt there are others.'

She shook her head. 'Come on.' And suddenly she was the old Sally again, head up, decision made, uncertainties swept aside. 'Come on.' She stopped and turned. 'You will look after me, Colin, won't you. I . . .? I don't know but I need help with all this.'

He nodded.

Sally walked slowly to the door in the middle of the roof terrace, surrounded by planters growing small trees that helped to disguise the outline of the exit. The door itself was glass and steel, protected by an electronic lock. She pressed a few numbers into a keypad, buzzing the door open. She led him down a narrow but beautifully decorated staircase, open plan once they were below the level of the roof. He followed her as she walked slowly along the carpeted corridor, the smell of eucalyptus telling him that they were near the gym. She turned left when his instinct told him they should have gone to the right. 'You did say that you needed to know all of it. I think I should show you something. Down here.'

She walked down another corridor, reminiscent of a hotel. Pictures, soft carpeting, fire doors and somewhere he could hear the muted sound of a Friday night television show. They stopped in front of a picture of New York skyscrapers, abstract and colourful. Sally pressed a button and the picture shaded to white, then cleared. The first thing he saw was a blue coat on the white clothes stand, the woman heavily pregnant was sitting in an armchair, watching the television. The bed near her had been slept in but neatly made. It was light blue. Sterile. 'This is where they come to stay before they give birth. Adele was here for a couple of months.'

It looked like a room in the best of private hospitals.

She was talking through her tears. 'I had to show you that. I don't want you to think, think that anybody gets hurt here. Look at that, she is fine, her delivery will be fine – there is a birth suite next door – and her baby will be looked after by people who will adore it.'

Colin had noticed the theme of Sally's warped reasoning – if they pay for it, they will love it. 'You think that nobody gets hurt?' he asked gently.

'Nobody gets hurt in here. I was hurt out there in the big wild world.' She looked away. 'At first that was all we did. Took babies from girls that didn't want them. We were putting women with unwanted babies in touch with couples who desperately wanted children and I didn't see it getting any more than that, I never saw that. We were doing nothing wrong. But then Andrew started, well, it all started to slide. We were contacted by a couple who wanted a baby of their own. Nobody was to know their child was adopted, which was the usual story. They said they were in the process of adoption and people going through that process never get asked anything more than "how's it going". It's too sensitive.'

'So to the family, this was a process of adoption?'

'Yes, and no recourse for the real parents.'

'Bloody hell, do the children not have a basic human right to know who their parents are?'

'Real parents like Bernadette Kissel?' she snapped. 'My friend was adopted. Their birth mother tracked them down, asked to be pals, my friend met her to say thanks but I have a great life and I have a mother, thank you. Don't worry about me I am fine. Your mother is the one who washes your socks, not the one who gives birth to you. It's our western world that has got all that a bit screwed. Being a parent is not a God given right; it is a privilege that has to be earned.'

For the first time Colin saw a flash of something Sally was not in control of and he wondered what Sally's parents had been like, their reluctance to accept her decision to keep the baby.

'Then Andrew changed into somebody I didn't know.'

She switched a button, the glass clouded over again, the New York skyline reappeared. Anderson realized that the patient was unaware she had been observed. He had noticed the food on the tray was the same as that in the restaurant, Costello had been right. It was a damn sight more comfortable than the NHS hospital where both Claire and Peter had been born. But that wasn't the point. This was about Adele. And a girl called Orla. It looked like somebody had taken Orla downstairs and killed her. Downstairs from here.

'Sally, you need to get your story down. A child was abducted.'

'Sholto Chisholm.'

'And he has a mum and a dad, and a cot waiting for him.'

'He has a dad who sleeps with everybody in the tennis club. A mother who does nothing but moan how much her baby cries . . .'

There it was again, Sally justifying it to herself.

'He is a much loved child, he has a nursery that he has barely slept in. He keeps his mum awake all hours of the day and night. She is exhausted. But she would go to the end of the earth to get him back.'

'Yeah, Roberta.' Sally was in shock but she walked on, back to the studio area. She opened a door onto the gym, the line of running machines standing silent now looking out onto the city scape through the huge window.

'I need to make a statement. I need to tell you where the children are. And Sholto? Sholto Chisholm. Bobby's wee kid. I need my jacket, my keys. Oh Christ. Where is Andy? Don't let him come back here. Not until I can get away. Where is my jacket? My keys?'

'Calm down, Sally. We will sort everything out. Was that a genuine call on his pager?'

'What?'

'I'm just asking. Did you see it go? Or hear it?'

'No, I didn't hear it. Oh God!' And she was crying again . . .

'Are you sure he is gone?'

Her face fell. 'I need to get my jacket.' She was walking past the weights, all stacked neatly in their racks. She opened another door, the smell of ozone drifted out, the air damp and warm. The walls were lined with pine. Saunas? Whirlpools? Was this where the spa was? She stopped and turned to him, her head down. 'Colin, I am really sorry, I can't tell you how sorry I am.'

'About what?'

'What was that?' Out in the van they heard a thud followed by a lack of voices, a more worrying lack of noise. Then a deep ominous rumble.

'Fuck!' Bob Noakes jumped back, pulling his earpiece out before the volume was turned down.

Then the silence was total.

'Has that bastard turned the mic off?'

'Why would he do that?'

'Shagging her before he arrests her?'

'You'd think he'd have left it on, we could do with a laugh.'

Then they sat in silence.

'I think you should go in,' said Wyngate.

'He's not going to like it if he has pulled out his wire so that he gets a bit of nookie with his old bird in peace and quiet.'

'He wouldn't pull out his wire,' Wyngate said hopefully, acknowledging that it was not beyond reason.

'Aye, right, if I had a bird like that pouring over me.'

Wyngate called Costello. Her voice came back loud and clear.

'We have lost contact with Anderson, it's gone quiet.'

'Last time of contact?'

'Two minutes ago.'

'Was he with Sally?'

'He was. Andrew was called away.'

'I think we saw him come back in. I think we had better get in there. Mulholland is a man down.'

'Do you want us to—'

'No just leave him for now.'

He heard her move, walking quickly across concrete then her heels clicking as she went up the stairs of the Blue Neptune, barking out questions. 'Sally Braithwaite and the blond guy? Where did they go?'

'Roof top. You can take the lift,' the maître d' pointed, anything to get the scruffy cop with her stinking jacket out of his posh restaurant.

She rushed up the stairs and burst onto the roof, looking round, nobody was there, then suddenly Braithwaite was running up behind her pointing to the door. She held her baton tight.

'One nine three eight, the code is one nine three eight,' he said and Costello, nearest the key pad, hit the combination with her free hand. The door opened, and they rushed down the stairs, aware now of the loud rumble.

'Hydro pool!' shouted Braithwaite, pushing Costello out the way. She fell clumsily, stumbling into the side wall but she had heard a splash of water and Braithwaite shout something. It didn't sound good. He sounded scared.

Costello limped round the corner, moving as fast as she could, through a door into an area tiled and scented with ozone or chlorine. Two training pools, each three feet off the ground, one as still as a millpond, the other angry and turbulent.

Tumbling at the far end was Colin Anderson, submerged in the current, crimson jet streams trailing from the back of his head. Costello climbed into the pool, trying to stand up in it, waist deep, holding Colin's head above water as his body twisted and contorted to get away from her, battered by the force of the water. She braced herself against the low side and grasped the side of Colin's chest and pushed as hard as she could. Braithwaite seemed to be panicking in the corner, flinging open the door of a metal cupboard, looking for the right switch to flick among the bank of switches. Then Costello got a good grip, the water slowed and the noise was beginning to quieten.

Costello pushed Anderson's body over the rim of the hydro pool and his centre of gravity did the rest. He slithered onto the floor tiles, coming to rest face up, skin reddened by the pulsation of the water pressure, a small vein of red pooling underneath his head.

Costello knelt beside him, her face down at his, saying words in his ear, asking Anderson if he could hear her, feeling for a pulse.

She said she couldn't find one, so she started doing CPR, then turned him on his side, blood and water and all sorts spewing from Anderson's guts. She was shouting down her mouthpiece for an ambulance, not caring who heard.

'It's already on its way,' Wyngate was shouting back.

'Let me, let me, I am a doctor,' said Braithwaite, rolling up his sleeves but Costello pushed him away.

'I think you might be better restraining her . . .' She had seen Sally wild eyed and panicking out the corner of her eye but as she looked up, Sally's foot, clad in her black heels, caught her right on the temple, and Costello fell back onto the wooden side of the hydro pool, hitting her head hard.

Sally hurdled Anderson but slipped on wet floor tiles as she landed. Braithwaite lunged at her as she tried to regain her balance, but she twisted through his arms, then hurtled to the stairs, heading towards the roof terrace. Costello managed to dodge out the way as the bulk of Andrew Braithwaite followed his wife, screaming her name at the top of his voice.

The sound of his deep voice, shouting, 'Sally, no! No!' followed him up the stairs and out the door.

Wyngate looked at his older colleagues. 'Do we go in now, or do we sit here and keep listening in case they need us.'

Bob Noakes' answer was to rip the wires out the recorder, as his mate opened the back of the van and within a minute they were gone, running back down the lane to get to the front entrance of the Blue Neptune. It was a long way round. The cars based at Glasgow Central would get there first.

Wyngate followed them out the back door. It had all gone quiet over the air and he had no real idea of what he was doing next, thinking about Anderson, hoping that he would be OK. The boss had always bounced back, he was sure he was going to bounce back this time.

He tried calling out over his mouthpiece but nobody responded. He listened to his airwave radio, a lot of panic and chatter and lot of screaming for ambulances. He kept hearing the code for cop down, and he wondered who it was. Which one it was. He was thinking, hearing sirens in the distance when a body battered into the cobbles beside him. It shuddered a little before coming still. Wyngate looked at it, blonde hair webbed against the dark stones underneath. He looked up, realizing the body must have come from the top of the Blue Neptune.

'Costello? Costello?'

The figure lay motionless, blood spreading. He bent down to touch her shoulder, his mind slowly numbing with what he was seeing. Then he saw the shoe that had come loose as the body had fallen, strappy black high heels. Not Costello then. His mind cleared, hair too long, more red gold than white gold.

'Not Costello,' he sighed, his relief overwhelming. People were streaming into the lane now, attracted by a single scream. He heard somebody start to shriek and lifted up his radio, trying to be heard above the fray.

Suddenly everything started to happen at once, Costello was doing CPR trying to keep the rhythm right, tears streaming down her face, 'He's not breathing, he's not breathing' she kept saying out loud until a first aider appeared and then an ambulance man. O'Hare appeared from nowhere and pushed the first aider aside.

'How long was he under the water?'

'A few minutes?'

O'Hare shook his head. 'Let's get him out of here, we can work on him better in the ambulance.'

And they rolled the inert, soaking body of Colin Anderson onto the stretcher.

'Keep him on the oxygen, let's see if we can get something going, we will still work on him.'

'Did you find a pulse?'

'No.'

'But we will keep at him.'

Costello realized she was holding Anderson's hand until he was carried to the lift door, that slowly closed over, leaving her behind.

Waterlogged, Costello walked down the hall, and squelched her way back up the single set of stairs and onto the roof. She felt she was on automatic pilot.

Did that just happen?

Did all that actually just happen?

She saw Braithwaite sitting on the ground under the wall, hands on his head, crying his eyes out.

'She went right over the top. She jumped right over the top.'

Costello was stunned. She sat, sliding down the wall to sit beside him and stared straight ahead, registering nothing.

TWELVE

Mulholland and Wyngate were both back in the interview room. It was two o'clock in the morning. Andrew Braithwaite looked as if a strong whisky might be welcome. Mulholland's leg was strapped, he had refused to stay at the hospital and Wyngate had realized that he, nominally, was in charge.

'I'm afraid Sally has been lying to you,' Braithwaite said after listening to the recording.

Wyngate pushed across a cup of black coffee. 'It looks like she's not the only one.'

'How is Colin? Is he doing OK?'

Mulholland looked at Wyngate.

'No, not really. How long have you known him?'

'About twenty-five years, but there was a twenty-year gap in the middle of that.'

'He is on life support.'

'Good God.'

'His wife and children have been in to see him.'

'Yes, I think Brenda has taken them back home, you know. It could go on for a long time,' added Wyngate.

'So, Mr Braithwaite. Andrew. You have heard what Sally had to say?'

'Yes. Where is Sally just now? I mean, where?'

'She is being taken care of, you know as well as I do what happens with bodies. There will be a post-mortem then we wait and see. O'Hare will try to hurry it through. Can you talk us through what happened on the roof?'

And he did, sobbing frequently. Wyngate began to get emotional, recalling the horror of the noise when she landed, the sickening thud. Mulholland called a halt to the proceedings, there and then. They might not have had a lot but they did have time.

Braithwaite's story was a simple one. Sally must have bolted after hitting Anderson and had ran across the roof. Whether she meant to stop or whether she meant to jump was unclear to him, but he had caught her before she reached it, and she had pulled free leaving him carrying an empty sleeve. *If only he had held on.* And she had run away from him, tears blinding her, right to the rail, and went over.

'She didn't stop to think about it?'

'I don't know. How could I know? Oh God, what am I supposed to do without her?'

'Do you want a fresh cup of coffee?'

Wyngate went out the room, and saw, to his surprise, that the ACC was behind the glass.

'Once you get his statement, let him go,' said Mitchum.

'Let him go?' Wyngate was incredulous.

'He is guilty of many things but not murder. And he has just lost his wife.'

'But Sally said on the tape that she only brokers deals. Then we have a dead girl. And an abducted—'

'I know what she said, but then she flung herself off a roof and innocent people tend not to do that,' said Mitchum, reinforcing his thoughts with a tone of authority.

'Is that the right thing to do, sir?' Wyngate said, then remembered who he was talking to. 'Sorry, sir.'

'We need to let him go, we need to investigate further. Process him then release him. He has other things to attend to. And so do we. I know you are rudderless at the moment with Anderson in intensive care and Costello at the hospital, so you can take it from me, in my capacity as the most senior police officer. Now get on with making the coffee and get one for me while you are at it.'

Noakes had been going through the gym, room by room. They had found Miss Bluecoat and she had been removed from the premises in the middle of the night and he was finishing that corridor, opening doors, looking in cupboards, finding, he suspected, the instruments of an abortionist. He was at a walk-in linen cupboard, marked 'clean (not sterile)' and he rummaged around in the shelves of fluffy blue towels and folded dressing gowns. At the bottom, at the back, was the folded body of a woman. He called for assistance as he placed a finger on her neck, feeling a faint pulse. She was curled into the corner, her head down as if she had been sheltering or hiding from her attacker. Her knees were drawn up, her hair down and lying over her face. Only a sliver of her cheek was visible, it was deep purple and swollen. He could see a ligature round her neck, narrow, brown, deep into the skin of her neck, leaving it white and puckered. There were slight traces of blood on the hands that were pulled up in front of her face. When had she realized it was all going wrong? Had she started praying?

He knelt down, getting closer, hearing a conversation in the gym, help was coming. He tried to see behind her fingernails, had she scratched her assailant? He shone his torch on the chain round her neck, slight and silver with a butterfly clasp at the front, around which was attached some dark hair. It didn't look like the woman's straight dark hair, this was more like fluffy wool.

Black fluffy wool. He'd make sure that the preservation of evidence was at the forefront of the mind of any medical assistance.

It was a question more often asked in jest than in legal history: did she fall or was she pushed? And there were many factors to be considered before any definitive answer could be reached. The height, weight and momentum of the victim as they went over the top and the horizontal distance they landed from the drop point.

Professor O'Hare knew a whole team of people with very accurate computer algorithms who worked that kind of thing out, but so far all he knew was here in front of him in the form of a forty-three-year-old female, white, slim but well-nourished with good muscle tone. There was evidence of some surgery on her right knee which was not recent and old scarring to her right shoulder. He knew from palpating the rib cage and the skull that there was a lot of internal damage, her ribs compressed easily and with a familiar scrunch that showed the bony cage was no longer intact. A large part of her parietal bone had moved and disrupted the brain tissue underneath which was commonly found when impacting concrete at speed. She had probably died when she hit the tarmac. There had been no time for her to bleed out, although the blood in her spleen and her liver at the time of impact had flooded into her abdominal cavity, all of which was fairly typical. He didn't need to wait for the toxicology results, he had eyewitness evidence that Sally had consumed a few glasses of wine and brandy but that she was not drunk. With her rather low body weight it would have been enough to upset her balance. Experience told him that it was odds on that she was pushed, experience and the deep red abrasion she had on the side of her pelvis. He had looked at the photographs of the rooftop terrace. Sally was fit so she would have gained speed and gathered momentum but as she came to the rail she would have put her hands out to stop her. It was one of those infallible human instincts and even if that hadn't stopped her, the rail would have hit the front of her pelvis and in someone so slim that would have been metal on bone, but there was no evidence of that. The evidence was at the side like someone who had stopped and half-turned to face their pursuer, maybe to fight back or plead for their life. It was not for him to speculate. The certainty was that the rail had caught her on the hip under her centre of gravity and one small nudge to the upper body would have sent her over. He knew before any of Mathilda's staff ran their computer program that she would have landed relatively close to the side of the building. And that meant she was murdered. Then he remembered he wasn't allowed to have a professional opinion nowadays, it had to be backed up by a boffin staring at a screen, so he got on with his job, selecting his scalpel, ensuring the recording device was picking up his dictation, and he started with the Y incision.

Braithwaite nodded, a silent thank you for the coffee. 'I heard what she said on the recording and she is not being entirely truthful. And yes, I have lied all the way through this. You need to understand that I love . . . loved Sally. I love the ground that she walks on and, well, she is, was, vulnerable, more vulnerable than you might think. She needed money, she needed money because of me.'

'Why?'

'I like to gamble but I am not very good at it. You know that the billionaire Joe Aspinall had a selection of busts made from marble. He called them *The Great Gamblers*. That kind of gambling is admirable, fearless and it's in my nature. I will gamble on anything, even my career. I like to win, I lose with a degree of philosophy.'

'And Sally?'

'Sally didn't lose the baby that resulted from the rape. She sold it, that part of what she said is absolutely true.'

Mulholland leaned forward in his chair. 'Sold it?'

'It wasn't like that. A friend, a good friend had been trying for a baby for years. Nothing happened. They tried to adopt and that didn't work. They were offered a child that was older, but she wanted a child to be seen to be her own, so the two women came to some arrangement, like a surrogate. Sally, three months pregnant, the other woman announced she was pregnant, and the two pregnancies – the real one and the false one – went along hand in hand until the day came and the baby was born. Abby went home with a new baby girl and Sally got money to go back to uni and continue her studies. And I think she wanted to get back to Colin. There was always a wee spark of something there, you see. Even back in our uni days I used my medical knowledge to edge him out; it was me who helped her get fit, me who strapped her knee. And later she couldn't get together with Colin because I knew. I knew what she had done, and that brought us close, and we have remained so ever since. I was bound to her because of my gambling and I needed her money, and she was bound to me because of her big dark secret. Then we heard Colin had joined the police, we knew he was bright, and we kept our distance.'

'But continued the baby selling.'

'Brokering, I tend to call it. And I trained as an obstetrician. It wasn't difficult.'

'And she gets the women through the gym, the Pilates, the yoga class?'

'Yes, all fair, all above board. And she is the one who makes that initial conversation. It's something women talk about.

God, at one point, a woman came to the Pilates class believing that it was the class who had got her friend pregnant.'

'It's not legal.'

Braithwaite waved the objection aside. 'It's a floating loophole. That's all it is, nobody gets hurt, and everybody gets looked after.'

'I think Orla Sheridan might disagree with that.'

'Sally became odd. I don't know where she was that night we got drunk at my house. You need to find out what happened to Orla.'

'We are getting to the bottom of it,' assured Mulholland, rubbing his leg.

'She was back in the Blue Neptune building on Wednesday. And I think you should be looking for a woman called Valerie Abernethy. She was there last night, I let her into the building. Sally might have harmed her, but if you could find her and make sure that she's OK. Please.'

'We will. Do you know Valerie socially?'

'Vaguely. She hinted that she wanted a child but would be considered unsuitable for adoption, her age was against her. I think it was one of those things that can surface in a women's psyche. She was supposed to be investigating why, or how, a woman called Diane Speirs got pregnant. And that led her right to me. By sheer bad luck, Valerie knew Diane and knew that Diane had suffered bilateral ovarian cancer. Then it turned out Val wanted a child. I thought she was genuine but Sally thought she was investigating us. And I believe she was, at first—' he took a sip of coffee – 'but it resonated with her. Val saw the good in what we were doing and was going to let us be, as long as we gave her a baby.'

'And what happened to Valerie?'

'I don't know. What did happen to Valerie?'

That was almost too glib. Braithwaite went on. 'Sally was very suspicious of her, it all started going wrong in her head. So if something has happened to Valerie then . . .' He shrugged and whispered, 'I think Sally killed Orla. I don't know when or how but Orla wanted more money. There was another girl, Sonja. They had found out about each other and seemed to think they had hit on a gravy train if they gently blackmailed us, threatening us. No way Sally was going to have that.'

'Sholto? What happened to Sholto?'

'I have no idea, honestly, I have no idea.'

'Are you telling us that Sally killed these women, not you?'

'Yes. On the night Orla was murdered, Colin Anderson was out at my house, getting blind drunk on the sofa.' He rubbed his face, as if trying to erase the tiredness. 'I had difficulty walking never mind driving. Sally took a very long time to come home from work that night. And Colin Anderson knows that, so I hope to god he pulls through. He's my alibi.'

THIRTEEN

Saturday 14th October

Costello had to replay the short message on her phone before she realized who it was. Her heart sank, but what could she have done about it anyway, in the midst of all that had gone on. She couldn't be everywhere at once. She read the sign on the hospital wall telling her, in many languages, to turn her phone off and she called Dali on her home number, the phone being answered by a much younger voice that echoed all over a house, 'Mum it's for you', and then the phone was clattered down. Dali had come to the phone stressed and breathless.

'Hi, it's Costello here. I can't say much but whatever was going on at the Blue Neptune is over. For good.'

'That's good.'

'Well, we will see. But I am phoning about Malcolm, the boy I told you about.'

'The boy behind the bins? Yes?' The voice was immediately more alert.

'Can you get a call made out there, a welfare check to see how he's doing. He called me and left a message while I was . . .' She paused. 'Tactically deployed but I have been warned off going near the house by the powers that be. And there is a connection between Malcolm's mother and the Blue Neptune so my hands are tied.'

'I'll get somebody to pop out. What did he say on the phone?'

'He just said, "you said I was to call you". Then he waited a bit and said goodbye, that was all. He didn't sound distressed, more detached than anything.'

'Beyond fear? I'll deal with it. I'll try to action something but it's a Saturday.'

The phone went down, leaving Costello to send a text before she walked through the double doors of the hospital.

It was strange to think, those little tubes keeping somebody alive. Costello wouldn't have believed it, but they had agreed that it was the high pressure of the water going up Anderson's nostrils, racing down into his trachea and into his lungs, bursting delicate vessels and making them bleed. It accelerated the damage of oxygen deprivation. It took people a long time to drown. Not so long when the water was being fired into them.

So now there was a machine that hissed and puffed, Anderson's chest rose and fell. There were another few bits and bobs of machines that clicked and whirred. Small pads fixed bits of wire onto his skin.

Costello had told them back at the station, both Govan and West End, 'All we can do is wait. He knows we are here and we know that he is getting all the support he needs.'

Brenda was with Claire and Peter up at the terraced house. David was with them. They were waiting. From Wyngate's brief report, the person who seemed to find it hardest to accept was Andrew Braithwaite. He was still numb from the shock of Sally's death. Incredulous that within a few minutes, one was dead and the other hanging onto life by the slimmest of threads. Not so difficult to accept, Costello had replied, if the survivor of the three is a cold-blooded killer.

Costello stayed at the far end of the corridor, sitting behind a vending machine, but able to see anybody going in and out of Anderson's room. She was tired, leaning back against the cold metal of the machine, her eyes almost closed, but in reality fixed on a small mirror placed on the seat she was resting her feet on.

A cleaner was slowly arcing the mop back and forth across the floor, leaving no trail of water behind it. It certainly wasn't dirty after the length of time he had mopped it.

It was the fifteenth time the double doors opened, a click and a hum, as the palm hit a switch and the electric motor whirred into action. The cleaner looked up and went into a coughing fit. Costello recoiled in her seat, dipping her head slightly to see what was going on at the other end of the corridor. She picked up her phone. And they waited until the door into Anderson's room had opened and then closed over, giving them all a little glimpse of the man lying on the bed covered in a light blue sheet, in the dim light, his face covered in tubes and wires.

'This is going to be a nightmare,' Mathilda McQueen, the forensic scientist, looked round the small room next to the birthing suite, hands on her hips looking like a two-year-old in a dolls house. 'How am I supposed to make sense of all this?'

She opened a fridge, full of specimens and dishes, and then looked at a freezer, locked with a colour-coded electronic lock. 'Do you think anybody will tell me what I am looking for?'

Gordon Wyngate was sitting on a stool in the middle of the birthing room, spinning round. He seemed not to have heard her.

'I can't believe he did that.'

'Did what?'

'The ACC. He just let Braithwaite go.'

'Well what did you expect him to do?' She opened a few drawers and looked in. 'Can you look round and gather all the computers? We need all the records. I know he was an unethical bastard but even unethical bastards are good at defensive note taking.'

'Do you think if I had looked up I would have seen him on the roof, pushing her?'

'No, Wyngate, I don't. You need to look at the bigger issue. Two people involved in this each doing a very good job of blaming each other and that makes "beyond reasonable doubt" very difficult to prove if they ever get Braithwaite to trial. That is why the ACC told you to let him walk. For now. And I am sure you are familiar with the three greatest defences: I wasn't there, it wasn't me, and a big boy did it and ran away, or in this case, my other half did it and jumped off a tall building. You need time to get more evidence and that is our job, so you can either sit there and twirl round on that seat like a four-year-old or start collecting the computers and laptops. So, hop to it, now.'

Wyngate slunk off the chair and started walking towards Sally's office. It seemed a good place to start.

*   *   *

The cleaner laid his mop against the wall. Costello slowly got up from the chair and made her way quietly across the corridor to the room where Anderson lay. His visitor was sitting beside the bed. Costello clicked in her earpiece. The cleaner did the same, both listening to what was being said, picked up by the microphone on the bedside table by Anderson's head.

She could make it out quite clearly. A deep, resonant voice was asking how the patient was doing, just popping in to say hello, how nice it had been to meet up again and how tragic it all was. The cleaner, a big DS from Stewart Street, built like a brick shithouse and the only guy they could think of who would take Braithwaite down, looked at Costello and shrugged. The doctor wasn't incriminating himself in anyway at all.

Then his voice went quiet almost as if he was whispering into Anderson's ear. Slowly, quietly, closer. Then one of the machines stopped going ping, as if it was malfunctioning.

A male in a nurse's tunic came round the corner, not hurrying as much as he should be. He opened the door to Anderson's room just as Andrew Braithwaite stood up.

Costello reached for the light switch and turned it off. The bright blue fluorescent gel on Anderson's neck glowed brightly. As did the fingers of the tall, bearded man, easily seen in the dark.

'So, you touched the pipe then touched his neck. What were you trying to do? Give him a reassuring hug or trying to strangle him?' Costello asked.

Braithwaite moved quickly towards the door. Costello sidestepped to let him through. The other cops, one dressed in a nurse's tunic and one dressed as the cleaner gave chase. The nurse would catch him, the cleaner would hold him.

'You OK?' Costello asked Anderson.

The 'patient' sat up in the bed, rubbing his neck, then looked at the gel in disgust. 'These pillows are bloody uncomfy.'

'You have bigger problems than that. I photographed your bare arse hanging out that hospital gown. That's worth a few bob at the Christmas party.'

They heard a squeal and a thud, a scuffle and some swearing.

'I hope they don't rough Braithwaite up too much, they are busy enough in A and E as it is.'

'I heard about your subterfuge, congratulations,' said Mathilda McQueen.

Costello was at the door of the lab, frightened to go in in case she touched something she shouldn't. 'I never thought Mitchum would go for it, but our luck was in. He was really bored at a dinner party when I phoned him. If he had been enjoying himself he would have said no. I had a bet with Colin that it was Sally. He said it was Andrew. I owe him a curry. But we are doing a small re-enactment of Sholto's abduction, with somebody of Andrew's build, let's see what wee Mrs Carstairs says. I can't help thinking that she would have mentioned a big man, a large man, something like that if it was Braithwaite she saw. So it could have been Sally with an anorak on. Anyway,' Costello stood aside and introduced the woman standing behind her, 'this is Dali. I think she is the one you need to speak to.'

'Hello.' Mathilda lifted a computer disc and a stack of A4 papers an inch high. 'The tech boys have copied these from the computer in here and in Sally's office. I am sure it's the files on the women, the surrogates and the intended parents. There are DNA records there as well, from a reputable clinic in London. There will be stored samples around here somewhere. And that business that passed as minor cosmetic surgery, more often than not was abortion. It's all there. All in there behind the closed doors and the lovely pictures.'

'We will throw the book at him,' said Dali.

'There's a queue,' said Costello.

Dali said thank you. 'How many do you reckon? In all?'

Mathilda shook her head. 'That's over to you. But I think five, maybe six a year, in the most recent years.'

Dali opened her mouth, the closed it. 'Can I take these?'

'You can take copies. But feel free to have a look through them here.'

'Gordon Wyngate is doing me a huge spreadsheet to keep track of it all. What a lovely young man he is, so helpful.'

'You can have him if you want; he's a bloody liability to us. Him and that cripple Mulholland,' said Costello.

'We will leave you to it. Can I have a word?' Mathilda McQueen edged Costello towards a side room and closed the door. The worktops there were so spotlessly clean it looked like a showcase kitchen. 'We have a bit of an issue, I need to talk to you first. The DNA on sample TZ395 is one we haven't tracked down yet, but it is probably from one of the surrogate mothers. She will have donated a child. It's close to the bottom of the list so I think it's recent.'

'Do you want me to track her? Dali might be better and—'

'It's more complicated than that. I know exactly who she is, but not her name.'

'And?' Costello was growing impatient. She knew scientists always had to be this way, check, check and double check, think about all the possibilities. Evidence didn't 'fess up to them the way the guilty did to the police. And here was Mathilda thinking slowly, making sure that A would lead to B and never jump to Z the way it sometimes did in an inter-view room. The way it did the minute Andrew Braithwaite put pressure on Anderson's oxygen tube.

'Listen to this. Sally Logan was raped in 1992. We now think that she gave birth to a child and sold that child, a daughter. I think we have that on the recording.'

'Yes.'

'How old would that woman be now?'

Costello did a quick count. 'Twenty-four, twenty-five?'

'And if Sally was telling the truth, the father of that child was the rapist.'

'Yes. Oh, you beauty . . .' Costello could tell what was coming next.

'This is where we get complicated. There is one batch of DNA here that matches Sally's on the maternal match.'

'You are kidding?' Costello thought that through. 'So you are suggesting that her own daughter comes back here, pregnant herself, and offers her baby to be sold, just as she was?' She leaned on the worktop, thinking. 'Maybe not so odd. Sally said she sold the girl to family friends. So if that child got pregnant all these years later and . . . well maybe her parents suggested the Braithwaites as an answer. Which means—' she pointed her finger at Mathilda – 'that in your hand we have the DNA of the rapist, that 24-year-old woman had the rapist for a dad. Please tell me that *is* what you are telling me.'

'Well I ran it on the database.'

'And you got a match.'

'I did.'

'Oh I am so loving this. Wait until I tell Anderson.' Costello almost clapped. 'And working the other way round, if I am following the DNA right. The baby is missing, maybe because it wasn't worth taking, because it had a faulty chromosome. I am guessing at that. All the others match up but not TZ395 so that sample is—'

'Little Moses.'

'That's all I can think of.'

'You can check that with the hospital later, but we are sure about his Y chromosome?'

'He's on our database, you have a name? You beauty, you absolute beauty. Please tell me he's alive and fit for prosecution.'

Mathilda's face paled.

Costello breathed out. 'No? Oh Christ, was it Andrew Braithwaite's baby all along? That was why she couldn't abort it? I wonder if Andrew knew. Shit,' said Costello. 'Shit. Shit. Still, Dali needs all this so get it to Gordon and his glorious spreadsheet. We have to return Baby Sholto to his mum and dad.'

'No, Costello.' Mathilda put her hand out and held onto Costello's elbow. She didn't let go.

The journey to Balcarres Road was in silence, they had so much to say to each other but this wasn't the time. Now was the time for Archie to tell Abby about her sister. Valerie was barely alive when she had reached the hospital, and after all the work that had been done on her, it remained a question of time. The ruse of oxygen deprivation they had used for Colin Anderson was true for Valerie Abernethy. The ligature had been round her neck for a long time and they had no idea yet how much brain damage had occurred.

There was nothing else they could do, just wait.

Archie had phoned Costello and cried like a baby. She had
been his god-daughter that was all he had said and had asked
Costello to go with him to tell her sister.

Costello had offered to run him over to Edinburgh first, her
flat, pick up some things she might need, things she may
recognize. Archie said Valerie had a cat who she adored. He'd
like to bring it back and make sure it was OK.

Costello understood that, the simplest of things can make
sense of madness.

And she had walked in the flat with a sense of wonder at
the size and the light, the minimalism, and the white floors,
and walked into the estate agent who was selling it. Valerie
had told him she was going away. Sure enough, there were a
few items packed, but only a few.

Costello spotted the small ebony vase on the tall table, and
the photograph sitting behind it. The woman she had seen
with Archie, her arms round another much younger woman
with fair hair. Then a darker woman, with a closer resemblance
to Valerie, close enough to be sisters. In between, dark-eyed
and spikey-haired, was Malcolm.

She pointed. 'Who is that?'

Archie snuffled, the way people do after a bout of tears.
'Abigail. Val's sister. Those are her kids. Mary-Jane and
Malcolm.'

'Come on, she needs to be told,' Costello had reminded
him, her mind chasing connections that she could not make
connect. She kept totally quiet about her own agenda, what
Archie didn't know couldn't hurt him.

Costello pulled her car up outside the big house. It looked
cold in the daylight, the grass too neat, the pebbles on the
drive raked into lines. Costello could tell Archie was impressed.

They walked up the path at the front past the monkey puzzle
tree, Archie taking the lead, telling Costello that she was to
be quiet and speak when she was spoken to. 'We are here to
inform Abigail Haggerty of her sister's condition. And that is
the only reason why we are here,' he snapped, as if he had
sensed she had an ulterior motive.

She snapped back, 'Look you, if I find any evidence of

criminality towards a child, I will do my job. If you decide to turn a blind eye, that is your call. Mr Walker, you were at the meeting with Dali.'

He continued to walk ahead of her, ramming his hands deep into his coat pockets, his little legs striding out. Hitler used to walk like that.

He knocked on the front door, an authoritative rat tat tat tat. If it was possible for a knock to sound aggressive rather than sympathetic, this was it. Nobody answered. He knocked again, staring at the door willing somebody to respond. Costello sidestepped onto the front lawn, neatly edged and bordered with white stones. The neatness was at odds with the harsh voice that had shouted from the gap in the door, when was that? Three nights ago? She took a few steps back, craning her neck to get a better view.

'What are you doing? You can't go looking in people's windows.' Archie looked at her then slapped his side as though calling a disobedient dog to heel.

'You can when a minor phones a police officer for help,' she said, vaguely. 'The TV isn't on.' She stepped forward into the bright white bed of stones, noting the precise row of green plants, all folded over and fixed by red wire ties, nestling into themselves against the first frost that may be with them any day now.

She leaned forward, stretching up on her toes, not caring about the indents her feet were making in the small white stones. She pressed her ear to the glass, and heard the rhythmic thud of a bass booming from inside the house.

'There is someone in there, or at least there is music in there, but I doubt it's so loud they can't hear the front door. Give it a good bash.'

She stepped back on to the front steps and swung on the handrail, ready to go round the side.

'Costello, you shouldn't be harassing these people, they are not suspects. I am here to inform them of . . .' Then he remembered why he was really here, and the news he was going to break and he fell silent. 'My god-child.'

He turned around but Costello had gone.

Costello had walked round the back, looking in the kitchen

window, the glass panel of the back door that opened into a utility room. She held her hands up to the glass, cupping her fingers to get a better look inside, her breathing making white clouds on the clear surface. There was no sign of life.

She moved round to the next one, aware that Archie was moving in behind her.

'What is it, Costello?'

'I am not happy about this.' She dashed to the next window, she could only see the upper reaches of the hall from her lower viewpoint. She looked round the garden and saw the small green food bin. She pulled it over and stood on it, raising herself up on the sill, lifting her weight on her stretched arms.

'What do you see?'

'I thought you were only interested in telling Abigail about Valerie.'

'But what do you see?'

'It's a very tidy house, look at the garden, at the flower bed, all squeaky clean, it's obvious the person who works here is a psychopath. Bit like you, as neat as a band box until one wheel falls off the bus and it all goes to pot.'

He ignored her but provided her with a steadying hand as she clambered up further.

'Excuse me!' said a rather cross voice over the fence, loud but the screechiness lessened its volume. 'Excuse me, can I help you?'

'Great, another bloody neighbour,' muttered Costello as she half climbed, half fell down. 'Police, we are the police.' She began digging in her pocket for her warrant card.

'Can you prove that?' the talking head asked, but a little more politely, probably had clocked the small dapper man with the steel grey hair. He looked as though he would panic if he had a broken nail. 'Oh, I mean, do you have a card or something? This is a neighbourhood watch area,' she laughed a little, a coy giggling little laugh for a woman on the wrong side of fifty. 'They always say to ask for some ID.'

'Yes, of course. Here it is.'

Costello jogged across the back path and on the grass, up to the hedge. Archie watched her, thinking how competent she looked in her dark suit, the small flat-soled boots, the bulky anorak, her flat blonde hair and the small pinched face. 'There you go.' She waved it at the woman's face, too close for her to see it. 'Have you heard or seen anything odd around here, last night or this morning?'

'What do you mean by odd?'

Costello stood up on a low wall that ran the length of the bottom hedge. 'We have concerns about the boy.'

'Do we?' asked Archie, not too quietly, not caring if the woman heard. That was not why they were here. All he got in response was a withering glance from both women.

'Ignore my junior. Did you hear anything?' Costello jerked her head towards the house. 'You know, in there?'

'It was bad last night, worse than ever. We have called the police but nobody does anything.'

'Common complaint. When did it stop?'

'About one this morning. I can't sleep, you know, when they start arguing, it's upsetting. When both kids were there, it was really awful, but the girl has left home now so that's not so bad.'

'Are these the children?' Costello showed her the photograph she had lifted from Valerie's flat, still in its frame.

'Yes, that's Abby, Mary-Jane and Malcolm. I don't know the other lady.'

Costello slipped the photo back into her jacket. 'And the noise stopped . . .?'

'Around one a.m. Something like that.'

'Stopped?'

'All fell silent.'

'Just like that?' Costello snapped her fingers.

The neighbour looked worried now. 'Yes, just like that.'

'Or did you hear a door slam or a car drive off?'

'Well, yes, it was his car. I saw it leave, we sleep at the front,' she said by way of explanation.

'And have you heard or seen anybody this morning?'

'No. No. I don't think so, I have been out but no I haven't seen anybody. Nobody at all.'

'And the car that left, how many people were inside it? Could you see?'

'No, sorry it was too dark. Everything is OK, isn't it?'

'Don't worry, we'll get to the bottom of it.' She turned to
Archie and said, very loudly, 'Walker? Could you go and see
if there is a car in the garage?' And then to the neighbour, she
asked, 'Did they have one car or two?'

'Oh, just the one. A Volvo, I think. Abigail doesn't drive.'

'Thanks.' Costello turned her back, trying to think why a
GP wouldn't drive, and jumped off the wall. She went up to
the back door and gave it a good push while turning the handle.
She wasn't surprised to feel it swing slowly under her hand.
She let it open, releasing the vapours of Persil and floor cleaner.
It looked a very clean utility room.

'There's no car in the garage, is there?' she shouted to
Archie.

'No. What are you doing?'

'Police work, it's what we do.' She let the door close slightly,
cutting off the sight line of the neighbour. She heard Archie's
breathing as he approached the steps. He stuck his head in the
gap of the open door.

'Come out of there, we have no permission.'

'Do you smell that?'

'What?'

'That.' She crinkled her nose, reaching into her pocket for
the spare set of gloves and the shoe covers she always carried.
She slipped them on.

'What smell, Costello?' She could hear the tremor in
Archie's voice.

'That smell, bleach or something. Somebody has taken the
time and care to tidy up.'

'It's a utility room, Costello, that's what people do.'

'You stay there, don't move, get your phone out. Do not
walk in here.'

She walked across the white tiles of the utility room floor,
through the kitchen and turned back into the hall. She could
see the glass on the white PVC front door, a small side table
sporting a landline, a few books and a rather weather-beaten
cheese plant. She looked at the magnolia wallpaper going up
the stairs. She could make out the marks more clearly, much
more clearly than she had from the window. The usual bumps
of family life. She stood on the corner listening to the music

on repeat. It was the same song, recognizable, 'The Clapping Song' floating down from somewhere upstairs.

She called out hello, knowing that nobody was going to answer. She called to the front and then to the back, still nothing. She stayed still, trying to sense where the smell was coming from. She looked closer at the wall, placing her plastic-coated feet carefully, checking where her weight was going, no creaking. She was sure the house was empty though, they had made enough of a noise outside to alert anybody.

And the music, the door. The fact that the back door had been left open. The house had been staged. Or was she wanting to see things that were not there? Too many horrors in the last few days. Was every baby she saw now a commodity, every child a potential Kissel case? Did she want Abigail to be involved with 'criminality', to use one of Archie's stock phrases? If he knew the family so well, if they were so precious, why was he not in here making sure that Valerie's sister was OK, surely he knew her equally as well. Yet he was standing outside on the step like a naughty child, too wary to come back into the room.

Maybe that was it, maybe it was all about Archie.

The mark on the wall had been wiped with a very wet cloth, the staining spread as it was being cleaned. She knew that pattern, the mark of it like a faded comet. Somebody with blood on their shoulder had come down the stairs, then realized they had left a mark on the wall and come back to clean it off. She pressed her gloved fingertip to it. Round the outside, it came away dry but the centre was still wet.

Down the stairs.

They had a stain on their shoulders, enough to be easily transferable as they came down the stairs. But who? And whose blood?

She got her phone out. Ready. She stepped back down two stairs to the bottom hall. He, she was sure it was he, had been moving at speed, getting closer to the wall, heading for the door now on her immediate right. She opened that door, into the living room; perfect. The dining area beyond. The kitchen was the same. She looked at the sink, seeing a pattern of dark stained drops that may or may not have been paper from the blood being cleaned. That could wait.

She called out, 'Are you still there?'

'Yes, what are you doing?'

She went back out to the hall, upstairs slowly, one step then catch up, the next one then catch up. She dialled Archie on her phone, hearing him outside as she heard him through the earpiece.

'I want you to stay outside.'

'I am right here.' She could hear the neighbour standing close, asking if everything was OK.

'I'm going up the stairs.'

'Why, what have you seen?'

'I'm investigating.'

'Well be careful, very careful.'

His voice faded. She could only hear him over the phone now, as she stepped onto the top landing with its oak wood floor, a keyboard tucked into a recess on the wall. She noted the fold away chair stacked beside it.

The smell was stronger up here. The bedroom door to her left was open. If the next-door neighbour slept to the front, the chances are that Abigail did as well. To her right was the window she thought she had seen Malcolm wave from that night, a small face at the window. He could have said something, he could have asked for help.

He had phoned her. Why did she not get back to him?

But why did he not ask for help? Because victims never do. They are trapped, physically, emotionally and psychologically, conditioned to respond as they are told to. Nothing can make them truthful, they live with their own truth.

Something had happened here. A suitcase opened, not filled, but an attempt. At flight?

She pushed gently on the door, it squeaked eerily. She saw the posters on the walls, the picture of the Lego model of the Millennium Falcon. The duvet cover on the bed was smooth. Lying on top of it was a Celtic top, a pair of black leggings, the socks, the shoes. The left shoe at the bottom of the toe of the left sock, the neighbour sitting likewise. As if the body had slipped out the clothes, leaving them behind.

Costello stopped breathing for a moment.

Then she crossed the hall to the small room at the front and there they were. She couldn't make it out at first. The narrow bed with the suitcase sitting open on it, then at the end of the bed, a bundle of clothes, like somebody had woken up and tossed the duvet off the end of the bed and left them there.

That was the first impression.

The second was of Abigail, lying curled up.

The third was of Malcolm.

She had no idea how long she stood there for, looking. She knew, had known this was going to happen. She had felt it in her bones. She had told Dali, they had discussed it. She had even requested a welfare check.

They always thought they had tomorrow.

Well they didn't.

She had walked right up to the end of the bed. The blood spattered on the walls, the piss on the floor, the deep mineral stench of the blood with the sweeter, mulchy smell of faecal matter. But there was mess everywhere, human tissue, hair, blood, bone on the floor, the walls, the duvet that hung over the end of the bed, some of it had hit the ceiling, some had even spattered on the suitcase. The mirrored wardrobe had a rose spray spatter.

And she looked. Abigail was there, on her side, her arm up and over the smaller, less substantial body underneath. His blood-stained swollen fingers still gripped the stained purple silk of her blouse.

She heard somebody whisper her name.

Then again.

She turned round, looking behind her. Nobody there. She checked in the mirrored wardrobe. The blood splattered reflection was on her own.

The phone was speaking to her.

She replied, 'Hi Archie. You need to come up here. Now.'

Costello had her head in her hands, sitting on a stool in Anderson's kitchen.

'How's Archie?' Anderson asked.

'He's asleep at home, under sedation. I'll pop in and see him on the way home. How are you?'

'My throat feels as if I've been gargling sandpaper. But I am fine, you don't need to look after me, I have a houseful of folk here. Any news on Braithwaite?'

'He's not confessing, but he must have felt the squeeze being put on him, Sally freaking out, thinking she recognized Mary-Jane or Adele or whatever it was she was calling herself. And then Valerie was coming closer, ever closer and him wondering what she was really up to. In the market for buying a baby or was she testing the water for a prosecution? Braithwaite had no idea what she did or did not know. It could have been a fishing expedition. I mean, there was no way she was going to get a baby herself, not with her alcohol abuse. And they would have not sold a child to her for the same reason. Sally would have told her that. And there would have been a scuffle. Being refused a baby, Braithwaite had conjectured that blackmail wouldn't have been far from her mind. Sell me a baby or else. Braithwaite was sure that Valerie had gone a fair way down that road. She had sold a lot of her stuff, she was planning to move. That fits in with some odd conversations Valerie had been having with both Archie and her boss. And then Braithwaite saw the whole thing tumbling down around him. She's still in the hospital.'

'Still hanging on.' Anderson nodded. 'It seems so desperate. All these women who seemed to have everything were all squirming with their internal pain. But I guess you never know what's going through anybody's mind, it's all the suffering of strangers. Everybody lives in their own private hell. It's just that some of us know it.'

'You are real ball of fun today,' Costello said, biting her lip, then falling silent.

'I'm sure that was entrapment, what you did to me.' Anderson put a cup of tea in front of Costello, trying to get her to talk. He had listened to the horror of the house, now known as the monkey puzzle house. She was off that case, she had been told. Twice. So he was now trying to get her to talk about the Blue Neptune, they were walking a fine line.

Braithwaite was sharp, and he had Sally lined up as fall guy – and he pardoned the pun – as she could have been responsible for it all, except the attempt on Anderson's life.

If it had been that.

Now Braithwaite was saying that as a doctor he was palpating Anderson's neck. It was shite, of course, but it might be enough to muddy the water. And his defence team was quoting all kinds of entrapment.

Costello was perched on the breakfast bar seat and she pulled the plate of HobNobs closer. 'Nobody asked him to come into your room, to try to strangle you,' Costello answered. 'That was what he was trying to do, all those pictures we got with his hands fluorescing with Claire's paint. I think we got the evil bastard. That's all that matters. I don't think Wyngate or Mulholland are going to forgive us for a very long time though. They really thought you were a goner.'

'Nice of the ACC to chip in, telling them Braithwaite was to be released,' Anderson laughed, then remembered the horror that Costello had witnessed and why she was here, curled up on top of a high stool, her feet resting on the top bar so that her knees were almost up as high as her chest. A protective posture if ever there was one.

She looked very tired and very vulnerable. It was on the front of every Scottish national. The Monkey House of Horror.

'I'd have loved to have seen Wyngate's face, trying to tell the assistant commissioner how to do his job.' Costello took a bite of her biscuit. 'And I thought Braithwaite would stick around, check your vital signs. Try killing you by doing something – I don't know – sticking an elbow in some nerve that stops your heart instantly. I mean, he didn't even question how quick O'Hare got you out of there, or even the fact he's a friggin pathologist.'

'Give him his due; he had just pushed his wife off a roof so he was a tad preoccupied.'

'Are you sad about that?'

'Never go back, Costello, you have always said that. There's a reason why the past is behind you.'

She sighed. 'Still, glad you didn't drown. Just feel bad that we didn't get to Malcolm in time. The crime scene people had almost finished by the time Dali's welfare check social worker arrived.' She shook her head, trying to break free of the horror of it.

He went very quiet. They sat for a while, the faint beat of music in the distance, somewhere on the two floors above them.

'Was it awful?'

'It was.'

'You couldn't have stopped it. You, Dali, the combined might of the social services couldn't have stopped that from happening. Sad but the only person responsible for the death of Abigail and Malcolm Haggerty is George Haggerty.'

'Well, that is not true, his alibi checks out, totally, it wasn't him. Seemingly,' said Costello.

'So I heard.'

'It checks out. He wasn't there.' Costello spoke without conviction. 'Dali is right though. What is the point of it?'

'Well, Claire would say that it is the starfish. You only save what you can save.'

Costello wasn't listening. 'Any more on Braithwaite for Orla? Sholto?'

'All they have is his access to Sholto at the Blue Neptune. We have hairs from Sally's jumper on Valerie's necklace, black vicuna.' He shrugged. 'Easily planted. We need to hope that Valerie wakes up and can remember the details of her attack.'

'He was that good. But we do have his palm print that matches the print you found on the side of the car in the underground car park. He cleaned the one on the car in front of him, but forgot to do the car behind him. That puts him there. The oil and the indent on her thigh puts Orla's body there. And his only alibi for that night is me. And I was so pissed I fell asleep really early on their sofa. Not like me to go out like that, like a light.'

'Had Sally warned him you were coming? All it would take was a wee bit of sleeping tablet then he was clear to do as he wished. And so was she. He admits he fell against the car when he took Orla up from the car park. He denies killing her.'

'Water under the bridge and time will tell. If anything, he'll go down for murdering Sally. Mathilda and her crew will get to work on the forensics dots. She's so good, you know.'

'Doesn't let anything past her,' agreed Costello, formulating what she had to say in her mind, then being unable to say it.

Another silence fell between them, slightly more tense this time.

'Have you had your pep talk yet?' asked Anderson.

'Oh yes, I have a team counselling me now. But I'd rather get the bastards. Valerie will wake up. Braithwaite will go down for a long time. George Haggerty is still out there. And I will get *that* bastard.'

'He has an unbreakable alibi, Costello. He was on his way to see his sick father. That's where he was going at that time of night. It wasn't him.'

She bit her lip. 'Except there is no such thing as an unbreakable alibi. I will leave the force tomorrow, I will go after him. That will do me far more good than any counselling.'

'I believe you.'

'And I was thinking.'

'Never a good sign. And I have been thinking too. Nobody had ever run the rapes of Sally and Gillian together through a spreadsheet, I don't mean HOLMES, I mean a human eye. Both raped, both had ligatures round their neck, both had violence perpetrated to their person, after the event, to the left shoulder. That's not normal, that's a signature. He will not have stopped, he will still be out there doing it. I think . . . Well, I'm not sure what I think or what I want to think.'

'He could be dead.'

'Or progressed to murder.'

'What's your thinking?'

'That instead of cold case shite, all this review, you pull it all together. You have more clout now, you have suffered again in the course of your duties.'

'I was hit over the head by Andrew Braithwaite who was skulking in a corner after pretending to be called away. I wasn't mauled by a serial killer.'

'Well actually you were once we prove it, but that is beside the point. Tell them you want to head up a task force. With me, Wyngate, Mulholland – the old team. We work much better together than apart.'

'And they will listen to me, like that?' He snapped his fingers.

'You have been mauled by a serial killer. The ACC signed off on that plan of action.'

'Only because you suggested it!'

'See teamwork. They will agree to anything you ask now.' Then she was laughing. Then sobbing.

'Why is it such a big deal, Costello? They will get who killed Abby and Malcolm, give them time.'

'But do you think that was his first? Do you really believe that? That wasn't a domestic, that was ohhh . . . so much more. That was slaughter. The way the boy's clothes were laid out, that was a message. I just don't know who it was for.'

'For who?'

'I don't bloody know.' She wiped her face. 'But there is a connection that I can't see. Valerie wanted a child. She was doing the whole wearing loose clothing thing, preparing to be to be pregnant in inverted commas, to buy a baby. Because she knew her sister had done the same thing? Abigail's eldest child was purchased, not conceived.'

'Surely Mathilda will be looking at all that.'

'God, yes, you should see the spreadsheet. Wyngate is in his element.'

'What happened to the woman in the blue coat?'

'Oh her, Emma? She's driving Dali nuts. Had her baby, can't decide whether to keep it or not. But a tabloid has offered her a load of money for her story so she's weighing up her options. Her baby too, is a commercial enterprise. By Christmas Emma will have a workout DVD and will be in the jungle eating kangaroo testicles. I see where Sally was coming from, you know, and they drifted into this mess.'

'Andrew led her into this mess.'

'And she followed.' Costello was firm.

Silence fell again, listening to the odd sound of movement upstairs. Costello had hoped they would be alone.

'Anyway, you are fine, the plan worked out. He had you convinced though, Braithwaite. He had us all convinced. Nothing a defence council likes better than somebody else to blame. He will go down for murder for Sally though, I am sure of that. And the little matter of his offshore bank accounts that are stuffed to the gunnels, all that stuff he told the tape about being a gambler was a load of lies. He was rolling in it. Him. Not them, not him and Sally.'

'So she believed his gambling story?'

'Who knows, but it's a great way to explain why he was always skint. Colin?' she looked upwards.

'Yes.'

'Is Claire upstairs?'

'Yes. With David no doubt.'

'I need to ask you a personal question and I need you to be honest with me.'

He looked at her, seeing she was serious. 'OK.'

'Did you and Sally ever have a relationship that went beyond friends?'

'Why is that of any interest to you?'

'It's complicated. This girl. She might be calling herself Adele—' she held out the photograph taken from Valerie's house, now out of its frame – 'that girl. She's the elder child of the Haggerty house and we cannot trace her.'

He looked at the picture, then up. Costello was staring at him as if she had never seen him before, her grey eyes scanning his face, memorizing every detail; his blue eyes, the high cheekbones, that fair skin that turned gold in the sun.

'There is no easy way to say this. But we think, we know, that she is your daughter.'

Anderson sat down, laughed, then stopped laughing. 'That's shite. How do you know this?'

'At least that's a better answer than "this is not possible". Mathilda and I—'

'What has it to do with her?' He was angry now, he took a few deep breaths. 'Sorry, I think I see where this confusion has come from.'

'There is no confusion, the DNA doesn't lie. You, me, all serving police officers, have their DNA on the system for exclusion at crime scenes. When Mathilda ran the sample, yours showed up as a familial, paternal match. Exactly. We looked as Sally had said the father of the baby was her rapist. And yours came up as the match. If I look at the timelines,

I'm sure it wasn't the rapist's baby Sally was carrying. It was yours.'

Anderson shook his head.

'Sally wasn't put down to your year when she was attacked. She was already in your year because of her knee surgery. You knew her, that's why you were interviewed after she was attacked, remember? They asked you to account for your movements. Because some of your acquaintances thought you were a couple. You were right up there as a suspect.'

'That can't be right.'

'It is right.' Costello was adamant. 'Mathilda got it double checked. The sample at the lab. A sample from the mortuary. Your cheek swab. You and Sally are the parents of this girl.'

'Oh my God. So Sally and I have a daughter. Is that what you are telling me?' He whispered it, his eyes flicking to the ceiling as if Claire might hear. 'Where is she?'

'Colin, we don't know. At the moment we don't even know her real name. Mathilda and I are on it. We have a picture and her DNA.'

'Adele. Do you think it is Adele . . . that was the only one Sally mentioned by name.' He ran the top of his finger over the face on the picture. 'Bloody hell.' Then his face fell, eyes narrowed. 'Do you think she's still alive?'

'I did think about not telling you, in case she wasn't but . . . well, it will all come out, won't it.'

'Do I tell Brenda? And Claire, Peter . . . they have a sister.'

'Colin, don't go rushing into this all red roses and *Little House On the Prairie*. You don't know what this girl is like, you don't know anything about her. We don't even know if she's still alive.'

'Except that she's my kid, and she was sold. Sold?'

'Sold because Sally couldn't keep her. You heard what her parents said, she was sold because Sally wanted her to live. She couldn't bring herself to abort your child, bloody sure Andrew didn't want it around if he knew it was yours, and you have no idea what she and this child have been through.'

'She was sold.'

'Well, if you are going to be all Pollyanna about it, there's another logical conclusion to all this.'

'What?'

'Well, there's more.'

'What? What could be worse than that?' He looked at her face.

'It does get worse. One thing is that the woman who bought Adele as a baby, was called Abby and was the same age as Sally roughly. Sally told you that. Adele would be about twenty-four now. And we have an Abigail, with a twenty-four-year-old daughter, called Mary-Jane. Who wanted to be a singer, like . . .'

'Adele?'

'And if she got pregnant, it's not beyond possibility that Abigail might have directed her daughter down the same route that she went. George was not going to give Mary-Jane the time of day, so maybe Abigail thought she was doing the best thing. Think how she must have felt, finally getting pregnant after all she'd been through. Especially if you think how badly George treats Malcolm, and that boy is his own flesh and blood so Abigail might have thought it best if Mary-Jane went to the Braithwaites to be "looked after".'

'That's all supposition.'

'The neighbour recognized the photo immediately as Mary-Jane. She hasn't seen her for months. Long enough to go away and give birth.'

Anderson dropped his head in his hands. 'Poor kid, Jesus Christ.'

'Think about the timing of the birth and the abduction. There's . . . well . . . another DNA issue. The match of Sally's grandchild if you like. Adele's, Mary-Jane's baby. We have treble-checked this. Mathilda sent the original sample to another lab for checking. She was desperate to avoid cross-contamination. She has checked and double-checked until we are sure, but whatever way you look at it . . .'

'What?'

'Baby Moses. His mother is your daughter. Congratulations, Granddad.'

'The wee Down's baby?'

Costello nodded. 'The wee Down's baby. Sorry to put that all on you. I thought better me telling you than hearing it from Stuart or Bruce.'

He smiled at her, his eyes now glistening with moisture. 'Yeah, rather you than anybody else. God, woke up this morning as a dad of two, going to bed as a dad of three and a granddad. This will take some getting used to.' Then his eyes creased. 'But you don't know where Adele is?'

'As far as we know, five weeks ago she walked up Sevastopol Lane and gave birth to Moses. We don't know what happened to her after that. We are finding it difficult to find anybody to ask.'

Colin folded his arms. He swallowed hard. That look of steel hardened in his blue eyes.

'But we will find her, Colin, we will.'

Thirty minutes later Lorna McGill and Mulholland walked up the path of the house, through an overgrown garden. The front door was old and painted many times over. A large brass knocker hung in the middle with nine thick glass panels and a curtain behind, preventing anybody on the step from looking in.

'Look at this place, this garden, I would have given my right arm to grow up in a place like this.'

'Sholto is not their baby, Sholto has a mother and a father who are waiting for him. He doesn't need all this.'

'But what about wee Little Moses, who is going to look after him?'

'He will be adopted eventually.' Mulholland kept his lips sealed, the DNA results were not public knowledge yet. And they were still looking for Mary-Jane, also known as Adele.

'Aye after years going through the state system, going from pillar to post being unable to form long-term friendships and relationships. That's what does all the harm. Could we not just take Sholto away and give them baby Moses instead?'

'Moses has family,' said Mulholland, feeling a burst of paternal loyalty to Anderson.

'I have the same amount of paperwork to fill in as you do, so the brief answer to that is no. We need to let the wheels of justice take their course. Roberta and James are waiting for Sholto. Imagine what that woman has gone through.'

'But we are doing the same to them.'

'Not their baby. Small detail, but true.'

'Do we just go in and do it?'

'We do. Nothing else for it.'

They heard a dog panting at the back of the door, a male voice shouted, 'Hold on, I'll get it' and told the dog to get out the way. As the door opened a large golden retriever rushed out, panting, tail wagging. Lorna immediately bent down to pat it on the head.

Mulholland held up his warrant card. 'We need to have a word.'

The man who opened the door aged about ten years in one glance. He stepped forward and closed the door a little behind him. 'Please. My wife, please.'

'The baby is not yours, you know that.'

'He is ours. We adopted privately. So there is a misunderstanding.'

'Have you read the newspapers, Mr Ingram? Then you will know why we are here.'

'I'm Lorna McGill, I am a social worker and—'

'We were turned down for a baby by you lot, considered too old. Too old? Look what we can offer.'

Mulholland had to agree but thought it best to say nothing. They were not Sholto's parents.

Ingram opened the door wider and they walked into the hall. Standing at the bottom of it, outlined against the light in the doorframe was a thin woman, dressed in leggings and a T-shirt, a baby in her arms. She was dangling a pair of blue fluffy leggings in the baby's face, he was gurgling and kicking his legs in appreciation.

'Isobel?' Ingram said gently. Her eyes went from her husband to Mulholland to Lorna and then a tear started to fall. She muttered one word.

'Please?'

The nurse had left him alone at first with this tiny little person. He didn't know, but perhaps he would spend the rest of his life with him. Moses opened his eyes, blue like his granddad's, so clear the likeness now they knew. A warm blue and a crinkly little smile. His overlarge tongue protruded slightly. Anderson

stuck his tongue out in return. It seemed appropriate. Moses'
arm waved in the air, vaguely at Anderson. He looked like a
drunk trying to hail a taxi. Anderson held up his little finger
and Moses' hand opened like a starfish and grasped at it tightly.
And with remarkable strength.

'Hello grandson,' Anderson said, aware his voice was
breaking. The baby was so small. The door opened quietly
behind him, Brenda came in. and stood at the side of the cot.
'So it's true then.'

'Looks like it.'

Then both stood in silence looking at Moses still holding
onto Anderson's finger. He knew he was holding his breath,
not knowing which way Brenda was going to jump. This was
really nothing to do with her. She could be very black and
white.

'You forget they are so small, so helpless,' she said, running
the back of her hand over the baby's forehead, lifting the curl
of blonde hair. 'You had a curl like that, I remember your
mum showing me a photograph of you sitting in your nappy
in front of a coal fire.'

'No central heating in those days. We thought we had it
tough.' Moses gurgled a little. 'God knows how tough he's
going to find it.'

Silence fell between them again as they listened to Moses
quietly crooning, kicking his legs as if he wanted the blanket
off.

Brenda took a deep breath. 'The kids are outside, they didn't
know if they should come in or not.'

'I wasn't sure if . . .'

'Sure of what?' Brenda looked at him, her head down, eyes
studying him from under her eyebrows. 'Not sure if they want
to meet their baby nephew?'

So Peter and Claire came in and fussed and bothered over
him, Anderson stood back in the corner of the room, trying
to stop the lump in his throat from choking him, as they
chatted about where Moses was staying, fighting over him.
What they needed to buy, and if they were still going to call
him Moses as somebody had pointed out that was not his
name. He had no name.

And he was intensely proud of his family, his open-hearted loving family. If he could do it for them, he could do it for Moses.

After a few moments Dali came in, slithering through the door as easily as a large lady could. It was the first time he had seen her without her great blue duvet jacket. She smiled at him and folded her arms over her huge chest, letting her forearms rest there.

'It's lovely, Mr Anderson, just lovely.'

'It is, isn't it?'

'And you have no idea how much paperwork you have to go through, this one almighty legal mess.' She seemed to take some delight in this.

'But he is mine, the DNA doesn't lie. In law, I mean.'

'It will be fine, complex but fine.'

'Can we take him home though?'

'Legally you can, seeing you are who you are.'

'I've been trying to find a nurse who will tell me how he is, if we can take him, medically.'

'There was a bloody meeting at the corner of the corridor with five managers, I had to walk round them.' Her brown eyes crinkled mischievously. 'As I said, that's the problem with this case, too many chiefs, not enough Indians.'

'Is that racist?' smiled Anderson.

'Probably.'

And then Moses started crying.

FOURTEEN

Costello got out the car, closing the door carefully. She stepped back a little onto the road, smoothing down her black coat, grasping the handbag under her arm. It was a dull day, with a light breeze blowing in from the east. The wind carried with it a bitter chill, as befitted the sad occasion.

The funeral of Mary-Jane Haggerty, aged 24. A dog walker had found her body in a car, her own small Fiesta. She had been curled in the driver's seat and had been there for a few weeks by the state of her decomposition. O'Hare had found a single injection site in her neck, he thought she had suffered an air embolism that had been administered deliberately.

And Archie Walker was after Braithwaite. He had known Mary-Jane as part of Valerie's extended family. And Costello was banned from that investigation.

Adjusting her hat to obscure her face, Costello walked through the gates of the cemetery, having parked her car a couple of streets away to be anonymous in a line of residents' cars. She had no intention of joining the cortège or attending the service. She intended to watch them as they came in, see how Haggerty behaved and how the family – the two families – reacted. Then, as she moved her handbag from one side to the other, she realized her hands were empty, she had forgotten the flowers. They were still sitting in the boot of the Fiat so she hurried back and quickly retrieved the wreath, a circle of intertwined orange and crimson flowers; the colours of Partick thistle.

She held the wreath close to her chest, protecting it from the wind as she returned through the big gates, keeping to the path away from the vehicle access, so nobody in a car could catch a glimpse of her. She'd be just another woman in black. At a funeral.

There was already a crowd of mourners at the doors of the crematorium, a gathering in black, seeking shelter from the wind. Costello walked on, briskly, making it quite clear to anybody who was watching, that she was headed elsewhere.

She had no interest in this funeral, which was true. She had never met the deceased alive, she was more interested in who was attending.

Trying to appear inconspicuous, she strolled slowly round the older gravestones, reading the engravings that hadn't been weathered away. She studied the tall stone with the one-winged angel on top, and the gentle indents of an ornate carving which would be lost in the next years. The stone was for Donald McPhail and his 'beloved wife Elizabeth' who had gone now to lie in the arms of the lord. It was too cold to do the maths but they had both lived a good long life, buried in the days when a memorial in death meant they had been something in life. She wondered what Mary-Jane's family would get to remember her short time on this earth, all of twenty-four years. And who was 'her family'? Who would do it for her? The man who had brought her up, George Haggerty, or her biological father, Colin Anderson.

It was Colin's DNA that had been the blueprint to her existence but it was George Haggerty who had helped with her maths homework, who had taught her how to ride a bike and who had broken her nose. Twice.

Costello stood at the side of the tall headstone with its slightly faulty angel, leaning against it slightly, the soft, brittle moss crackling under the weight of her shoulder and flaking onto the black wool of her coat. She was leaning more than the deceased might think appropriate due to her heels sinking into the grass, so she apologized. The wind was bitter here, as she was exposed on the rise of the hill. She explained to Donald and to Elizabeth, and to herself, hoping they would understand. They had lived long lives, hopefully untouched by violence. Mary-Jane's short life had been full of it.

Aware of the little crowd stirring, Costello turned as the hearse arrived. The mourners, about thirty of them in all, began to thread themselves along the back of the car park, respectful but not crowding. Costello felt her stomach tighten as George

Haggerty got out the lead car. She scanned her eyes over the crowd, Colin Anderson was not amongst them. Maybe he had decided he had no place here, he had not known his daughter in life. But Costello did watch carefully as George remained at the door of the limousine, helping out an elderly woman. His mother? Older sister? Dressed in very formal black, her face covered by a dark veil that blew and billowed in the wind, the old woman carried herself with the grace of a princess. Costello thought she would be getting good wear out of that outfit, seeing as George had murdered his wife and his son, and was now burying his daughter. It was difficult to fathom how they could all be there, so accepting of this farce, or were they questioning it just as she was.

Another car followed, pulling slowly and silently into the car park, then another car behind that, all three were black limousines. It was a good send-off. Three women got out, dressed in the way of the young, more like a wedding than a funeral; high heels, long glossy dark hair, thick black eyebrows and all sharing the same pout. As they stood, almost posing, the back of the hearse was opening up to reveal a wreath of pink flowers, lying on top of a white coffin. George Haggerty had been watching that but turned to the three women and gave them a little smile, they raised white hankies to their eyes. The doors of the second limo opened.

Anderson was here after all. She recognized him immediately, the tall blond man who emerged as the door was held open by the driver, even though he was dressed in a black suit, well cut, a Crombie coat to keep the wind out. Brenda followed him out in a long dark coat, her auburn hair now tinged with grey that softened and lightened the colour. Then Claire got out, wearing a black trouser suit and polo neck, with David Kerr. Anderson gave his daughter's boyfriend help out the car, handing him his crutches as the boy got to his feet. Then came Peter, almost as tall as his sister now. He was a wee kid when Costello had last seen him, a wee kid with a gap in his teeth who ate Milkybars and giggled a lot. Then she noticed the other girl emerging from the car, and it took Costello took a moment to recognize Paige Riley who was looking around like a startled fish, mouth gaping open.

So this was Anderson's little social project, this was Paige the junkie transplanted to a middle-class life where you attended funerals for people you had never met and you had to behave yourself.

The runaway ex-heroin addict scrubbed up well. Costello had to give her that. Anybody would have bet a thousand pounds that Paige would have been in a coffin long before Mary-Jane. Except Colin had intervened in Paige's life, he didn't get that chance with his eldest daughter.

The crowd shuffled around slightly as the coffin was pulled from the back of the hearse. Dad, biological dad, and a brother she had never met, lifted her body in its wooden shroud and carried her through the dark doors of the crematorium, the mourners following behind.

Costello thanked the McPhails for their support and walked down to the main driveway of the cemetery, working her way up the hill and to the right, to the grave where she was going to leave the wreath, that of Alan McAlpine, DCI of the Strathclyde police as they were. Joining him in his eternal rest was his wife, Helena. Costello placed the wreath on top of the short grass and stood back considering the black marble stone, how faded Alan's gold intimation was compared to Helena's more recent. She was thinking about her old boss lying there, on his side as he had requested, so he could look at the view over the campsies for all eternity. Silly bastard.

Bastard. Hard wee bastard, flawed enough to understand the flaws of others, unlike Colin Anderson, her current DCI, who was Maria Von Trapp in comparison.

'I hope you like the flowers,' she said, her words caught and spread by the wind. 'That bastard Haggerty wouldn't have you fooled for a minute.'

DCI Alan McAlpine remained silent.

By the time she had walked around a little, stopping at the stones of those who had died before they had lived a life, the service was over and the funeral was breaking up. Mary-Jane was on her way to the flames, once there was a trial, her brother and mother would be out of cold storage and be able to join her. As the mourners made their way to a local pub, Costello made her way back behind the gravestones, mentioning to the McPhails that they had the best spot. She wouldn't be the first to stand here and she wouldn't be the last. How many ex-wives had hidden here, how many mistresses, not allowed to mourn the man they loved?

She was watching George Haggerty, a weasel of a man talking to Brenda as if they knew each other well. They had obviously met at the hospital as Moses continued to thrive. How did they reconcile the complex family entanglements? Perfectly well from the look of things.

She knew he was there before she turned round; she had caught the scent of his aftershave on the wind.

'Why are you here?' Anderson asked.

'It's a free country. And I wanted to see him.'

'George Haggerty did not kill Abigail and Malcolm.' Colin Anderson said it, for the hundredth time.

Costello was not listening. 'Yes, he did.'

'He did not kill his wife and his son. He was already on his way to the hospital to see his father; he's on the speed cameras all the way up the road and they were alive when he left the house. We have witnesses.' He had given her that speech a few times too.

She kept her back turned to him, looking at George, the little runt now talking to Claire, then David, looking as if he was asking about his crutches. Quite the charmer. 'Oh, he did it all right.'

'No, he didn't.'

'He did,' and she walked off, back towards the gates of the cemetery. As she walked she looked over her left shoulder, catching George Haggerty watching her, watching her walk every step of the way. He lifted both hands, quickly placing them both together palm to palm. To any onlooker he was slapping the cold from his hands, but she knew. Clap clap. The clapping song. Just what he had left playing in the monkey house of horror. Clap clap. She could have sworn he winked at her. She smiled back. Yeah, she thought, game on.